THE LOST DIARY OF LUCREZIA BORGIA

Deathbed Confessions of the Pope's Daughter

Johnny Teague

THE LOST DIARY OF
LUCREZIA Borgia

DEATHBED CONFESSIONS OF THE POPE'S DAUGHTER

Histria Fiction

Las Vegas ◊ London ◊ New York ◊ Palm Beach

Published in the United States of America by
Histria Books
7181 N. Hualapai Way, Ste. 130-86
Las Vegas, NV 89166 USA
HistriaBooks.com

Histria Fiction is an imprint of Histria Books. Titles published under the imprints of Histria Books are distributed in the United States and Canada by Simon & Schuster and worldwide through Unified Book Distribution. We appreciate your support of copyright by purchasing an authorized edition of this book and for respecting intellectual property laws by not reproducing, scanning, or otherwise distributing any part of it by any means without permission. You are supporting authors and enabling Histria Books to continue publishing books for everyone.

All rights reserved. No part of this book may be reprinted or reproduced or utilized in any form or by any electronic, mechanical or other means, now known or hereafter invented, including photocopying and recording, or in any information storage or retrieval system, without the permission in writing from the Publisher. No part of this book may be used or reproduced in any manner for the purpose of training artificial intelligence technologies or systems.

Certain characters in this work are historical figures, and certain events portrayed did take place. However, this is a work of fiction. Names, characters, places, and incidents are either the product of the author's imagination or are used fictitiously. Any resemblance to actual persons, living or dead, is entirely coincidental.

First Edition

Library of Congress Control Number: 2025933042

ISBN 978-1-59211-600-3 (softbound)
ISBN 978-1-59211-615-7 (eBook)

Copyright © 2026 by Johnny Teague

The Lost Diary of Lucrezia Borgia, Deathbed Confessions of the Pope's Daughter is dedicated solely to the Lord Jesus Christ, God's only Son, the Savior of the world. May He move us from empty religion to a full relationship with Him.

Contents

The Assignment 9

The First Visit to Santa Maria sopra Minerva 13

The Night Search 30

Presentation of First Thoughts 32

The Second Day of work at Santa Maria sopra Minerva 34

The Night at the Basilica 36

I Believe My End Is Near 42

The Diary of My Sins 44

Papal Inauguration 49

Orsino 54

The Family 59

My First Marriage 63

My First Marriage Soon Crumbles 70

Annulment 78

San Sisto 81

My Second Marriage 84

A Child is Born 92

The End for My Second Husband 95

My Third Merger 100

Guiseppe Takes a Break 110

The Departure for Ferrara 112

The Groom and His Father Appear 118

The Entrance into Ferrara..122

Cesare Strikes 127

My Descent 131

The Beginning of the End for the Borgia Reign...................................136

The Marquis of Matua Rises..146

The Duchess of Ferrara..150

The First Year as Duke and Duchess of Ferrara 153

The Brothers' Este Coup 159

The Warring Pope 163

Heartbreak...165

The War..175

The Time when Everything Changed 183

Leonardo and Federico Wait 187

The Wars Outside and Inside 189

My Final Requests 198

Guiseppe Set Free 202

The Assignment

It had been an exciting four years since Guiseppe Campise had discovered the lost diary of Mary Magdalene in his private dig in the ancient village of Magdala on the Sea of Galilee under the supervision of his heroes and superiors, Father Virgilio Canio Corbo and Father Stanislao Loffreda. They had given Guiseppe, their foreman, liberty to pursue his own digs in his off-hours, knowing he longed to one day lead an excavation team of his own. Guiseppe's dream was realized in March of 1976. He had become known in archaeology circles the world over, simply for following a hunch on the shore of Galilee. His face had graced the covers of *National Geographic*, *Time*, *British Archaeology*, *American Journal of Archaeology*, *Antiquity*, *Israel Exploration Journal*, *Archaeology*, and *Biblical Archaeology Review* magazines to name a few.

On February 12, 1981, Guiseppe was called to the Palace of the Pontifical Institute of Christian Archaeology to meet with its rector, Father Antonio Ferrua. Father Ferrua was a famous Jesuit archaeologist in his own right, accredited with finding the bones of Saint Peter. Guiseppe was nervous to meet the world renown lead of the Catholic Church's archaeology department and confidant of Pope John Paul II. As he rushed to the meeting, a thousand fears crossed his mind — had he made some mistake, was the diary of Mary Magdalene a forgery, was he right to grant so many interviews, had he said something heretical, or had he somehow offended the beloved pope?

When Guiseppe Campise arrived, he was told to wait in the outside foyer. Father Ferrua was on an important call with Pope John Paul II. Campise could not believe it. He was about to visit with the man who has the direct line to the Vicar of Christ. Campise had seen the pope numerous times in the Vatican Square, from a distance. He admired this pope more than any before. Here was a man who seemed to have the respect of the world. The longer he waited, the more nervous he became.

Finally, after about twenty minutes, Father Ferrua walked out. He had the look of a pope. Unlike, the kind, approachable appearance of John Paul II, Ferrua looked worried. He walked as if he carried the weight of the Church on his shoulders. This brought greater anxiety to Giuseppe. Father Ferrua issued an order, "I am ready for you now. Come with me, Mr. Campise."

No hand was extended. Guiseppe took no liberties. He followed quietly into a spacious office. On the walls were articles about the Saint Peter discovery. Huge maps lined the walls noting several of the digs Ferrua had led. As the rector sat in his high-back chair, behind a desk the size of most formal dining tables, Campise sat opposite in a low-back, shorter chair. He felt inferior, as if he did not belong. He wondered if this was the purpose in the distinct difference between the two chairs.

There were no pleasantries exchanged. Father Ferrua went straight to the point, "Mr. Campise, I am glad you could meet with me today. We have a huge problem in Rome today which I am sure you are aware of if you follow the daily news. The Red Brigades, the far-left terrorist group, are threatening not just the safety and peace of Italy, but the historical sites of our faith. As you know, the Vatican City is well fortified, but there are many relics exposed beyond these walls. We have called every trustworthy archaeologist within the Church's purview to help locate and secure these artifacts. Pope John Paul II has given me unlimited resources to get this done in rapid order. This is why I called you in today. Mr. Campise, will you work for us over the next two years? I believe this will provide time to at least prioritize and secure the items most vulnerable."

Guiseppe Campise, once the foreman, was being called by the Church to lead. He could not keep his eyes from glancing at the framed portrait on the desk of the Pope, when Father Ferrua said his name. He was flattered but could also feel the gravity of the offered assignment. The time between the rector's statement of need and Campise's response seemed like a half-hour, but took only a second before his answer, "Yes Sir. I will consider it an honor to serve in this capacity. Where would you like me to start?"

Father Ferrua let out a short sigh, followed by a faint smile, "Thank you Mr. Campise. I am sending you to the Santa Maria sopra Minerva Basilica for your first assignment. As a matter of priority, we need to gather the relic of Saint Thomas Acquinas, his arm bone, along with the body of Saint Catherine of Siena. The history of this basilica warrants further research to ascertain what lies within and below the historic structure. Basically, I am sending you to find what you can with no other guidance then this. You will have full levity and unlimited funding, of course within reason, to do as your experience dictates. You followed your instincts upon finding the lost diary of Mary Magdalene, as I did in finding the body of Saint Peter."

Campise was pleased. He had never had a blank check given to him for the work assigned. Fathers Corbo and Loffreda always worked on limited budgets. As their foreman, Campise further restrained his expenditures to allow for any unknowns. He gave the rector his promise to do the best he could to please the Institute. Father Ferrua sat silently. Campise wondered how much he would be paid, who he would be allowed to hire, and what method would expenditures be covered. Never being in this position before, he was afraid to be so forward. He figured he would ask one of the rector's attendants when the meeting was over.

After a long pause, Guiseppe stood to leave. Father Ferrua stopped him, "I do have a side venture for you to pursue if you do not mind. It is not to be documented. You will appreciate my curiosity. This basilica was built upon or near the former temple of the Egyptian goddess Isis. The basilica is named sopra Minerva, meaning "upon Minerva." Minerva was the Roman title for Isis. Roman general Pompey built the temple in honor of this goddess of war. Prior to this, Alexander the Great prayed fervently to this same goddess whom the Greeks called Athena.

The temple was destroyed by Pope Zachary around 750 AD. Upon the temple to Minerva, a convent was first built, followed by a Gothic Church. There is a belief, though highly unlikely, that General Pompey had the remains of Alexander the Great buried beneath or near the temple since Alexander attributed much of his success to this goddess Minerva or Athena. Many say Pompey felt he had the ultimate relic to sustain his power — the body of Alexander the Great."

Guiseppe's heart pounded. This endeavor met his chief passion. He was ready to hug the rector's neck and run straight to the basilica with his tools. Father Ferrua could see the delight in his new-hire's face. Not letting Guiseppe speak, the rector said, "Most believe the temple was not directly under the basilica but somewhere in the front courtyard, perhaps beneath the elephant and the obelisk or in that area. You will need to see if it is possible to excavate from underneath the structure and out into the courtyard. Because it was built upon other ruins, there will be some support for tunneling, but there will also be some instability. It is a wild consideration, but one I would like for us to undertake in addition to identifying and transferring the true relics of the Church."

Goosebumps covered Guiseppe Campise. His heart was pounding all the more. Because the rector had been so entrusting, Guiseppe felt free to ask about his pay, his expenditures, and the laborers needed. Father Ferrua called for his attendant to reenter the office. He let Guiseppe know all this would be taken care of by his chief of staff, but in an almost coded statement, he said, "Any work on my special assignment needs to be initiated by you alone, after hours. I want updates with each step you take."

Guiseppe stood in agreement. It was only then that the rector extended his right hand. Guiseppe returned the gesture. Father Ferrua then warmly overlapped his confidant's hand with his left as one would a special friend. They had known each other for only minutes, but they had contracted on a secret mission. The close circle of archaeologists was all about secrets — contemplating them and pursuing them. The exciting secrets underground truly were the motivation for this tedious occupation. Walking out, Guiseppe offered a silent prayer to the Lord, "Thank you again Father that you let me do this, that you called me to this. I pray you will be glorified in everything I do."

The First Visit to Santa Maria sopra Minerva

As Giuseppe exited the rector's office, he was met by Ferrua's attendant who handed him a large envelope with the papal seal. He was told that everything he needed would be inside. A bank account had been opened in his name with a scant reference to the project. It read, "Campise — Minerva relics." He was told his starting budget had already been deposited. More money would be added as needed. His pay would be directly deposited into his own account. Every receipt must be kept. Expense report sample forms were enclosed along with a flash drive for electronic filing. His credentials were included along with keys to the Santa Maria sopra Minerva. The necessary security codes were enclosed. His identification card was inside with his picture already emblazoned onto it. The floorplan of the basilica was included. His duties were itemized except for the one Father Ferrua communicated only verbally in his hearing. Guiseppe spent the rest of the evening reviewing the files, the history of the basilica, as well as making a rough draft of his strategy to achieve his assignment.

A point of confusion came to the archaeologist as he perused the documents for his task. Identifying the relics was a museum curator's job or that of an auditor. Moving them to the Vatican was an assignment best suited for one of the cardinals. Should any of the caretaking priests of the basilica ask his credentials, they would be surprised to see a man of his profession assigned to such a duty. His only answer would be — archaeologists are trained to handle ancient artifacts with care. Due diligence, patience, and meticulous care to preserve were the vanguards of his field. This would suffice. The secret assignment of the rector was the chief reason why only an archaeologist would be given this chore. A dig from the Santa Maria sopra Minerva to the elephant and obelisk and below required a special skill.

Campise could hardly sleep. He poured over the documents and especially the external and internal footprint of the edifice. About 3 AM, he realized he had given no thought to the relics. He was enamored by the excitement of being the first to possibly uncover the remains of Alexander the Great. Finding the lost diary of Mary Magdalene was an eternity-shaping discovery by Guiseppe. No find would ever match finding the diary of one so close to the Savior which led to the greatest discovery any human can make — meeting and receiving the Son of God into His Life. He knew nothing else would ever compare in significance to that.

From a pure archaeological point of view, nothing would be greater than to find the body of the young and great Alexander. In his mind, Father Ferrua, a famed discoverer in his own right, had no real concern for the relics at all. He wanted Guiseppe to do what he could no longer do himself. Guiseppe's reputation as an inquisitive foreman who gave full allegiance to his employers was the most important credential the rector needed.

Campise tossed and turned for about another half-hour. He decided to give up any attempt to sleep. He got up, drank some coffee, slid on the clothes he had worn the day before, and sleeked off to the Basilica of Santa Maria sopra Minerva. The church opened at 6:55 AM. He felt this was an odd time for opening, why not 7:00 AM or 6:30 AM, but 6:55 AM? He would ask the caretaker when he was comfortable. Arriving at the church, an hour and fifty-five minutes early, he thought of using his key and code, but decided against it. It would be better to be introduced to the priest over the facility, than barge in unannounced with the access he had received.

Giuseppe felt sad at the thought of wasting almost two hours milling around, awaiting the doors to open. But when he reached the courtyard, all concerns for idle time were arrested by the strange elephant statue with the Egyptian obelisk sitting on its back. He looked at the distance between it and the front of the building. He began to calculate the distance and tools needed to tunnel to this statue. The archaeologist began to wonder what was beneath the ground where he stood. He looked up at the elephant. For a minute he felt it looked down at him, gave a wink, and then looked forward and to the right again. It was as if it knew why Guiseppe was there and was willing to assist anyway he could. Goosebumps appeared on his arms again with a sensation that something supernatural was within reach. He felt very similar when he found the clay pot in the old cistern in Magdala.

The past of this place raced through his mind. This was pagan ground. Around 50 BC Roman general Pompey had a temple built on this very site to the Roman goddess Minerva. This was the goddess to whom Alexander the Great attributed his many successes. Alexander's body was initially interred in Memphis, Egypt, then relocated to Alexandria, Egypt. It was there Pompey visited to pay homage.

Many Roman emperors had visited his tomb in Alexandria including Julius Caesar, Caesar Augustus, and Caligula. There was a superstition surrounding the body of Alexander the Great. Many believed whoever visited his tomb would find victory, whoever possessed his cadaver would be unvanquishable forever. References to the body of Alexander the Great and his tomb in Egypt suddenly disappeared from the historical record soon after the Roman Emperor Caracalla, better known as Marcus Aurelius, visited the tomb. It is not a far reach to conjecture that Emperor Caracalla stole the body and moved it to Rome to ensure future success.

Campise began to feel what Father Ferrua felt. The likelihood of this being the site of the great general was compelling. But, why the secret? If Emperor Caracalla felt his dynasty would remain only as long as he held the body, it made sense to conceal the location of the prized relic.

The archaeologist looked up at the obelisk. It was brought to Rome by Emperor Diocletian. Many obelisks were located, in the first century, on these grounds. This one on the elephant's back was dedicated to an Egyptian goddess by none other than Pharaoh Hophra who reigned in Egypt from 589 BC to 570 BC. He challenged Nebuchadnezzar during his reign but was beaten back and defeated as God foretold through the prophet Jeremiah in the forty-fourth chapter:

'This will be the sign to you that I will punish you in this place,' declares the Lord, 'so that you will know that my threats of harm against you will surely stand.' This is what the Lord says: 'I am going to hand Pharaoh Hophra king of Egypt over to his enemies who seek his life, just as I handed Zedekiah king of Judah over to Nebuchadnezzar king of Babylon, the enemy who was seeking his life.'

The elephant was carved around the 1660's. The obelisk was then set upon it to make a statement. The elephant is the strongest of all animals. To the friars of the church, the obelisk represented wisdom. They were placed together in the piazza of the church to state a strong mind supports sure wisdom.

Campise was amused when he walked behind the statue to see the tail of the elephant slightly off center. He had read the sculptor, over an argument with the friars, displaced the tail to mimic the elephant emanating gas toward the office of the church leaders.

The question to be discovered; was this statue located on this spot as a marker for something of greater value below? The Egyptian obelisk could tie the movement of Alexander the Great's remains from Egypt to this spot in Rome. As the obelisk made its journey, so had Alexander. Every restraint was needed to keep

Campise from digging right there in the open. He would not allow himself the luxury. This was to be a covert operation.

Studying the elephant and the obelisk more, he noticed a drainage system ran to the bottom of the monument from the north and the south sides. Draining grates touched both sides of the monument on the brick pavement of the piazza. Guiseppe knelt. He took his hat off, and looked down into the grates to see how deep the sewage system ran. It appeared to be around two meters deep. He began to reason how this could enable an easier dig beneath the monument, especially if he chose to do it from outside the basilica. He would need to get some city approvals, but he felt Father Ferrua could obtain whatever permissions he needed. Again, an outdoor dig would raise questions. If there was drainage below, existing tunnels could be used to access this spot.

As the archaeologist lifted his eyes to look at the elephant. He was struck by the way the trunk of the elephant ran horizontal from its face, northward, then turned a right angle pointing to the sky. The end of the trunk narrowed to a point like that of a finger. This pointy end of the trunk was perfectly in line with the northwest corner of the obelisk, and in perfect alignment with the saddle.

Excitement filled Guiseppe's heart. He looked at the elephant's face again. It seemed to smile at Guiseppe. The elephant was looking toward the north, in the direction of his trunk which was pointing upward. The whole picture was as if the elephant was carved to say, "I have marked the site where the great Greek is buried. The point of my trunk marks the exact center of his tomb beneath me."

He began to question himself. He knew the tendency was to read into the digs whatever one wanted to see. Rationalizing one's task makes the tedium more bearable. Still. Guiseppe's trained eye was discovering solid evidence to justify the secret project.

As Guiseppe faced the façade of the church, he was disappointed. This was an ugly building. That aside, Michaelangelo's magnificent statue of Christ the Redeemer was proudly housed within its walls. This basilica housed three or four popes. He could not remember the number. It held the remains of Saint Catherine of Siena, minus her head. She was an industrious woman who worked relentlessly to reunify the Church during the 1300s. Saint Catherine took the Herculean task upon herself to bring the Catholic Church, being led by two popes in two locations, into one Church with one pope. She never lived to see the fruit of her labor which was realized in 1417 with the election of Pope Martin V, but her contribution resulted in her sainthood and high regard. Guiseppe never knew the church had been divided. Yet, he could relate to Catherine of Siena. He was taking on a Herculean task in the cloak of night. His hope was his efforts would be crowned with success. As one who was accustomed to finding treasure in the unlikeliest of places, he was pacified.

Time flew by as did his thoughts. He heard the deadbolt of the massive doors slide followed by their creak as they were pulled open with great effort. A priest in simple daily clerical attire systematically put the stops in place at their base. Without acknowledging the first guest, he assumed a tourist, he briskly walked to light candles in the entry way. Guiseppe followed close behind. At first the young priest ignored him, but noting he had a relentless follower, he turned in silence half-expecting to be irritated with what would follow. Guiseppe introduced himself, "Father, I am Guiseppe Campise. Father Ferrua has assigned me with the task to secure this church's relics from the dangers seen in Rome of late. I am taking the day to familiarize myself with the grounds. Is this, okay?"

Campise wondered why he asked, "Is this okay?" He had the full authority to be there. Asking if it was okay opened a problem should the priest say, "No. it is not okay." Not far from this contemplation, the young priest responded, "I am not in a position to grant you this right. You are free to walk as a tourist or to pray as a worshipper. Anything beyond this will have to be approved by my supervisor, Father Sullivan."

Guiseppe said, "Very well. Can you take me to Father Sullivan?"

The priest replied, "He is not here. He should arrive sometime this afternoon."

"Very well, I will do my best to not distract or trespass beyond what a normal tourist does", the archaeologist answered.

With that, the young priest left Campise alone to his survey. He was excited to be inside. He was also glad to have arrived early enough to walk the site with few distractions. The style of the church was Gothic. The floors were marble. Each step he took was followed by an echo rolling down the voluminous structure.

The floorplan itself appropriately formed the shape of a cross. From the entrance, he could see the high altar featured at the far end. On each side, there were six smaller chapels to the right, six to the left, with an apse before the high altar extending farther to the right and to the left beyond the six chapels on each side. He decided to take an inventory of the six chapels to the right first, then the apse to the right. The high altar would be the midpoint. He would circle back to analyze the apse to the left, followed by the six chapels to the left, returning to the entrance where he started.

To the right, he saw the first chapel. It was dedicated to the baptism of Jesus. The next three chapels to the right held nothing familiar to Campise. The fifth one was dedicated to the Annunciation of Our Lady, the mother of Jesus. The sixth chapel was a private one originally for the Orsini family. The name was familiar to this tourist, but he was not sure why. The parents of Pope Clement VIII were buried inside as was his brother. Guiseppe was not sure who this pope was. He made a note to research him more.

The next little room had an intriguing painting of Saint Lucy and Saint Agatha. These two women were martyred for their faith. In the painting, Saint Lucy is carrying a platter with her eyes on it. Saint Agatha is carrying a similar platter holding her severed breasts. Guiseppe made note to learn more of these two as well.

Time was passing quickly. There was a small crowd of people walking around the spacious church taking pictures, reading displays, kneeling in different chapels praying. He thought it was a small crowd, but the way the church was laid out, there was no telling how many people were present at any given moment. Most were reverent preventing any break in Guiseppe's thoughts.

To the right of the transept was the Chapel Carafa named after Cardinal Carafa. This was one of several hallowed rooms. Inside this chapel was a key relic Guiseppe was to gather in the days ahead — the arm bone of Saint Thomas Aquinas. Looking to the right, Campise saw the masterpiece, "The Triumph of Thomas Aquinas." The depiction held the tourist spellbound. This was what Campise loved about Rome, the Church, and the Vatican City. The painted, sculpted, and architectural works of art were the best the world had to offer. Everywhere he turned, he was captivated. He was like a kid in a toy store, full of wonder. He spent his life digging long hours, days, weeks, months, and even years. Occasionally, he unearthed things wonderful to behold. In Rome, sights of awe were prevalent.

In "The Triumph of Thomas Aquinas", the famous Italian artist Filippino Lippi depicted Thomas Aquinas passing judgment on two adversaries — one who denied the Deity of Christ, the other denying the Trinity. The good doctor holds a book in the painting which says, "I will destroy the wisdom of the wise." Guiseppe remembered the Scripture which states something like "the wisdom of the world is foolishness to God." Laying prone behind the two adversaries is Satan with the caption, "Wisdom conquers malice." Two young boys are noted in the crowd before the great theologian Aquinas, one is Pope Leo X and the other is his cousin, Pope Clement VII taking note. Guiseppe knew both popes were entombed in this church near Saint Catherine of Siena. The painting was an amazing tie between Saint Thomas Aquinas and the popes. To the left of this work of art is the tomb of Pope Paul IV.

Guiseppe lingered in this room for over an hour. He thought of how Pope Leo X and Pope Clement VII are pictured at the feet of Thomas Aquinas. They were there and not Pope Paul IV because the painting was completed before the latter mentioned had assumed the papacy. Knowing a little history of all three popes, Campise believed they each should have sat at the feet of Thomas Aquinas through studying his works. All three would have benefited greatly from applying those truths expounded by the great doctor to their papal reigns. As a Catholic, and now a Christian, archaeologist Guiseppe knew the best manual for a vicar of Christ is God's Holy Word which served as Aquinas' source material along with creation.

Moving closer to the painting, Guiseppe was a great admirer of this artist. The one painting of Lippi's which Guiseppe loved more than any was that of Lucrezia Borgia, the mysterious, often vilified daughter of the licentious Pope Alexander VI. He had read many books on Lucrezia. Some accused her of murder through a poisonous ring. Others believed she served as pope during her father's illnesses. Her sexual affairs were notorious. Her three marriages were politically arranged to grow wealth and power for her father, for her brother the wicked Cesare, and for herself. The victims of these shenanigans were the three dotes she married, so the stories go.

The rector's protégé had known nothing of Santa Maria sopra Minerva a week ago. Suddenly, he found not only was he familiar with the contents inside, but the persons represented or entombed in this basilica. They were all from a time of great interest to Guiseppe — the Renaissance era. During this time, the papal regimes was filled with nepotism, a thirst for wealth, a quest for power, and a desire to use the church to fulfill selfish desires.

Speaking of nepotism, Pope Leo X was cousin to Pope Clement VII. Both were housed in this lavish structure. Cardinal Carafa was buried in the room adjacent to his nephew Pope Paul IV. Pope Clement X's two relatives were buried in this place. Pope Clement VIII's parents and brother were given extravagant places in this basilica as well. Opulence was given to the clerics and their families far above those of the worshippers and theirs.

Guiseppe could not quit thinking. In just a few hours of touring this place, he realized even this church was filled with contradictions. Two women who sacrificed their lives for the Lord were depicted next to those who sought to profit at all costs. Saint Catherine of Siena who did all she could to unite the church is entombed with men who spent their time tearing the Church apart for their own gain, killing those who got in their way. Then he remembered the name of the church, Santa Maria sopra Minerva. The church bore the name of the pagan goddess. The whole area was filled with pagan temples which were finally destroyed by Pope Zachary in the mid-700s AD. The temples were gone, but the idolatry and debauchery continued for centuries to follow. At times they would be put down. Other times, they would be resurrected.

Sometimes the sinful excesses were replaced by others. Pope Alexander VI, Pope Julius II, Pope Leo X, and Pope Clement VII sought political fiefdoms. They spent extravagantly. The church suffered spiritually. Of these four, only one had a semblance of concern for the things of God, and that was minimally seen in Clement VII. Pope Paul IV sought to undo the extravagances, seeking to emphasize an ascetic life matching that of Christ, along with reforms in the quest for renewed orthodoxy. Unfortunately, his methods were harsh. As a result, he continued the papal abuses but for the opposite reason. And he villainized the Jewish people, ostracizing them from the community of Christians, forcing them to wear identifying badges to denote their race.

The state of Ferrara under Lucrezia's husband's reign embraced the Jewish people. His father before him nurtured this love for the Jewish people when other states forced them to leave. In Ferrara, Christians coexisted harmoniously together with their Jewish neighbors. When under attack, the Jewish people did all they could to defend their state. Guiseppe came back full circle to ask a question, "Why am I really here?" He had the stated assignment to secure the relics from this place. He knew the true purpose was to try and find the tomb of Alexander the Great. But there seemed to be a deeper reason for his being there. God works all things for our good. He would search for the purpose God intended.

Going to the next chapel called the Capella Altieri, Guiseppe found the tomb of bishop Guilauma Durand. He had never heard of the man before, but as a first-time visitor himself, he quickly found a reference guide to this person's life. Bishop

Durand was an advisor to several popes in the late 1200s, teaching them canon law and its application which enabled them to better guide the church. What caught the archaeologist's attention was Durand was rewarded the governorship over Romagna. His territory came under attack on several occasions. Sometimes he defended it with diplomacy. Other times, he and his citizens were required to take up arms.

Romagna would later become a state conquered by Cesare Borgia, Lucrezia's brother. After his acquisition, Cesare defended Romagna from outside attack through arms and brutal violence. He felt diplomacy was useless when arms and chicanery were available. The region was productive in many aspects but poorly organized until Cesare took it over. Alfonso d'Este never liked his brother-in-law, but he respected how Cesare could administrate, the one virtuous gift he inherited from his father, Pope Alexander VI. Administration was also the valuable trait Lucrezia learned from her father which helped her protect Ferrara as duchess when Alfonso was away. Again, Guiseppe felt he had entered the world of Borgia for some Divine reason.

As he walked out of the Capella, a strange excitement consumed him. The tourist Guiseppe saw the high altar of the basilica. Approaching the climax, the featured attraction, he stopped to admire the statue of Saint John the Baptist. He was delighted to find the sculptor bore his first name, Guiseppe Obici. To the left of the statue, but at the center of the altar, lay the shrine of Saint Catherine Siena, the patron of Italy and the co-patron of Europe. Encased in a gilded metal box with arches like windows, was the marble vault encasing her body. The vault was lit. The carving of the vault was done by another Guiseppe, Guiseppe Fontana. Campise was surprised how many Guiseppe's were tied to this shrine. He had the feeling again this was meant for him.

There were cushions on the step leading up to the memorial. Guiseppe Campise could not help but sit and think. The vault was carved into the likeness of Saint Catherine as she would have appeared laying on the funeral bier, her head on a marble pillow. Every detail of her face was represented. He felt as though he had been transported back to 1380. He tried to imagine the people coming by to pay homage to this solitary figure who championed the unity of the church. She died at the prime age of thirty-three. Her last words were those of the Lord, "Father into Your Hands, I commit my soul and my spirit." The tourist could not look away. He felt a deep love for this sainted lady. He asked, "Why couldn't her spirit of sacrifice and piety be instilled into the popes and religious leaders of that day?"

An immediate, "Shhhh" was heard. He looked to see the young priest who had opened the doors that morning walking by just as he spoke. Guiseppe did not intend to say those words out loud, but in the emotional moment, he forgot he was not alone in this church. Tourists were everywhere. He was one of perhaps several hundred. There was a lady next to him before the relic, on her knees praying to this saint. The rest of the tourists seemed to be there for the architectural beauty.

As he walked behind Catherine's vault, he found more people kneeling, writing down their prayer requests. They then inserted the little pieces of paper into an opening at the back of her vault which floated down to rest upon the marble likeness of her body. They waited for their longings to rest upon her, then prepared themselves to wait a little longer with the hope she would receive their prayers and lift them to the Savior on their behalf. They would then solemnly move backwards still on their knees with their faces fixed on her to resume their desperate yearnings on the cushion from where they started.

Though this was a house of prayer, few were there to pray. Campise was saddened of how many of the churches in Rome had devolved from houses of prayer to sites to see. He had no idea the thoughts of those all around. He wished he could hear what each was thinking, to engage them, to answer, to correct, or to speak of God. He wished to know where they fell on the spectrum of belief. On the left end would be those of no interest in the things of God. On the right end would be those who were devout lovers of God. At the midpoint of the scale, he imagined would be those who were merely inquisitive.

Beyond the high altar was the choir loft made of a deep brown wood. Above the choir were three pairs of stained-glass windows They were fabulous. The left set featured the preacher and friar Father Vincent Ferrer and the martyr Stephen from the Bible Book of Acts. Guiseppe found the pairing curious. He sat in one of the choir chairs, gazing upward, his right hand on his chin. Stephen was well known to him. He had been stoned for preaching to the Pharisees that Jesus was the Messiah. He was stoned while Saul, the future Apostle Paul, held the assailants' garments. Many believe Saul was the ringleader to Stephen's execution.

But why would Father Ferrer be pictured with Stephen? He lived in the mid-fourteenth century. He was known as a missionary and a logician. He had worked with Saint Catherine of Siena who lay below his stained-glass. Together, they worked to end the schism of the Catholic Church, seeing their work rewarded with the election of the unified pope, Martin V. It made sense for him to be featured in the basilica with Saint Catherine. They had labored hand in hand to rescue the Catholic Church which had been self-destructing.

But why with Stephen? As the archaeologist thought, he remembered Father Ferrer had a two-fold task concerning the Jewish people. His first concern was to stop their persecution. His second was to tell them of the Messiah, Jesus. As a gifted preacher, he led many to receive Jesus as their Savior, the fulfillment of the prophecies found in the Old Testament. It all made sense! Stephen died trying to convince the Pharisees of the truth of Christ. Father Ferrer carried on his work until the day he died. A great appreciation swept over Guiseppe for the features of this church.

To the right of the center stained-glass couplet, was another depicting Catherine of Alexandria and Catherine of Siena. Catherine of Alexandria was a young girl from Alexandria who was the daughter of the governor. She had a vision of Christ and made Him her Lord and Savior. She began to lead many to convert to Christianity. Roman Emperor Maxentius objected to the impact the teenage girl was having. He had her arrested and tortured to try to dissuade her. During her imprisonment, his own wife converted. In anger, he had her beheaded at the age of eighteen.

The center couplet was of Saint Dominic, the founder of the Dominican order and Pope Pius V. Two men who fell far short of the people represented to their left and right.

The giant papal monument of Pope Leo X to the left of the high altar needed to be studied. Speaking of the religious spectrum, Guiseppe would put Saint Catherine on the far right of the spectrum, labeled devout lover of God. To the far left, he believed Leo X would register — no interest at all in God. How could this be? The vicar of Christ, the representative of God's Son, had no interest in Father or Son? He led the church. He issued papal bulls. He was to intercede for the worshippers around the world. How could he pray to the One in whom he did not believe? Campise was sick to his stomach.

Again, the archaeologist recalled his studies of the Borgia family. Cardinal Rodrigo Borgia became the most powerful cardinal in his day up until he ascended to the chair of pope. He had multiple lovers, many illegitimate children, more scandals, matched only by the wealth and lands he took. Deaths followed everywhere he went, most at the hands of his son Cesare. Many said the former Rodrigo Borgia, the Spanish Pope Alexander VI, was good for the Church from a secular viewpoint. He increased the reach of the church. But as a spiritual leader, he was absent any capacity to lead in matters of Christ. Some said he had cut a deal with the devil to assume this lucrative position. His primary successor was Pope Julius II who was as evil as Alexander, and more warring.

When Julius II died, Cardinal Giovanni de Medici was selected with the hope he would bring peace. De Medici took the name Pope Leo X. He chose expansion like the ones before. His life intersected with Lucrezia Borgia on several occasions, but mainly through the governance of Ferrara and her husband Alfonso d'Este. At one point in the church war for control of the various states, Cardinal Giovanni de Medici was captured near Ferrara. Duke Alfonso d'Este could have placed him in the lowest dungeon or required his life. Instead, the cardinal was treated with respect and honor. Once he attained the highest position of pope, instead of rewarding Duke Alfonso for his mercy, Pope Leo X sought to take the dukedom from d'Este and give it as a favor to a family member. Thankfully, Pope Leo X never succeeded.

Over the term of Pope Leo X's papacy, he spent extravagantly. He drove the church to such debt that there was no money even for candles for his funeral. Candles were borrowed from other recent funerals. The tapestries were pawned to raise the money for a humble ceremony. He was then buried in a simple brick grave in Saint Peter's. Later, in the mid-1500's, money was raised to build an appropriate tomb for the pope in Santa Maria sopra Minerva.

Guiseppe, knowing the history, looked up at the monument to this unbelieving pope. Leo X is featured in the center. The apostle Peter is to the left, apostle Paul to right. Above the pope is a carving of him and Francis I of France. To the left is the baptism of Jesus. To the right is the miracle of Saint Julian. The tourist remembered a children's book of games as he looked up at the monument. The child's game was to choose what figure did not belong on a page — a cat, a dog, an elephant, or a candlestick. A child would delight to say, "The candlestick does not belong!" Looking at the pictures of past saints, Pope Leo X did not belong on his own memorial.

Walking to his right, the tourist marveled that the monument to Pope Clement VII was closely aligned with that of Leo X. In the center is the likeness of the pope.

To the left is the apostle Peter, to the right apostle Paul. Above him is the coronation of Charles V, the highly successful Holy Roman Emperor. To the left is a relief of Saint Benedict and Totila, representing a famous history of discernment. To the right is the relief of the battle with the Turks. The history represented on Clement VII was invigorating to this archaeologist, but he had no time to relish this portion of the past. He had a job to do.

Guiseppe looked down to pray. When he opened his eyes, he noticed several memorial slabs under which various notable people of the church were entombed. The tourist was shocked to see the slab directly in front of him. It bore the name and the body of the poet Pietro Bembo who died in 1547. The hair stood on the back of the tourist's neck. This was the first real lover of Lucrezia Borgia. He had read many of their written exchanges which Lord Byron said were the "prettiest love letters in the world."

The archaeologist wanted to know how all this could be He was randomly called by the rector, Father Ferrua, for a task of unearthing the body of Alexander the Great. The site would be the Santa Maria sopra Minerva, a church he had never heard of before his meeting. Like a man driving at a high speed on a major highway lined with trees which whisk by, historical character after historical character were racing by Guiseppe's eyes and mind from his favorite portion of church history.

Pietra Bembo was a known womanizer, but he finally found true love in the wife of another man, the Duke of Ferrara. Pietro risked much to be the lover of the Dutchess d'Este. Some say his father ultimately had him move from the state of Ferrara to prevent a midnight encounter with an assassin sent by the duke or from his wife's brother Cesare who had threatened her first husband and killed her second. Bembo adhered to his father's wisdom.

Time passed, Bembo became the secretary to Pope Leo X. It was while serving this pope that Lucrezia died at the age of thirty-nine. "So, this is the man who bedded Lucrezia Borgia, who wrote of her love and her beauty. This is the man who always seemed to be in the city of Ferrara when Lucrezia's husband was away on state business. This is the Bembo who received Lucrezia's nursing when he was sick, the lover for whom she wore his favorite dresses at state functions as a secret display to him of her steadfast love", the tourist mused. Two feet below him was the consort of Pope Alexander's favorite illegitimate daughter. Bembo was buried beneath Pope Leo X, his superior. In life and in death, the poetic romantic never reached prominence or real love because his fleshly frailties stunted his ascent.

Campise did not want to move from this spot, but he needed to finish his survey before the church closed. Afterward, he planned on returning with an instrument to look for secret passages beneath the floor and the walls. As he walked slowly from the high altar, he saw the famous statue by Michelangelo, "The Risen Christ", which he carved from one block of white marble. The feature of the church was Saint Catherine of Siena. Prayers were offered to her, but most adoration was reserved for this statue of Christ. Worship was offered only to the specimen of the art, the Lord and Savior Jesus Christ, God's Only Son

Guiseppe had a hard time taking in the beauty of this masterpiece as people took turns falling to kiss the Jesus statue's right foot. As one person moved aside for the next person, he noticed the bronze modesty cloth on the white marble statue. The tourist remembered what he had read the night before. Originally, Michelangelo sculpted Christ completely nude. Within a short time, the church leaders realized this was inappropriate. The phallus was removed and replaced with the modesty cloth.

Looking down, he saw the right foot of the Lord. The toe closest to the big toe was cracked with what appeared to be from erosion. He realized why as he saw one worshipper after another wet the statue with their acts of devotion. The kisses of worshippers upon the holy foot of Christ had taken their toll over the years. There had been a bronze sandal placed over this foot for a few decades, but it was ultimately removed for reasons unknown.

Again, the archaeologist bowed his head in gratitude. "The Risen Christ" statue included the Cross, the sponge, and the reed that held the sponge. Victorious was His resurrection. Guiseppe pondered as he watched pilgrims fall before the representation of Christ, "This whole city, the entire Roman empire was changed because one historic man from a small part of the empire lived a perfect life, died a sinner's death, was buried in a rich man's tomb with mourning heard late that Friday night into the early Saturday morning which followed. Many carried Jesus' blood stains on their clothing. Two smelled of myrrh which was applied to embalm His body. Women watched in inconsolable grief as the man they followed, the miracle worker they witnessed, was entombed. They thought He would never be seen again. There would be no churches had nothing happened on the third day, just regret, a footnote to history."

Guiseppe thought of the places he had dug for Fathers Corbo and Loffreda. He had seen mosques. He was reverent near Buddhist temples. He dug with men who had no belief in anything but themselves. He worked side by side with men who believed in every superstition imaginable. The archaeologist thought of how these false religions would be all which dotted the landscape, had something not happened over 2,000 years ago. The Risen Christ appeared. There was no other way to explain the spread of Christianity, the rise of churches, the beautiful contributions made by the followers of this risen one.

Guiseppe looked back to the high altar. He believed the more perfect place for this statue was front and center as the high altar. But the Risen Christ had been pushed to the side in this world, taken for granted. Pope Leo X pushed Him aside. Pope Alexander VI demanded the glory for himself. Lucrezia's father was the one who demanded his feet be kissed. They were kissed by Lucrezia along with every consort he could wrangle into his papal harem. Pope Julius II cursed, killed, and demanded loyalty only to himself. His heretical belief, "Let the Scripture be annulled. My word is what matters."

The archaeologist on assignment was sidetracked. His stated mission was to inventory and move the relics. The true mission was to find a way to dig underneath the elephant and the obelisk in the Minerva piazza. Ever since his encounter with the Risen Christ in Magdala, everything he engaged in took on deep meaning. He shook his head. He could chase down these thoughts when his work was finished.

The tourist moved past the tomb of the patron saint of artists, Father Angelico. Coming to the Capella Frangipane, he stopped when he read this chapel was dedicated to Saint Mary Magdalene. Had it not been for the discovery of her diary, Campise's name would not be written in Heaven, nor would he have been given this assignment. He moved on with gratitude and a quick bow of his head. At the Sacristy, he gazed upon a sculpture of Mary Magdalene. He continued his walk with a sweet fondness for the lady.

At the Chapel of Saint Dominic, he stumbled upon the tomb of another pope, one who had not been listed in his reading of the history of this basilica, Pope Benedict XIII. Leaning on his sarcophagus are two ladies. Thinking back to Pope Alexander VI, he chuckled thinking these might be two of his consorts. Instead, the tourist was delighted to see one of the ladies represented Purity. The other represented Religion. Planning to do more research on this pope, he hoped the display was not revised history.

The next to last thing Guiseppe noticed of significance was outside the Chapel of Saint Pius V. There was a memorial there to a nun by the name of Sister Maria Raggi. She had once been married but the Ottoman Empire killed her beloved husband. In grief, she fled to Rome where she became a nun. She was known throughout the city as the epitome of holiness. Some nuns were noted for the stigmata. Sister Maria Raggi was revered for a glow upon her face, reminiscent of Moses after seeing God. She walked with God. Her face showed it. She gave her life for the cause of Christ.

The words of Jesus suddenly began to echo in his mind as the steps of tourists echoed throughout the basilica, "If anyone would come after me, he must deny himself and take up his cross and follow me. For whoever wants to save his life will lose it, but whoever loses his life for my sake will find it. What good will it be for a man if he gains the whole world, yet forfeits his soul?" So many of these church leaders lived to gain the whole world. How many lost their souls? Yet there were many others entombed in this church and beyond who followed Christ, took up their crosses, and lost their lives just to find better ones which followed within Heaven's gates. Guiseppe sought to be found in the number of this latter group.

The last thing this tourist found tickled him with joy. In the Chapel of John the Baptist, a lady named Giulia Naro is entombed. She had the tomb designed and etched before her death. Then she died. The front of her tomb reads her name, her birthdate, but no death date. Her birth was in 1543. The current date was 1981. There was no way she was still alive on this earth. At her death, the family gathered, buried her, and gave her not another thought. Obviously, no one came to visit, or those who did, assumed someone else was having her final date etched soon. They passed like she passed. No concluding date was recorded for her life.

This was exactly a thought Guiseppe had for his own grave. He had purchased property for his and his wife's burial but had not yet purchased a monument. In visiting with his wife about what the memorial would look like and what it would say, he spoke of leaving the death date off. Those in Christ never die. They simply graduate to Heaven. Maybe Ms. Naro's date was not forgotten at all. Perhaps her family sought to make a statement — to be absent from the body is to be present with the Lord. All this was made possible by the Risen Christ.

The doors of the basilica were being closed. The young priest saw Guiseppe lingering. He was asked to leave, but Guiseppe showed him his credentials. He would be leaving to get some equipment and would soon return to do some work into the night. He asked if Father Sullivan had been in. The young priest said he had, but he neglected to let his supervisor know the man sent from the Pontifical Commission for Sacred Archaeology had requested an introduction. Guiseppe showed his credentials again to the young priest along with his key and the codes. The priest shrugged, "Do what you want. I am going home. Please don't let anyone in. And turn the lights off when you leave. Do not answer the door."

Guiseppe assured the priest he would honor this sacred place. He wanted to tell the priest of all his digs, of all the valuable artifacts he had handled, of the lost diary of Mary Magdalene, but that would be self-serving. Plus, the young priest turned to walk away. The conversation ended for him with "Do not answer the door."

The Night Search

It was 10 PM before Guiseppe returned to the basilica. He brought with him a new generation Ground Penetrating Radar (GPR) device which was experimental. His hopes were it would reveal any tunnels or vacuums below the church floor. Over the years, he was sure this structure like many in Rome was built upon previous ancient structures. If this was the case, there might be an opening leading from the church to the statue in the piazza allowing an unseen dig in search of the body of Alexander the Great.

Within an hour, he found what he was looking for. Moving the chairs for worshippers, he was able to find a void running from the high altar of the church to the front door. Opening the huge doors, Guiseppe prayed the piazza would be empty of people. He needed a little time to run the GPR from the door to the elephant statue to check for a continuation of the tunnel beneath. A young couple was walking in the moonlight at the far end of the plaza. He walked out, without his device, toward them. He gained the effect for which he hoped. The couple moved on down a side street, out of view. With their exit, the archaeologist rolled out the GPR. He was pleased to see the void beneath ran all the way to the statue.

Curious, he ran the device past the statue, in line with the church doors and the statue. The empty space extended beyond. It had a width of approximately one meter. The void continued in a straight line past the elephant and then terminated at a T on the west side, going to the right and left but not straight ahead. Guiseppe turned back toward the church. He was able to do his work unnoticed. He found his readings were consistent in his return. He rolled the Ground Penetrating Radar device back through the front doors, closing and locking them behind him. He then rolled it down the center aisle until he reached the tomb of Catherine of Siena. He rolled it around her, up a step, and proceeded to the back of the altar. The tunnel of some sort was there as well.

The archaeologist pulled diagrams from Rome's Metro which marked Rome's ancient underground components. Notations were made of an ancient sewage system as well as the oldest aqueduct ever found in Rome. Based on the documentation, Guiseppe surmised the tunnel running under the church was of the Cloaca Maxima, or the great sewer of Rome. Feeling there were pillars beneath the structure remaining from past buildings pagan, civic, and Christian, he believed there would be supports to dig beneath without fear of collapse. Making his notations, he prepared a report to inform the rector of his findings.

The next thing Guiseppe would need to decide was, where best to begin his dig. It made sense to dig on the ground beyond the front doors, but this would inhibit tourism and worship. Such an excavation would also raise questions which would demand answers from city leaders, religious leaders, and reporters. To dig inside the front entrance would not work either. The best answer he felt was to begin his dig in the back of the building near the loft between the memorials to Pope Leo X and Pope Clement VII.

Going back to the high altar with the GPR, he found an opening between the altar, the sewage tunnel, and the monument to Pope Leo X. With a wall scanner, Guiseppe found a cavity existed to the left of the monument, between it and the huge pillar which supported the roof over the altar. He figured he could cut into the wall, connect to the void beneath, and reach the ancient sewage tunnel running perpendicular from the center of the high altar. Once he was able to bore a hole into the sewage tunnel, he could follow it out to the courtyard. From there, he would see how best to plumb the depths below the statue in search of a tomb, hoping it to be that of the great conqueror. Once again, he made his notes for Father Ferrua. What Guiseppe was proposing would need approvals. If Ferrua was as close to the pope as thought, his permission would pass every objection. By 2 AM, Campise was finished for the night. Excited, he lugged his equipment back to his apartment which the rector had provided. All would begin with approvals granted. He hoped they would come in quick order.

Presentation of First Thoughts

Making his way to the rector's office to submit his work, Guiseppe was surprised to arrive at the office at the very same time as Father Ferrua. Before Guiseppe could greet the man, Ferrua said, "Come with me. I want to hear what you have found." Guiseppe followed.

Father Ferrua greeted his assistant and secretary. He then asked for he and his guest to not be disturbed. Entering the spacious office again, Campise did not feel as apprehensive. He belonged there. He was on assignment. Ferrua knew him by name.

As the door closed, Ferrua asked Campise had he come to any thoughts after one day. Guiseppe was excited to share. His insights poured out with no effort at all. He let the Father know of his survey of the relics and what would be necessary for their temporary removal. Impatiently, Father Ferrua said, "And, what about my personal request?"

Campise was glad to answer this. He let the rector know there was what appeared to be an ancient sewage tunnel which ran from the altar to the statue and beyond. He shared how he could begin excavation from Pope Leo X's tomb, go through what appeared to be an underground shaft from some type of third century construction. He could bore into the tunnel, and if everything worked right, crawl to the space below the statue. From there, Guiseppe could determine what was needed next. In a perfect world, the tunnel sat a few feet above the tomb of history's Alexander. If not, he would decide how to proceed with his GPR and some delicately executed discovery digs.

A smile broke across Father Ferrua's face. He obviously had not smiled much in his life. The look seemed foreign to his countenance. Campise believed visions of another find like Saint Peter's body were in the offing. If so, Father Ferrua and Guiseppe Campise would be the noted archaeologists adding to Ferrua's legacy and Campise's reputation.

"What's that in your hand?", Father Ferrua asked.

"These are the written notes which I have shared. They are accompanied with a request for permission to do what I have laid out."

Ferrua took the envelope from his new employee's hand. He quickly signed each page. Placing them back into the envelope, he handed the paperwork back to Campise with the statement, "You have your permission. Go to work. Requisition whatever you need along with workers. I will let the overseer of Santa Maria know I have approved your digging. I will not tell him why. You are not to tell anyone why. The discovery of the sewage tunnel and voids beneath are enough to explain the work. With Rome Metro looking to expand, due diligence to protect ancient artifacts and the stability of the building justifies the work. Keep me posted."

Father Ferrua looked down at his desk to begin going through the duties awaiting. Campise left with a smile. He never realized such a task would be this easy.

The Second Day of work at Santa Maria sopra Minerva

Guiseppe took a few days to gather the supplies he needed both for labeling, preparing, and transporting the relics as well as his night work of digging down from Pope Leo X's tomb toward what he hoped would be Alexander the Great's final resting place. Seeking to be frugal, he decided to initially hire two men to help with mission number one. He knew he had a blank check from the rector, but often people do not mean what they say, especially if the results do not warrant the expense. Guiseppe was not going to come out of this venture owing the Vatican money.

The archaeologist had worked with Leonardo Accardi alongside Father Corbo a few years back. He was delighted to find Accardi in between jobs, living in Sicily. After a quick call, Leonardo was on the train headed for Rome. He arrived 36 hours later, ready for work. While waiting for Leonardo's arrival, Guiseppe went to Father Ferrua's attendant for a recommendation. The rector had been pleased with the work of Federico Bandoni. It just so happened Bandoni was in the building next door. The archaeologist made his way over. Bandoni was ensconced in paperwork. When given the opportunity to do what he loved, he threw the paperwork in a packed drawer with more paperwork, grabbed his hat, and asked, "Can we start today?" Guiseppe was pleased. He let his new friend know they would start in two days, once Leonardo arrived and was settled in. Bandoni dejected, took his hat off, opened his drawer to resume his paperwork. He let Guiseppe know he would be ready the minute he was called.

On a Thursday morning after a nice time of getting acquainted over a hot cup of coffee, Guiseppe, Leonardo, and Federico made their way to the basilica. Inside, the new hires were in awe of the grandeur of the place. They especially loved the blue ceiling with stars giving them a feeling that Heaven was right above them. After a few moments of admiration, their foreman gave them the list of relics he had itemized. He asked them to go through the basilica on their own to confirm his list, as well as document how best to move them. Guiseppe let them know he was going to do some work around one of the pope's monuments at the high altar. He said they would perhaps be digging there in the days ahead as the Rome Metro was planning on expanding one of their underground lines. He was not comfortable telling them about the excavations for Alexander the Great. He knew Leonardo well enough, but it had been a few years. People change. As for Federico, he was not sure if the rector had confided the secret mission with him. He decided to wait until the relics were ready for removal before being more transparent.

The men went to work. Guiseppe knew it would take them the rest of the day to complete their task, and perhaps another to lay out the strategy. This gave him time to work on his own. He began his work to cordon off the area of his dig. Materials for a blue curtain wall barrier were brought in around 11 AM that morning. The two assistants helped Guiseppe construct the barrier. He then sent them back to do their work. Leonardo and Federico worked very well together. Guiseppe thanked the Lord for bringing the best two men to help.

With his work shielded from view, Campise brought in his GPR device to again locate the void near Leo X's monument and his wall scanner to determine the cavity behind the wall. Following the GPR to the area of the cavity below, he noticed a memorial slab adjacent to the part of the wall with the cavity. The memorial had no name on it. It sat catacorner, a few meters from the Bembo burial. There was a void where a body was to be placed. This was not unusual, but being up against the place where the wall had an opening seemed strange. Cutting into the wall and digging down through the floor afterward was not a task the archaeologist looked forward to doing, especially if there was electrical wiring behind the face of the wall. He thought, what if that memorial slab is an opening to the tunnel below?

With a mason's hammer and cold chisel, Guiseppe decided to free the slab from the ancient mortar but save its removal to when his cohorts had gone to their hotel rooms. The work was surprisingly quickly done. The only thing he needed was to lift the slab. He sent for his portable A-frame hoist which he would use later that evening. It was delivered within the hour. Guiseppe looked to find Leonardo and Federico. They paid him no attention. They were entranced in their work. As archaeological professionals, they took their assigned task very seriously, with the utmost concern to do no damage to the relics when the work began. This caution took careful planning. Again, Guiseppe was thankful he had been led to the right men.

The Night at the Basilica

At 6 PM, Guiseppe had a meeting with his two helpers. They did their work in record time. They estimated the planning could be completed within two more days without any unforeseen complications. The relics could be made ready to move within six weeks. The duration for the move of all the noted items would take approximately four more weeks with no unexpected surprises. They all said in harmony, "There are always unexpected surprises." The three of them began to laugh. Leonardo and Federico let their foreman know these were preliminary estimates at best. They would know more hopefully in two days.

The men were complimented for their work. The three exited the church. Guiseppe locked the door behind them. They set out for supper — the best pizza in the world. They never tired of eating pizza when within the confines of Rome. Perhaps it was the air, or the water, but there was something exquisite about pizza in this hallowed city. After their meal, Leonardo and Federico headed for their hotel. Guiseppe made like he was going straight to his apartment for rest. They planned to meet back at the coffee shop at 7 AM before another day's work.

Bidding the other two goodbye, Guiseppe took a circuitous route around his apartment back to the basilica to begin his secret mission. At 10 PM, Guiseppe found the Minerva piazza with few pedestrians. He took his key, unlocked the massive doors. He was shocked when a hand touched his shoulder. He worked around dead things every day, but he never got past the thought one might come back to life while he was working. Turning quickly, he saw an elderly man, not far from the grave himself. His name was Father Sullivan, the caretaker of the facility and the convent next door.

Sullivan chuckled at the trembling archaeologist, "Forgive my laughter. I love to see people startled in this place. It never gets old. Father Ferrua has told me of your work. I want to thank you for doing what you can to ensure the Rome Metro does not damage our structure. Also, I appreciate the care you are taking to move our relics to protect them from any attacks during these chaotic days. I pray they are not gone too long. Thankfully, after their relocation, no one touring will be able to tell they are not here."

Guiseppe held out his hand to shake Father Sullivan's. He assured him, every care would be taken. In the back of his mind, he wondered, if the priest was going to be in the basilica much longer. If so, he would have to do his dig another day. Thankfully, his concern was answered when Father Sullivan said he was heading home, "Don't work too late, but thank you for working so late. I admire that in a man. I will report this back to Father Ferrua so he will know he has a diligent hire. God bless you Sir."

The archaeologist milled around the basilica until he was certain the caretaker had left. Moving behind his screen, he pulled the A-frame hoist over the empty memorial slab. Freeing the remaining mortar away, he attached the metal line by the rubber clasps to the slab. As he cranked the hoist, the slab pulled back for a moment before releasing and rising upward.

To his surprise, and in answer to his prayer, there was nothing below the slab, not a crypt, not a vault, nothing but a deep tunnel which his GPR had detected. Guiseppe was ecstatic. Excitement filled every ounce of his being. He felt like he did the day he first removed the lid from the clay pot discovered at Magdala. This was the part the archaeologist loved. He grabbed a flashlight to look inside. There was a room immediately beneath the high altar, perhaps fifteen meters deep. He would need a tall ladder to drop into the hole. A ladder was the one thing he had not anticipated needing. He scurried through the basilica hoping to find one. He did not want to leave the church to look, and he was certain there were no businesses open for him to make the needed purchase.

After about a half hour, he found a janitor's closet. To his delight, there was a tall ladder inside. He wrestled the thing back to the hole behind the screen. He lowered it down and grabbed his flashlight again. His adventure was about to begin.

Once below, he saw a sarcophagus directly below Pope Leo X's monument. Etched in the costly material was his name. He had assumed the body of the pope was within the memorial, not beneath it. Curiosity made him want to open the tomb to see if the pope was inside. Respect outweighing his adventurous desire, he chose to leave it be. Looking in the opposite direction, he saw a one meter tall, one-meter-wide tunnel going toward the middle of the high altar. It appeared to branch to the right toward the front door and the elephant statue. His GPR seemed correct. Pulling the ladder away from the hole, he moved it to the tunnel which was three meters higher than the floor of the room below.

With flashlight in hand, Guiseppe began the crawl he hoped would terminate at the tomb of Alexander the Great. Making his turn to the front of the building, rats scurried through the ancient sewer system. He hated rats. Unnerved, he paused to gather his wits. Once they had run in the direction he was going, he continued his journey through the tunnel, grateful for the direction it ran.

About halfway to what he believed was the front of the church, he felt a slight tremor. Rome has historically been a place of frequent tremor activity. His prayer was this was not a foreshock to a major earthquake. Everything settled. Guiseppe continued his journey, but another tremor hit, this time harder and lasting longer. The archaeologist began to question whether he should continue. In his mental debate, he thought of how angry he would be to quit for the night, return to his apartment to find no further shifting activity. Such a premature retreat would have wasted a night. His anticipation of what he would find trumped any cautions he had. He began to crawl forward.

Making his way to what he calculated to be the front of the church, a big tremor hit. There was no debate. He scurried backward as fast as he could. Moving backward was more painstaking, then the move forward. His heart was racing. He was cutting himself, ripping his clothing, but he needed to get out. No one knew he was under the church if the worst occurred.

Reaching the high altar where the tunnel cut back to Pope Leo X's tomb, a devastating quake hit. Dust filled the ancient sewage followed by loud sounds of collapse. Guiseppe jumped from the tunnel into the big room beneath with a cloud of debris behind him, almost propelling him to the floor of the room below. His right arm was injured. As he writhed in pain, a deafening bang followed. All light went out. He had dropped his flashlight in his fall. It went out with the impact. Feeling around in the dark, he found it. He clicked it off, then on with his left hand. Nothing happened. He hit it against his thigh. To his relief, it came back on. Pointing up, he saw the memorial slab had been released from the A-frame hoist and fell perfectly back in place over the hole.

Guiseppe had a slight panic. At first, he feared he would run out of air, but realized the rats he had seen gave him some hope there was porous ventilation. But what if another quake hit, what's to say the whole room does not fully collapse on him? He moved the ladder hoping to move the memorial slab. Pressing his left shoulder from the ladder's rung, the slab would not budge. Its weight, he estimated, could be anywhere from 136 kilograms to 452 kilograms, from 300 to 1,000 pounds. Depending on the movement of the basilica floor, the memorial slab could have been jammed in place. He had no cell phone. He never liked carrying anything in his pockets when doing his job. He had no watch. And no one knew he was down there.

The trapped archaeologist began to wonder. What if the two men meet in the morning to find Guiseppe absent? Would they assume he was sick and go back to their hotel? No. Leonardo knew Guiseppe well enough to call his cell. If he did not reach him, he would continue to try. Best case scenario, Leonardo would assume Guiseppe was back at the church working. They had no idea where his apartment was. Only Federico knew Father Ferrua. He might give his office a call. The truth was, only Father Ferrua would know Guiseppe's secret mission, and night work.

The trapped man prayed. Two hours passed. No more tremors. Guiseppe decided to look around at the damage below. The sewage tunnel was completely collapsed. He was so thankful he had gotten out before the cave-in. A second longer, Guiseppe Campise would have been buried alive except for the Grace of God. Gratitude filled his heart. Yes, he was afraid, but compared to what could have been his fate, he had a good chance to survive this geologic incident. Were others hurt above? He had no idea. Did the church structure survive? He was reasonably sure it did. His right arm was bleeding. He sensed a slight swelling, but nothing serious.

There was comfort Father Sullivan had seen him in the basilica before he left for the night. Surely, he would notice the tools. But wait, the screen Campise constructed hid any sign of tools or activity. Just then, Campise remembered a verse he loved, Isaiah 41:10, "So do not fear, for I am with you; do not be dismayed, for I am your God. I will strengthen you and help you; I will uphold you with my righteous right hand." If ever there was a time to remember a verse, it was then. Campise thanked the Lord for His watchful care.

As a strange peace swept over him, Campise decided to see what he could find in the room of his temporary imprisonment. He shined the light back from the collapsed tunnel to the memorial slab ceiling, then toward the sarcophagus of Pope Leo X. To his surprise, the lid had been moved slightly from the body of the burial container. He had been respectful not to try removing the lid earlier. The earthquake had moved the lid for him. Moving toward it, with bleeding hands and arms wiped clean on his clothing, he turned the flashlight to peek inside. Guiseppe saw an old dusty coffin. The lid to the coffin was slightly open. He laid the flashlight on top of the lid and pushed as hard as he could with his left shoulder. The grinding screech of stone moving over stone put his teeth on edge, but he was successful in unveiling the contents inside.

Traditionally popes were buried in three coffins — one of cypress, one of lead, and one of walnut. Leo X was buried in one of cypress only. Guiseppe wondered why, but then remembered this pope had drained the papal treasury. Candles had to be borrowed, tapestries pawned for his burial.

The skeleton of Pope Leo X bore the papal tiara upon his skull. His remains were dressed in his papal robes with the red chasuble. Yes, the relic was there if this pope was worthy to be called that. Leo was not worthy in Guiseppe's opinion. On his right boned finger was the fisherman's ring. A tube was tucked by his side with, what Guiseppe assumed, was a list of his accomplishments as pope.

Everything he saw was according to tradition, but one thing. Beneath his right hand was a book of sort. At first, he thought it was the Bible. But it was too small, too rudimentary to be a Bible from what he saw. He wanted to pull it from the pope's clutches but argued with himself not to. He pulled the ladder toward him, sitting on the fourth rung to think. Having lived in the late 1400s and to early 1500s, Guiseppe could not believe he was actually looking at the body of this pope from so long ago. A historical figure lay right before his eyes, at least what was left of him.

Thankful he was not claustrophobic, the archaeologist looked for a way out. Digging with his hands, he hoped perhaps just the entrance of the ancient sewage tunnel was blocked. Sadly, his digging led to more debris, predominantly ancient rock and mortar. Seeing no way through, he turned his attention to the slab blocking his exit. He climbed the ladder, lowered his left shoulder again, bent his head out of the way, and pressed with all his might. There was no give in the heavy stone ledger.

Turning his flashlight back toward Pope Leo X, he decided, "No one will know what I do down here. I am going to see what is in this pope's right hand. Who knows, maybe all this occurred so I could read whatever he holds. If it is a rudimentary Bible, it will be a way to pass time, as long as my flashlight batteries hold up."

Descending the ladder, he reached into the coffin. He lifted the pontiff's arm by the garments, pulling the book. It had decaying stains on the leather cover, but anything was better than rats. Opening the book, he read, "To His Holiness, Pope Leo X, From Your Humble Servant, Duchess Lucrezia Borgia."

Guiseppe almost passed out. His heart almost beat out of his chest. A momentous sensation permeated his being. Was this another life-changing event? Two in one lifetime? He had discovered the lost diary of Mary Magdalene. Now, in his hands was a book from the infamous Lucrezia Borgia! He fell to his knees, clutching the book in his hands. He gave God thanks and prayed for what he was about to read, if discernible.

His thoughts were racing, "Is this why I was randomly yet Divinely assigned this task? Could it be that Alexander the Great was not God's intention? Did I not notice everything in this church had some relation to my favorite ancient curiosity, the Borgias? The vacuum I sought was at no other place than Pope Leo's monument. The void below contained his tomb. I was going to pass this up, but an earthquake hit. The earthquake locked me in here. The quake slid the lid off the pope's sarcophagus. In my boredom, I was led to investigate this tomb further. None of this could be a coincidence. God is involved in all I do. He is watching over me. He leads me by His Design. He blessed me with my last and first discovery, is this the next?"

Campise bowed his head. He prayed, thanking God for all He is, all He does. He asked God to guide him, to show him what it is He wanted Guiseppe to see, what He desired for the world to know about this pope or about the duchess of Ferrara. Closing his prayer, he gently opened the book. Written in Italian, Guiseppe was thankful no interpreter was needed. And, the pages were worn, but the writing was pristine. Glancing through, this seemed like some deathbed confessional to the reigning pope. Guiseppe moved the ladder to a corner of the room. He placed his flashlight on one of the rungs, positioning it against the wall to hold the light directly on the pages before him. Contented to pass the time away, he began to read.

I Believe My End Is Near

This has been a terrible pregnancy, but why would I be surprised. Every pregnancy for me has been death defying. Each time new life has been conceived in my womb, my life was threatened by the one I carried. I would be driven to my last breath as each of my eight children pressed for his or her first breath of life. There is something within me letting me know this may be my final lap of life. My 39th birthday was two days ago. I doubt I will see the next one.

I am bed stricken almost entirely. Attendants are with me around the clock. My dear husband, Alfonso d'Este seldom leaves my side except to eat or to catch a few hours of sleep. We have decided to name our baby Alfonso Cesare if it is a boy after my husband and my dear brother. If the child is a girl, we have decided to name her Isabella Maria after my grandmother and the mother of our Savior. This will be our seventh child together. I am amazed at how I have grown to love Alfonso d'Este. He was my third arranged marriage by my father when he was Pope. I was merged into marriage at his whim. I felt it necessary to find true love outside these arrangements. The men I married did the same.

I grieve as I ponder these acts of infidelity. I am haunted by what my family and I have done over these years. I feel God's judgement upon my life is near. I am too stupefied in the head to write what will follow, but I must get my confessions to the Holy Father, Pope Leo X, before it is too late. I am a Christian now. I could not always say that. I am a sinner still. I have always known that, but we were so frivolous in our past walk, so covetous of what this earth could give, that the thought of sin and its folly, not to mention its consequence, never played a role in our decisions.

Today the remembrance of my trespasses against God are nearer my bed than Alfonso or my attendants. My father's secretary, Monsignor Hieronymo Ziliolo, has graciously agreed to write my confessional to God and the Pope. He has seen many of our failures of character. He too has given his heart to Christ in recent days. With that said, I am not afraid for others to read what I am confessing. Our True Father says we should confess our sins one to another. My sins were against

God, but they also harmed many others. I seek absolution. I am repentant. I beg for forgiveness. I am trusting Jesus to cover over my multitude of sins. I pray He will bring every one of them to mind. May God have mercy on me. As long as I am able, I will recite to Monsignor Ziliolo my evils as well as the circumstances surrounding them.

The Diary of My Sins

I was born Lucrezia Borgia on April 18, 1480. I was the third illegitimate child of Cardinal Rodrigo Borgia and his primary mistress, my mother, Vannozza Cattanei. She was the favorite of my father's harem of mistresses. He had several children with different women before my brothers and me were born. He would have more afterward.

Father arranged a marriage for my mother to marry a man named Domenico d'Arignano in 1473 through a political deal. Though married and intimate with the man, she carried on her affair with my father, often staying weeks at a time under his roof. Mother had my brothers Cesare and Giovanni while she was married to Domenico.

Domenico died at which time she and Father conceived me. A few months after my birth, Father betrothed her to a man named Giorgio di Croce in another political maneuver. Political favors were given. Loyalty, power, land, and money were received into Father's household.

There was an ecclesiastical reason for marrying Vannozza beyond the political and monetary reasons. The Church had imposed mandatory celibacy upon its clergy 1,100 years before. The priests, cardinals, and popes observed such publicly, but privately carried on with many mistresses or concubines feeling they were being Biblical in the process. Though never acknowledged, many in power knew. The king of Naples reported the Holy City was being filled with sons and daughters of the cardinals. It was said to be rare to find a Curia member without one.

Of course, the question would be why would a woman like my mother subject herself to such treatment? Why would she be willing to have a relationship with my father after she was married off and while he was carrying on with other women? My father was handsome beyond measure. He was ambitious to a fault. He was gregarious, of good humor, and always carried the most winsome of smiles. His voice was strong. Father was the best public speaker I have ever heard. He mesmerized every crowd. And, when he looked at women and spoke, they melted under his spell. I had seen women, in private company, literally disrobe at his veiled suggestion.

I believe Mother was no different, but why would she continue in such a relationship while being sold by my father to the next highest bidder? Mother was as good at using as being used. It was an economic deal, one not much different from a local prostitute but with higher rewards. She became a huge landowner, compliments of my father. She gained a steady flow of rental income from the houses and inns she obtained by his grace. In addition to what she gained from my father the Cardinal then Pope, she acquired more wealth from the husbands to whom she was sold.

I did not know my mother well. She favored my oldest brother Cesare but had little to do with me. Most likely because there was no political advantage to be gained from a daughter other than what selling her could bring in our male-dominated society. As mother was sold, I soon willingly would be as well. Father's bewitching power held sway over his daughter as effectively as over his mistresses.

I was raised in the household my mother shared with her second husband, Giorgio. A little after six months, Father lost interest in my mother after she turned 40-years-of-age. I was sent to live with my father's first cousin, Adriana de Milla. She was a 39-year-old widow. She was extremely wealthy thanks to father's contacts and the benefits from their mutual uncle Pope Calixtus III. Father cherished her loyalty. He also appreciated her complicity in his dalliances. Adriana assisted the cardinal in his affair with her son's wife, 19-year-old Giulia Farnese Orsini, while keeping her son occupied in their country estate located in Bassanello.

Adriana took great care of me during my formative years. She served as my teacher, my caregiver, and my chaperone. My father never neglected me during this time. Adriana and I spent many months at a time in his palace. My brothers Cesare, Giovanni, and me were loved by him as if we were the only three children he had ever sired.

Father saw to it that I was educated for a time in the Dominican convent called San Sisto which fronted the Appian Way. I have learned over the years this convent was different from many. Most seem contented to teach religion and observance of the Church's rituals. Other than this nod to piety, most convents believed a woman could be immoral, sin, please whatever power there was over her, however that power sought to be pleased. These indiscretions had no bearing on one's standing before God and the Church. To them, mass, confession, giving, having the relics and pictures of the saints like Mother Mary bridged the chasm from mankind to God.

The San Sisto convent was unique. It was here the nuns taught what true spirituality was all about. When I attended, I felt they were prude. Cloistered away from the real world, I deemed them naïve to the ways of the Church and the world. Their way seemed fine for them. The spiritual nurturing was a rite of passage for me as a young girl, nothing more. In later years, when times were hard, I found myself finding asylum in that place. It was in that convent, I felt God. It was there I could find my true north. God's Spirit moved in their sanctuary, and it was there I could find calm in the storms of life.

Father believed our success in life was partially determined by what we learned. He had been well-educated at an exclusive preparatory school and then at the University of Bologna. He had his sights set on creating a dynasty of some sort as he continued to climb the ladder of the Bride of Christ, His Church. I attained mastery over several languages including Italian, French, Latin, Greek, and Spanish. I learned to write poetry. Music and poetry became my passion. I was taught how to speak publicly. I was fluent in business. I learned how to manage. I was given responsibilities beyond peers of my age. These sharpened my leadership skills.

Father was blessed to be born in the town of Xativa in the kingdom of Valencia to a prominent family — Borgia. When his uncle, Alfonso de Borgia became cardinal and made the move to Rome, Father was on his heels seeking power and prosperity. Not long after the move, his uncle, the cardinal, became Pope Calixtus III. Alfonso was chosen as pope by the conclave as a compromised choice. The two vying Italian parties would give no concession, so a non-Italian pope was chosen to prevent further schism in the Church. The newly vested Spanish Pope quickly made Father a cardinal at the tender age of 25-years-old. A year later, he was made vice-chancellor of the Catholic Church.

After his uncle died, Father continued to serve in the Curia overseeing the affairs of the Roman Catholic Church through the reigns of four subsequent popes: Pope Pius II, Pope Paul II, Pope Sixtus IV, and Pope Innocent VIII. It was here Father gained rich benefices of property, power, influence, and income. He acquired important papal fortresses. He eventually built his primary home, one of the finest palaces in all of Rome. Father had over 113 household servants at his disposal in that residence. His income was fed annually by his three bishoprics of Valencia, Porto, and Carthage. Every facet of his wardrobe, his palaces, and his stables were adorned by silver, gold, and silk. All totaled, Father had become one of the wealthiest cardinals in the world.

In less than two years after his uncle died, Father obtained more than wealth. He was on his way to being one of the most powerful men in the Holy See. Sadly, his actions were anything but holy. Much to the dismay of Pope Pius II, Father had a garden party in the Italian town of Siena. It started the way it ended — a drunken orgy with many lewd women of the town copulating with several of the priests and cardinals. One said that if all the children conceived during that party were to take on the roles of their fathers, there would be an exponential increase in priests and cardinal ministers in the Church.

Pope Pius II when he heard of the gross display of immorality from those within his Holy Court, he wrote a sternly worded letter to Father accusing him of acting in a way unworthy of the office for which he was invested. He demanded Father act in a way consistent with his appointment. The Pope followed with a warning that another hint of such activity would come at a cost too great for Father to bear.

The Pope's letter elaborated further on the debauchery by stating Rodrigo had women there whose husbands, fathers, and brothers were not invited to attend. News of the drunken orgy was not privy to the Pope's ears only. It had spread by the tongues of Italians everywhere. The lewd event was attributed to one man — Rodrigo Borgia. Pope Pius II explained the impact Father's actions had on the Church as a whole. He said that the people with their tithes see their money was not being spent so the clergy could live blameless lives reserved for Christ. Instead, the sacrifices of the faithful were being used to make the Church's office holders rich so they had money to gratify their illicit passions. The publicly flaunted sins by Church leaders brought contempt from princes and laity alike. Such conduct daily diminished the authority of the Church bringing dishonor in this world and torment for the next. Pope Pius II closed his letter with the admonition, "A cardinal should be above reproach and an example of right living before the eyes of all men."

Father survived the remonstrance, but his actions were not deterred. He had enough power to hold his place. He did learn to be less overt. In the Pope's presence, he was the picture of piety. Behind his back, he scoffed that such a man known for erotic poetry and writings would dare seek to correct one who merely put into practice what Pius II only fantasized in print. Four years later, Pope Pius II was gathered to his fathers. The reprimand was quickly forgotten.

During the last days of his papacy, Pope Innocent VIII made a significant acquisition for the Church — a fragment of the holy lance which pierced the side of Jesus. On May 31, 1492, he presented the relic to the gathering on the square below the Vatican portico. My father, Cardinal Borgia, the vice-chancellor, had the privilege to hold it above his head for all to see below. The crowd celebrated with shouts of exultation. The pope was dead less than two months later. The man who held the holy spear would soon be named the Keeper of the Keys.

Papal Inauguration

When I reached the age of twelve, my father Rodrigo Borgia became Pope at age sixty, on August 11, 1492. It was one of the most memorable days of my life. I saw Father put on his papal vestments overwhelmed with joy as he proudly proclaimed, "I am pope and vicar of Christ!" Many said he was elected by the conclave through the movement of the Holy Spirit. In reality, many critics let me know later that my father paid over 150,000 ducats and hundreds of promised appointments to be named Pope Alexander VI. Part of the 150,000-ducat fee was for the votes of two hesitant cardinals.

Church bells rang all over Rome. Shops were closed as were the outdoor markets. Every human with any sense of the Church's importance lined the streets to see the grand entry of the new pope. Multitudes flocked to Saint Peter's to join in the new installment. Italians were optimistic. But King Ferrante of Naples told his wife that this new pope would mean a wrong turn for all Christendom.

Regardless of the doubters, his Holiness, my father, rode into Rome triumphantly. Thirteen splendidly dressed squadrons of men in shining armor on colorfully decorated horses led the way. The cardinals wearing their crimson robes, rode on great mounts draped in white. A count bore the pope's standard on his shield with the keys of Saint Peter forming the backdrop of a grazing red and gold bull. The streets and buildings were adorned with flowers and tapestries. Cannons were fired as the new pope entered. Following the procession was the main attraction, Pope Alexander VI, his chosen name in remembrance of Alexander the Great. The masses lining the streets cried out "Borgia, Borgia" as he entered. Plastered throughout the parade route were slogans such as, "Caesar was great, now Rome is greater: Alexander reigns — the first was a man, this is a god."

People saw Father's face as he followed the procession. His was one of elegance, of tenderness, and of dignity. He purposely made eye-contact with thousands of admirers as I watched. Each felt a personal connection with their new pope. He was vigorous and hardy. Their hope was he would hold this position for a long time to come. Their hearts were filled with joy. Their expectations were of good fortune for them and their families. An odd affinity burgeoned within the breasts of most women. They revered him as both a father and a lover. Behind his countenance was the desire to be obeyed as the former and serviced as the latter. He sought not to be the conduit of God's Blessings to others, but the recipient of all this world could bestow.

Jesus rode into Jerusalem on a donkey greeted by a massive crowd shouting, "Hosanna! Blessed is the One coming in the Name of the Lord. Blessed is the coming kingdom of our father David. Hosanna in the highest!" He came humbly. He came dressed in the clothes of a carpenter. He had nowhere to lay His Head. He came to save the world. He came to serve, to wash feet.

I was delighted for my father, yet in hindsight, I am ashamed at the difference between the Christ who came and the Vicar of Christ installed. Somewhere along the way, the Church lost its way. The spiritual nature of the role was cast aside for the political. Power was sought over piety. Positions in the Church were given not to the Bible scholar, or the righteous servant, or the one who had done the most for the poor, but rather to those who displayed loyalty to the Pope, who had political connections to add to the wealth of the enthroned, and those who could be trusted to keep secrets.

What the Catholic Church saw on the day of inauguration was the emulation of the political and war heroes of Greece and Rome, of Alexander and Julius Caesar. It was no accident my father chose his new name, Alexander. No thought was given to Christ's true representatives, the saints as written in Hebrews, chapter eleven: "Others were tortured and refused to be released, so that they might gain a better resurrection. Some faced jeers and flogging, while still others were chained and put in prison. They were stoned; they were sawed in two; they were put to death by the sword. They went about in sheepskins and goatskins, destitute, persecuted, and mistreated— the world was not worthy of them. They wandered in deserts and mountains, and in caves and holes in the ground. These were all commended for their faith, yet none of them received what had been promised. God had planned something better for us so that only together with us would they be made perfect."

The Pope, my father, was seen as Jesus' representative, as one holding His Place with all authority. But the splendor and wealth were quite the opposite of the One he was chosen to represent. Isaiah wrote of the Lord's Christ before His coming,

"Who has believed our message and to whom has the arm of the Lord been revealed? He grew up before him like a tender shoot, and like a root out of dry ground. He had no beauty or majesty to attract us to Him, nothing in His appearance that we should desire Him. He was despised and rejected by men, a man of sorrows, and familiar with suffering. Like one from whom men hide their faces He was despised, and we esteemed him not. Surely, He took up our infirmities and carried our sorrows, yet we considered Him stricken by God, smitten by Him, and afflicted. But He was pierced for our transgressions, He was crushed for our iniquities; the punishment that brought us peace was upon Him, and by His wounds we are healed."

Unlike the suffering servant, my Pope Alexander VI was handsome beyond measure. He was tall. His complexion was fair, his eyes black, his nose appeared as a hook. So athletic was he at age sixty, that even with weight gain, he was able to hunt over long distances, stalking animals of prey superior to men half his age. He was humorous. He could lift me from any level of sadness with a simple visit. He was a great dancer. He carried himself with joy regardless of the burdens of his position. He smiled continually. So magnetic was he, a glance toward a woman would melt her heart. Ladies in the kingdom gladly attended his private quarters considering it a blessing to service one so great. I believe they felt they were giving an offering to God Himself as they met the sensual needs of my benefactor.

Yes, my Beatitude was despised by some. He counted it envy. He grew the power of his office far beyond his predecessors. His powers to appoint, to grant, to reward were often used to ingratiate the most vengeful enemies. It is said that if one seeks to do as they wish, they should not be born a woman. I am a woman. I was used by father to grow his power, to ally his opponents.

Once Father was established in his Vatican surroundings, he sent for me and Adriana to live in the Palazzo Santa Maria in Portico. We were not far from Father. In this location, my pope housed his papal harem. I grew to love these ladies and to understand them. Together, we accepted our roles in the papacy: Adriana, her daughter-in-law Giulia, my mother, myself, the ladies of the Palazzo Santa Maria bordello.

How did I moralize such things? I was taught such things were in keeping with the Holy Writ. King Ahasuerus in the Book of Esther was one example. He had accumulated a huge collection of virgins to become his consorts. He had a chamberlain who watched over the royal harem assigning each to their night of passion with the king. My father had the same. Esther served her role. Through her, a whole people were spared destruction. The others kept the king happy benefiting the nation.

They say the pope's vocation is a stressful one. In my day, Father was not only overseeing the affairs of the Church, but he was also to watch over the state of the world. He was the one who kept nations at bay. He was the one to settle disputes. It was his duty to assure justice throughout the world as Christ's vicar. As Moses needed Aaron and Hur to hold his hands up during a grueling battle, the women in our court assured ourselves that we were doing the same.

My appearance was different than many of the girls of the court. I was a little taller than most. My hair was blonde which attracted many an eye. My eyes were blue, and still are. I was slim in face at the time. My body matched but with two distinctive curves. Father said I was well-proportioned. My teeth were blessed to be straight and white, unlike so many in those days. In fact, the pope boasted that I was the one who attracted him the most.

It was not necessary to say, sexual activity was the norm to which I was raised. When one's parents have no qualms of sexual forays, even participating in them for the children to see, the youth often follow suit with keen curiosity. Following my convent instruction, I kept myself a virgin for marriage, but I explored with many of my childhood friends. Adriana was good at answering my questions. The truth be told, she enjoyed such conversation. Her daughter-in-law Giulia spoke of such things as a delicacy to be devoured.

Adriana and Giulia laughed about the clumsy sexual advances of other men, but both revered Father as an object of highest reverence. They whispered what he liked. They spoke of bawdy interactions they had with him alone and in the company of many women of our house. As an innocent youth, I felt sorry for Adriana's son. The more I was exposed to this way of life, the more I lost those feelings of pity. I am saddened to dictate these were the things I accepted as right. Pleasing my father and building a kingdom in this life were all that mattered.

I speak these things to set the table for my own actions which followed. I pray God and Pope Leo X do not think I lay blame for my intentions and actions upon others. I was born in sin, conceived literally in sin. But inside, I was already a sinner looking for my opportunities.

I reflect on the high position my father held. The pope was regarded as the spiritual leader of not just the Church but to the world. I shudder to think of how Father abused this sacred position, using it for his own pleasure.

Early on in his life, his ambition overrode any devotion to God. When his uncle, Calixtus III died, the conclave met to choose the next pope. Father held his vote until he could discern the inevitable successor. When it was clear Pope Pius would be selected, Father threw his lot behind this man. I rejoice Pope Pius II was chosen. He sought to live out the role God had given him even though flawed himself.

When Father was asked who he had voted for, he made it clear he voted for Pope Pius II because he wanted to be on the good side of the man to retain his position as vice-chancellor. It was a good choice but only by God's Hand. If the devil's own advocate had been the leading candidate, I firmly believe Father would have voted for him to keep his position, wealth, and power. I know this is harsh, but it is the truth. How can I say anything else knowing I will stand before the Father of Heaven and earth soon?

My brothers Giovanni and Cesare were the closest semblance to a real family I had. We called Giovanni, Juan. Of the two, Cesare was the driver. He was the lead. He had ambition like our forebearer. His mind was as sharp as Father's. Often, even as a young man, he would question Father's actions with me and Juan. He would tell us what he would do and how what our father had decided to do would not work as well. It was surprising how right my brother was. Where our father was loving to us, my brother was freely accessible. He taught me how I should dress, how I should act, and when I should speak. He seemed to have a desire to see me elevated as only men could be in society. Father treasured the relationship I had with my brother.

Orsino

In 1489, at the age of fourteen, Cesare was sent off to Sapienza of Perugia for a higher education. Juan was soon to follow. I missed my brother very much. I longed for his return for every special occasion. That same year, Adriana's son, our playmate Orsino was married to the lovely Giulia. He was only thirteen years old. Giulia was fifteen. I was nine, about to turn ten. Their fathers had arranged the marriage when the two were mere toddlers. They saw the marriage as a merger to benefit both.

I do not think there was a girl as beautiful as Giulia. She was dark complected but had long flowing hair which reached almost to her feet. After the wedding, she and I spent many days treating our hair. I was naturally blonde. Giulia chose this color for her own as this was the most desired by men. Whether blonde by birth or blonde by choice, the goal was to become even more so. Exposure to the sun helped greatly, but this made our skin dark which was not desired. The ideal was to have the whitest skin and the blondest hair. A countess developed an alternative to avoid exposure to the sun. She prescribed two pounds of alum, six ounces of black sulfur, and four ounces of honey mixed with a hint of myrrh. It was then diluted for easy application.

Giulia was like an older sister to me. Her mother-in-law Adriana called us both her daughters. What amazed me was how men looked at Giulia. In a crowd of women, the collective eye of the male sort was drawn to one focus — her. Even Father would pause to look. He would stop midsentence, silently smile in adoration, then continue his address. He would often wink at Adriana each time Giulia was present. It would take a while for me to understand why. Had it not been for his paternal affection, I would have been neglected with Giulia nearby. Granted, he was sixty. She was fifteen. Father cared nothing about a girl's age. Copulating with beauty was one of his chief passions.

What men cherished, Orsino, my friend, paid no mind. He was an awkward boy in his teens. He seldom thought of girls. He never saw me as a female but as a friend. I saw no difference either at that age. The only distinction a child gathers at a young age is how one dresses. I played with Orsino and his toy warriors. He played with me and my dolls. One minute we were down on the floor of Adriana's playing, the next minute he was being suited with a groom's wardrobe. It was almost that sudden.

I could tell he had no desire for marriage at that age. His desire was to follow as a solider like my brother Cesare. When men of all ages lusted after Giulia, Orsino barely understood the strange attraction. On the day of their wedding in the Vatican on 20, May 1489, my childhood friend was terribly upset. It was the most awkward thing I had ever seen. My friend, a few years older than me, was being married and given a job as a commander over two men with a pay to support his wife. It was a civil wedding, so no consummation was allowed. That would be a year later.

With the marriage, Orsino changed. He was constantly troubled. He wanted to play with me and our other friends, but he was forced into the life of an adult. A year later, he and Giulia were married in a religious ceremony requiring immediate consummation. Every man at the ceremony was envious of what the boy would soon unwrap. The newlywed couple lived with Adriana and me following the grand event. I was first exposed to marriage through them. Their marriage was not one of love and reciprocation. It was like being sequestered with someone in a room or sentenced with someone in prison. The roommate was not chosen, but the roommate was assigned. Orsino, though married to the most beautiful of women, resented the union perhaps because they shared no love between them.

Two years after their civil union, one year after their religious one, Orsino was given a greater command at the age of fifteen. He was sent off to war, leading twenty-five men. In the conflict, he lost an eye and was sent home. He was a broken man in his teenage years. Orsino's compulsions turned to the only place he felt there was real help — to God. He had been brought up in the shadow of the papal palace, exposed to the pope his whole life, yet the place was empty. He knew there had to be something more. He made it known that he would like to make a pilgrimage to the Holy Land. He had a hefty inheritance, but he had not reached the age to access the ducats. He petitioned his mother for it, but she declined. Adriana did not want her son to take such a journey at the tender age of fifteen.

Maybe Orsino was too young to make such a trip to the Holy Land, but he was also too young to marry or to go to war. His mother objected to neither of those. Perhaps his injury made her more sensitive to his frailties. She gave him excuses and delays hoping he would change his mind. Orsino would not. He left his mother, his wife, and our home to seek shelter at their family estate at Bassanello. From there, he corresponded with his mother to let her know if she would not release the 300 ducats for his trip, he would take a loan against their estate. She finally complied.

Once Orsino had the money, he changed his mind. He decided to stay in Bassanello. I did not admire him at the time. Now I do. My friend Orsino was faced with many pressures. He was married to a woman he did not choose. He was given an adult job against his will. He lost an eye doing a job he was assigned. The role of his mother was to serve the pope in meeting the pontiff's carnal desires. Everything in life seemed hollow. I think Orsino felt if only he could touch the realm of holiness, perhaps then, he would find the strength to move onward. He needed that grounding for which every soul searches.

My friend would return to the command and be promoted. He would serve proforma as a spouse for Giulia, but he refused to live in the lie. When he was not serving in his command capacity, he spent the majority of his time in the family estate of Bassanello. The foresight of my friend Orsino is one I have grown to admire more and more over the years.

The more my father came to see me, the more he saw of Giulia La Bella, "the beautiful one." With the help and consent of Adriana, father gained La Bella as a mistress. Adriana betrayed her own son for ease. Her daughter-in-law and my father would have a child together. To cover over the matter publicly, Orsino was attributed paternity. In return, he was given the position as mayor of Carbognano to live life the way he sought. Giulia later used her influence to get her brother Alessandro made a cardinal with all the benefices which came with it.

After many years of benefits, Giulia and Father ended their relationship in a quite hostile manner. Adriana, ever Father's ally, was able to negotiate a peace protecting my father and guarding her daughter-in-law and grandchildren's positions.

This is the life I grew up in. Every mass at Saint Peter's Square, I would see thousands of devout Christians seeking forgiveness, calling upon the Name of God. They felt with the pope's blessing and intercession, all things would be available to them, so they revered my father. Little did they know he was going through the motions. He was having orgies. He was fathering children with women of all ages, wives of other men. It was all perfunctory.

I grieve in what the Church became. Make no mistake, I loved my father. I cannot explain how I could after all he did to others, how he used me. Yet, in his own way, he did his best to love me. I loved my brother Cesare. He was my strength, always my advocate, yet he was the most devious of men. I must not see these two I love through my human eyes, but through the eyes of the One who is ever True. They called my father holy. Yet, there is only One who is Holy. Jesus, not the vicar, taught us what the vicar should be in the twenty-third chapter of the Gospel of Matthew:

The teachers of the law and the Pharisees sit in Moses' seat. So, you must obey them and do everything they tell you. But do not do what they do, for they do not practice what they preach. They tie up heavy loads and put them on men's shoulders, but they themselves are not willing to lift a finger to move them. Everything they do is done for men to see: They make their phylacteries wide and the tassels on their garments long; they love the place of honor at banquets and the most important seats in the synagogues; they love to be greeted in the marketplaces and to have men call them 'Rabbi.'

I was taught to read and write. I was taught to think. Everyone has this right. Each should take advantage of the opportunity. The best thing I have ever read, which unfortunately was taken up late in life, is the Word of God. When we read God's Word and then look up from the page to see what is going on around us, we are able to discern what is right and what is wrong, what is performance and what is sincere. I now see too late what my father was doing. The Apostle Paul gave instructions to his pupil Timothy on how an overseer should behave.

Here is a trustworthy saying: If anyone sets his heart on being an overseer, he desires a noble task. Now the overseer must be above reproach, the husband of but one wife, temperate, self-controlled, respectable, hospitable, able to teach, not given to drunkenness, not violent but gentle, not quarrelsome, not a lover of money. He must manage his own family well and see that his children obey him with proper respect. (If anyone does not know how to manage his own family, how can he take care of God's church?) He must not be a recent convert, or he may become conceited and fall under the same judgment as the devil. He must also have a good reputation with outsiders, so that he will not fall into disgrace and into the devil's trap.

My father was not qualified to be an overseer, or a pope, much less a father. He was not beyond reproach. He was not faithful to any woman. He was not temperate. He was not self-controlled. He was not respectable. He loved to drink. He loved money above all. He fell into the devil's trap and liked it. Regarding his family, as far as my biological siblings go, he managed only to make us into his image.

The Family

My greatest memories in my short childhood were with my brother Cesare. I loved Juan (the familial name we gave Giovanni) but Cesare and I resented him to a degree. Though Father loved us all, it was clear he loved Juan the most. If his position was in jeopardy and Father could spare only one child, Cesare, Joffre, and me would be sacrificed. Juan would survive.

Our father's love for Juan was unexplainable. He was the least ambitious of the four of us. To be honest, he was quite lazy. He cared nothing for position or power or money. His life was lived to satisfy his palate for women and wine. Father would have to cajole him, push him, force him to take on responsibilities within his papacy. Father had an older son from a different woman named Don Pedro Luis. Father was able to barter a position for him in Spain as the Duke of Gandia. He died suddenly. Father quickly sent Juan to take over this dukedom.

Joffre was the youngest of our siblings by our mother Vannozza. Father did not treat him like Juan, Cesare, or me. Over the years, I believe it was because Father was not sure if Joffre was his son or mother's husband's. I suppose I was not close to Joffre because he was the youngest, and because he spent more time in Mother's household than our own with Adriana. Did I love him? Yes. But to be honest Orsino was more like a brother than Joffre.

Cesare on the other hand should have been Father's favorite. He was mine. I have never seen a more handsome man in my life than my brother Cesare. He and I loved each other so much that many speculated our relationship was intimate and sordid. I believe it could have been if I would have allowed it. As we developed in our youth, Cesare and I confided as to the changes our bodies were going through. Curiosity would sometimes lead to voluntary exposure for comparison. Where Orsino had no interest in the differences between his playmates, Cesare was enamored by the distinctions. He once shared with me that he loved me more than any woman in his life. I am not sure if he saw me as his sister, or as his mother (since ours was so distant), as a wife, or as his true love. He sought out not just my opinion in his life, he fought for my approval. Perhaps I was the one person he saw as his foundation. I do know we trusted each other beyond question.

Father and Cesare never realized how similar they were. Being on the inside, to me the only difference between them was Father knew how to cloak his ambitions. Cesare flaunted his. He once confided in me his belief that his life would be cut short. As a result, he sought to make the most of his life, to get all he could, and then defy death's call.

Cesare thrived in his education. He was a sponge. Two learned men were visiting with Father while we were sitting in the room. Cesare played games with me. Juan paid the adult conversation no mind. As soon as the men left, Cesare conversed with Father in detail concerning his conversation with the men. We were all surprised how he was able to do one thing, engage with one party, while knowing what was going on in another. At the universities he thrived. He could hear a lecture once and retain all that was taught.

My favorite brother was not only tall and handsome, but his body was also a chiseled masterpiece. He won every athletic contest. His endurance in hunting was unmatched. He could ride a horse better than any peer. He even taught himself how to bullfight. He was an expert marksman. One would think I am prejudice because he was my brother, but what I record has been written by many on the outside.

Dear Cesare's personality had no lacking. He was gregarious, joyful, and fun. He could play pranks on our friends and receive back the same with a jovial appreciation. Everything with him was upbeat. Even as I dictate my memory of him, I no longer feel sick or weak. His memory makes me want to get out of this bed, pregnant, and run through the woods to chase after him as we did as kids. In a large way, to me, he was perfection incarnate.

Our father made constant references to God publicly, but he never instilled anything of faith. He never broached anything regarding ethics. His concern was do whatever works to attain our goals. I never saw him pray in private, not even before a meal. His one religious anchor was a superstitious reverence for the Blessed Virgin Mary.

My brother Cesare had no religious bearing at all. He never spoke of God, never considered God, never feared Divine Judgment for his actions. I never once heard him pray publicly or privately. He referenced God in some public addresses but only to placate those who felt such was important. He believed this life was all there was. Other than his love for me, he had no regard for another human life beyond his own. He cared nothing for his children or his consorts. He had no love for Father other than the position and the benefices Father as pope could bestow. He did not desire to be a priest but to be a king decorated with conquests, land, and riches. Even as children, he played the warrior, the king, and the executioner.

To a degree, Cesare was my king for most of my life. Father was my pope in position or out. Whatever they desired for me to do, I did. Many would say I was a queen, but within our household, I served gladly as a pawn. The accusations of incest have been a constant by our adversaries. I will admit, had Father wanted me to sleep with him, I most likely would have but reluctantly. If my brother pressed me, I more readily would have submitted. I would have done whatever was required to show my love and submission to the two most important men in my life.

Morality was relegated to what made us happy. Whatever it was we wanted at the time, that was declared morally right. If others prevented us from fulfilling our desires, those human barriers were in the wrong. This is a confession. I replaced God with my chosen familial hierarchy. The consequences for prohibited idolatry haunt me still.

As a cardinal, Father had Cesare appointed as bishop of Pamplona. He was only fifteen years old. The diocese was not pleased to have such a young man as their religious leader, but I dare say Cesare was better equipped than most to lead even at that age, just not spiritually. When Father ascended to the papacy, he awarded Cesare his former position, the archbishopric of Valencia. The position granted him a large annual income. He was only seventeen years old.

Father did as many before. He rewarded family members while he was in the papacy. Juan was made duke, Cesare a bishop, even Joffre was made an archdeacon in Valencia. He made his sister's son a cardinal. He made a nephew the captain of his guard. His closest friends were given high positions in the Vatican. Legacy was sought through dynasty not through piety. As a result, nepotism was a practice for practically every pope.

Sexual deviance was often an attribute. Children born to previous popes were often called nieces and nephews to hide their sins. Some popes preferred sodomy, treating such fetishes as delicacies to have. Those who accepted advances knew such things were wrong, but also hoped naively for spiritual and physical blessings in return for their service to the pontiff.

My father carried on nepotism and sexual entanglements (minus sodomy) openly. It was not that he sought to be transparent and honest. Contrary to this, with great hubris, he dared any to bring a charge. Little effort was made to hide his orgies as cardinal. Only early on, did he reference his children as sons and daughters of a relative. He took full ownership once he was established.

He challenged the Holy Catholic Church to accept and promote us, his children. We were paraded as sons and daughters of royalty in whose relationships came great reward. Kings and queens, religious leaders, political leaders, and the wealthy vied for our hands in marriage. People clamored to please us so the pope could give positions, power, indulgences, and leniency. The Vatican became our ivory tower. Gifts dispensed brought greater power for the occupant of the chair of Saint Peter.

Nepotism was the fountain of our family's rise from obscurity. Our forefathers were landowners of insignificance in Spain. Then one day, our aunt married a man of nobility. This led to our uncle's promotion whose promotion led to Father's. As a cardinal in Spain, my father began to build powerful allegiances. When devout Catholic King Ferdinand sought to marry Queen Isabella, Father was able to gain a Bull of dispensation from his uncle Calixtus the pope. King Ferdinand did not forget the favor. He made our father a duke to add to his position as cardinal. Father took the two positions and parlayed them into even more gratuity.

My First Marriage

At the age of eleven, Father had betrothed me to the son of a powerful man in Spain. Father then had the betrothal annulled. He gave me no explanation because he did not believe he needed to. He immediately pledged me to another young man from Spain. His father was the Count of Aversa. Once he became pope, Father cancelled that one as well. Again, with no input from me. I had no objections.

While still eleven, the Pope pledged me to be married to a prince. He felt in his position, his daughter was worthy of none less. Giovanni Sforza fit the bill. Giovanni had been married before, but his wife died in childbirth. He was excited for a new start. He also felt I was incredibly beautiful (his words not mine). His family was of great renown. It did not hurt that he was also the nephew of Cardinal Ascanio Sforza who was very powerful in Rome. In fact, it was this cardinal's influence which helped father ascend to the throne of the Catholic Church. In return, he gave Cardinal Sforza his vice-chancellor position. I began to see the motivations for this union. Father could gain wealth through my hand, as well as favor in the Halls of Rome.

Even with my absence from the equation, Father's elevation of Cardinal Sforza was a punishment to their mutual enemy, King Ferrante, the king of Naples who fought my father's promotion. When he was unable to stop it, the king purchased two key castles near Rome with the help of the Orsini's to neuter the new pope. A rivalry against this king and the kingdom he ruled of Naples was born. Alexander VI solidified his strength with Milan and Venice. By marrying his daughter to the Duke of Milan's son, the lord of Pesaro, an alliance was welded with Cardinal Sforza's people.

The road to matrimony was very rocky at first. The last man Father betrothed me to, Count Gasparo, had not realized my pope had changed his mind. He and his father arrived in Rome to receive the pope's daughter as his bride. Giovanni was also in Rome to receive me as well. I was caught in an untenable situation from my father's maneuvers. The count made it clear he would not leave Rome without his bride, and if he was forced to, every nobleman and religious leader of Christendom would know the duplicity of this pope.

My pope had the contract between me and young Gasparo dissolved. In grief, my first suitor vowed not to marry for a year in hopes I would still one day be his. All of Spain felt betrayed by their countryman pope. To curb hurt feelings, Father gave the young count three thousand ducats for his grief. He accepted it with the hopes the money would be considered part of his future dowry. I look back and wish I would have said something to protect the people Father ground beneath his ambitions. I was young, but I was of the age of some discernment. I was more interested in being the center of attention. To my regret, I suffered from the same palsy as my forebear.

Giovanni was humble through it all, never taking anything for granted. He was of the mind to accept whatever occurred as God's Will. He did not realize it was the pope's will he had to worry about. He would learn this far too soon. He headed back to Spain to await a final decision. Two months later, our union was finally ratified by the Vatican. Giovanni Sforza received the dowry, thirty-two thousand ducats. My fiancé celebrated in his palace by throwing a grand celebration with dancing, singing, and merriment participated in by the whole city. I was only twelve, but I was excited. I thought of my childhood friend Orsino. Did he not understand the rite of passage is a joyous thing? Then I remembered where Orsino's bride resided.

Betrothed before my twelfth birthday, his Holiness provided a fabulous palace for me filled with the most extravagant furnishings of the land. It sat to the left of Saint Peter's Basilica. I went from being the one watched over in Adriana's household to being the princess of my own estate with Adriana working as my manager. Father conveniently made her daughter-in-law, Giulia, my lady-of-honor guaranteeing many visits to my residence which was called the palace of Saint Maria in Porticu. Orsino's wife, Giulia, lived near Saint Peter's for my father's pleasure alone.

I find it ironic how even at the age of twelve, my past, present, and future all assembled for that moment in time. I presided over my domicile betrothed to Giovanni Sforza while my former fiancé Gasparo was preparing to exit Rome. King Ferrante sought to break my engagement by offering his grandson, the son of the Duke of Calabria who would become my second husband. Unbeknownst to me, my third husband, Alfonso d'Este, came to call upon the pope with his first wife, Anna. Father chose to receive them in my palace as a matter of acknowledgement of my newfound role as a leader in the Church, one who had the ear of the reigning Church father. Alfonso d'Este was the prince of Ferrara, the most brilliant court of all Italy. If only I had known then what I know now, laying in this sickbed. I wonder what advice I would give myself. Perhaps none, other than to pay close attention to those around me and the mechanisms driving them to and from my presence.

Ten years before, the previous pope waged war on Ferrara. The Duke of Ferrara, Alfonzo's father, sought to build a strong alliance with Father to secure peace for his court. It was apparent, from the murmurings within the Holy See that his Holiness was seeking to build a monarchy, merging Church and State. If one is consumed with things of this world, nothing in this world will satisfy. The want for more, to reach higher, to gain power and more wealth becomes an unquenchable obsession. I suppose this is the great sin of mankind, thus the First Commandment, "Thou shalt have no other gods before Me." Father was successful in becoming the most powerful religious leader in the world. His next goal was to be the supreme secular ruler of the world through negotiations, through marriages, through intrigue, or even war. What if he would have obtained this? I tremble to think he would seek to rebuild the Temple in Jerusalem and declare himself God. My brothers and I benefitted in his wake.

It is said in the eighteenth chapter of the book of Ezekiel, "The fathers have eaten sour grapes, and the children's teeth are set on edge." Our father was consumed in his quest for power. Cesare's teeth were set on edge to assist and later be enthroned. By all means necessary was Father's mode of conduct. Cesare agreed wholeheartedly. My brother was made an archbishop, but he sought other avenues to power, even courting the King of Naples' daughter for a more expedient access. Why grovel and scrape to attain something when you can more easily marry for attainment? I had no objections.

June 12, 1492, was the date selected for our wedding. Father would have preferred it sooner, but Cardinal Sforza would not allow the marriage until his astrologers discerned what date would be most favorable. With the date selected according to the stars, my brothers Cesare, Juan, and Joffre joined the crowds to witness my nuptials. I was twelve years of age. While the Bishop of Concordia delivered the message, my father sat on his throne before us. Twelve cardinals were present as were many from the royal class. The King of France sent an envoy in his stead. All of Rome turned out as if to see a historical event — the marriage of their princess to the lord of Pesaro. I wore a gown worth at least 15,000 ducats, an immense sum unfathomable for the laity around us.

During the formalities, my groom and I knelt before Father, oblivious to what was being said by the bishop. We were enthralled with each other. My new groom could not stop smiling from ear to ear. His forehead was lofty. His face noble. His hair flowed more beautifully than any man's I had ever seen. He was gallant. His height struck me as that of a great military commander. I heard many women speak of his attractiveness. This was my husband. He was twenty-six years of age, yet he never acted as if I was an inexperienced child. His first wife died during childbirth. On a single day, he lost both his wife and his child. I was moved by his tenderness. The tears flowing down his face during the ceremony touched me dearly. Here was a man who had fallen victim to nature's sudden turn, nothing more. He was devastated but he resolved to love again.

My beloved honored my father, but it was not my father he wanted. I believe firmly, Giovanni would have chosen me had I been the chimney sweeper's daughter. He whispered in my ear, that he realized how precious to have one to exchange earnest pledges of companionship with until death parts the two. He let me know how he had learned the hard way to hold tight, to make the most of each day, to never let an evening pass without assuring his mate of his love.

Having loved poetry, for this event, I memorized my favorite love verses from the Song of Solomon. I did not know when I would have the time to share the passage, but in a private moment, I whispered into his ear:

The voice of my beloved! behold, he cometh leaping upon the mountains, skipping upon the hills. My beloved is like a roe or a young hart: behold, he standeth behind our wall, he looketh forth at the windows, shewing himself through the lattice. My beloved spake, and said unto me, Rise up, my love, my fair one, and come away. For, lo, the winter is past, the rain is over and gone; The flowers appear on the earth; the time of the singing of birds is come, and the voice of the turtle is heard in our land: The fig tree putteth forth her green figs, and the vines with the tender grape give a good smell. Arise, my love, my fair one, and come away. O my dove, that art in the clefts of the rock, in the secret places of the stairs, let me see thy countenance, let me hear thy voice; for sweet is thy voice, and thy countenance is comely. Take us the foxes, the little foxes, that spoil the vines: for our vines have tender grapes. My beloved is mine, and I am his: he feedeth among the lilies. Until the daybreak, and the shadows flee away, turn, my beloved, and be thou like a roe or a young hart upon the mountains of Bether.

My husband-to-be smiled as more tears moistened his face. His tears intermingled with mine as he pulled my face with his strong hands against his own. I had never known love like this. Giovanni's was not a selfish love. It was strange. I had only known of consorts and political unions. My father instigated this to be as much, but for Giovanni and me, love sprang from man's gyrations. As God spoke and light came to the darkness as sudden as His Voice commanded, love sprang from the dry soil of our origin. He was the illegitimate child of his parents. I was the same for mine. But our lives had never spawned anyone of illegitimacy. Thanks to the day of our marriage, I felt it never would. We had a chance to set things right. Integrity, uprightness was a thing of beauty, one I had never perceived.

Oh, that we could have rushed off to my palace which I would gladly resign as his. Sadly, there were obligations to fulfill. My father was the pope. The formalities were now my duties. His representative became my vocation. After our sweet private exchange, we were awakened to reality with the Cardinal's closing. We were back in the Vatican. It would be a long night before the consummation we sought. Father threw a lavish dinner in our honor. Afterward, we attended a licentious comedy acted out in our honor. For the first time, I realized how inappropriate the subject matter on the grounds where Saint Peter's bones rested. Never was what went on in this place acceptable to the dear Savior for whom it was supposedly built.

Such disrespect to the Savior was further aggrandized as my father showed his carnal affections for Giulia, my guardian and house manager, Adriana's daughter-in-law. Father's attention for me soon waned in his panting for the girl slightly older than me. He sought after her as a bull seeking after a female in heat. How ironic that Father's shield proudly displayed a bull. His edicts were called papal bulls. Why did she seek after him? I employ the explanation for her and every other woman and girl, they did so partially thinking they were pleasing God. The larger motive was financial.

I suppose also seeing how everyone bowed before the pope gave them a sense of power as he exchanged bows with them in his private chambers. Giulia was further encouraged as a holy concubine when Father appointed her brother Alessandro Farnese as a cardinal. The populace of Rome secretly called him the "petticoat cardinal" in the dark rooms of the Holy See. She would give birth to a daughter who was not immaculately conceived. Giulia, a friend my age, gave birth to my sister, the lust child of my father.

Gifts of great treasure were given to me and my beloved — gold brocades, gold rings with diamonds, rubies, and sapphires. Father awarded my Giovanni with a military contract to raise an army to lead. It would be funded by the Church. While the Romans went home to their hovels, we were celebrating upon the backs of their labors. They worked to survive. We partied upon their sacrifices to God. God was not honored, hardly referenced, and never revered at any of the pope's functions. Pope Alexander VI sat on the throne ornamented with a golden cape, having children at first sit on his lap to show his acceptance of all children as his to love. They were soon replaced by Giulia who seductively moved passionately upon his lap up and down, facing him, kissing him on the right cheek, then the left to the pope's pleasure. Peter lay beneath our ground having been crucified upside down on a cross. I reflect on this now when it is too late to undo what has been done. Giovanni and my hopeful future would soon be squandered at the people's expense, to Giovanni's heartbreak.

I lived in the middle of sin. I observed it daily by those considered most devout. This life became to me what a righteous life was to be. We even consoled ourselves with the fact that we hid nothing. Cesare, as illegitimate as I, was even legitimized by an act of the cardinals. In this religion, I saw sins expunged, illegitimacy removed, indulgences offered in advance. The law was what we determined. God's Word was revised with the pope's wink. Unaware, I was being desensitized to all morality and virtue. Some would lay this at the feet of my father. Others would say I had no chance. My mother was a willing conspirator. The cardinals' only objections were when their own fetishes were infringed. This is not to blame anyone. I willfully consented knowing in the back of my mind, such things were wrong. God's Spirit would compel me to move away from the darkness. I was not willing to let it go.

Father forbade our consummation for some unknown reason to me at the time. Giovanni was not to sleep in my bed until November. Neither of us felt this was right or fair. He claimed it was because of my age, yet he had no qualms copulating with a girl outside the realm of marriage. It was hard for my twenty-six-year-old husband to abstain. For about four days following the wedding, we toiled under the yoke of celibacy. Passion overrode parental obedience. We consummated our love without restraint. Though stymied at first by a vow to Father, my husband and I surrendered to the exuberance of sexual love unleashed. In our bedroom Giovanni and I rehearsed the lines of the Song of Solomon. We then acted them out in our chambers:

I am the rose of Sharon, and the lily of the valleys. As the lily among thorns, so is my love among the daughters. As the apple tree among the trees of the wood, so is my beloved among the sons. I sat down under his shadow with great delight, and his fruit was sweet to my taste. He brought me to the banqueting house, and his banner over me was love. Stay me with flagons, comfort me with apples: for I am sick of love. His left hand is under my head, and his right hand doth embrace me. I charge you, O ye daughters of Jerusalem, by the roes, and by the hinds of the field, that ye stir not up, nor awake my love, till he please.

I finally understood why the Shulamite begged the daughters of Jerusalem three times in this small book, "Do not awaken love until it pleases" (my personal application). Once the physical love is experienced, it becomes difficult to not want such an experience often. Giovanni and I were captivated by the love found in the marriage bed. I finally understood at the young age of thirteen what a great gift God had given married couples. Where those around me (the harem of my father in particular) recklessly cheapened the Divine gift, we enjoyed it with God's Blessing. Two illegitimate children partook in love as the God of all gods had designed.

We spent days in our bedroom, just he and I. Our servants brought food and water to our door. They would knock and walk away leaving the lovers to their delicacy. We would not rouse for work, for duty, for appearances, or even for my father. The Old Testament had allowed for men of war to have a complete year off from their nation's duties following marriage. God wanted a couple, in His Will, to enjoy Him and the mate He had predetermined. We were delighted in what He had ordained.

My First Marriage Soon Crumbles

Father was a king maker. He was also the grantor of kingdoms to kings. I look back surprised at how much weight he carried. He made Cesare a cardinal of Valencia. He made Juan a duke of Gandia. He established Joffre a prince. The pope chose King Alfonso to replace King Ferdinand over Naples which angered King Charles VIII of France. To strengthen his power over Naples, Father married my twelve-year-old brother Joffre to King Alfonso's seventeen-year-old daughter Sancha. They would reside in Sancha's palace.

As pope, King Ferdinand and Queen Isabella rendered submission to his authority because both were staunch Catholics. It was not long, however, Father's secular aspirations, tarnished his religious position. Queen Isabella particularly was offended at the avarice of the man who led the Holy See. She was repulsed her pope not only had illegitimate children, but that he promoted them to powerful and profitable positions. If that were not enough, she began to see firsthand the immorality of the pope's illegitimate son's behavior. The Duke of Gandia, my brother Juan, did not consummate his marriage with his lady prearranged. Instead, he spent the nights killing dogs and cats, visiting brothels, and squandering his benefices and the treasuries of his duchy. He was into gambling, drinking, and philandering. He spoke disrespectfully to those of high regard. He milked the privilege he was given until all in his vicinity hated him. The complaints reached the Queen who expected more of those entrusted with civil and religious positions. She felt being a Christian should be more than sacraments. She expected a Christ-like lifestyle.

When I heard of her criticism, I was offended. She was disparaging our whole family. I reasoned that we would not hold the positions we held, had God not been pleased with us. In hindsight, I realize we climbed the ladder of greed. Nothing to our rise was of God. We climbed to spite Him.

Things began to unravel for my marriage in August of that year. It made me thankful we had not waited for this month as my father had prescribed. A plague hit the city of Rome. I do not think it was random, looking back. I believe it was a warning from Heaven. One none of us heeded. Giovanni was caught in a precarious position. His family sought the overthrow of the reigning family of Naples even cutting a deal with King Charles VIII of France to take over. Father reinforced the status quo making his own agreements with Alfonzo the son of the previous monarch. This put my husband, whom he made an employee, in a bind. Giovanni received pay both from the Church and the State of Milan, his homeland. The pope pitted my husband against his own people. He was to choose — his papal employment and his marriage, or his State and his own people. The Sforza family had hoped my union with Giovanni would bring them support from the pope. Little did they know, Father's support was always self-directed. My husband left Rome to work out the matter with his conscience. He had my blessing. He used the plague as a good excuse.

In November, Giovanni returned to Rome to be with me, his wife. It was then, he and I made known our physical consummation to our families. Cesare was the only one who knew. He was always willing to keep my confidence. My husband shared with me his concern regarding Father's position on Naples. I broached my concern to Father, but he would not listen to what I had to say. He said he knew what he was doing, that I should trust him for the good of our family. Giovanni then took it upon himself to write Father for guidance. As was his custom, Father was cold to any dissent. Cardinal Ascanio Sforza was also consulted by Giovanni. He recommended that my husband and I move to Pesaro to be away from my father's whims.

With the plague raging in May of 1495, Father finally gave permission for Giovanni, myself, Adriana, and Giulia to take a trip to Pesaro. The destination was one I secretly planned to make my permanent home for the sake of our marriage and my husband's peace. I was thirteen years old, but Providence had blessed me with wisdom of one older. Orsino joined us in Pesaro to be with Giulia. Though she was openly my father's mistress, I was elated to see her resume her role as a loving wife to my childhood friend. It was funny how, out of the lair of sinfulness, true goodness raises its appeal.

We had not been gone long before Father became suspicious. He wrote to me. He separately corresponded with Adriana. He continued his love prose with Giulia. His recurring theme was for "his women" to return. He wanted Giovanni to stay in Pesaro to defend Naples against the French assault. His concern was perhaps for our safety, but I believe more out of fear we would begin to think for ourselves. The pope caught wind that Orsino was with us which he felt jeopardized his relationship with the man's wife. I believe he longed for me to return without Giovanni because my husband dared show a dual allegiance. His Beatitude was only content when everything went his way. He loved us, yes. But he loved only as much as a selfish person could.

What bothered Father most was for "his women" to be out of his direct command. He chose when we appeared. He often selected what we would wear. He told us who to marry. No one moved without his permission. Constant correspondence was required by him. Because our letters would normally take weeks to be delivered, Father, with Church money, paid couriers for the sole purpose of carrying our letters to and fro in a matter of three to four days.

Even so, in Pesaro, he had no reach. I was the countess of Pesaro, greatly received as my own woman. I had never seen a lord loved as much as my Giovanni. His vassals adored him. They responded to his faintest whisper. He treated them with respect. It was clear the love was mutual. No wonder Giovanni struggled to honor my father at the cost of these dear people. We were enjoying living our own lives. Giulia even left for her hometown with Orsino to check on her dying brother without Father's knowledge. When the pope heard, he was furious, "How dare Giulia go anywhere without my approval. How dare Lucrezia, you allow her to leave without my granting."

Father was like a child in a sandbox seeking to dictate what games would be played and who would play which role. At a distance, his juvenile hedonism was on full display. I believe he knew it too and was ashamed to display something so contrary to his public front. He did not care if Giulia ever saw her brother again. She existed to please Alexander VI, no one else. This was his attitude toward every pawn on his board, and every piece was a pawn with only one king. When he would send me a terse letter, I made sure to placate my father. Even knowing his nature, I did live to please him. I knew nothing different. He was my god. All I had, came from him. I ask for forgiveness for breaking the first command for the whole of my past unconverted life.

I later found that Father's whole foundation was cracking. France was on attack. The plague was threatening his life. His women were out of pocket exposed. Within his Cardinal delegation, many were being peeled off to call for Father's removal from the papacy. The charge was simony — selling something spiritual for money. It came from the Book of Acts where Simon Magus sought to buy power from the Apostles. He had relegated things of God and our Dear Lady to things to be bought and sold as commodities. Such was denied by my father. Yet, the charges were true. I did not see it then. As I was brought up, these were the things popes did. It was the reason people sought to be the pope, gave good money and made huge promises to attain the position. I have found people often accuse others of the crimes they themselves do. If a person's villainy works for them, they are happy. If the behavior inconveniences them, they are against it. Regardless, my Beatitude was losing his life's dream. He would do whatever it took to keep what was his, that is anything but truly seek God.

Giulia and Orsino were determined to resume their married life in Bassanello. Giulia even sent a letter to Father telling him this. She wanted him to know she was doing so of her own free will. Father, never one to be denied, wrote to her mother-in-law, to her husband, to their relative Cardinal Farnese, along with several others. He even threatened them all with excommunication and eternal damnation if they did not comply. Jesus said a man should not be afraid of one who can kill the body. All should fear the one who can destroy both the body and soul in Hell. My father did not have that power. I thought he did once. Again, I grieve of how distorted our doctrine became.

The young couple along with Adriana delayed as long as possible. The pope had one last threat to Orsino for which he could not ignore. He threatened the Orsini people if Orsino did not comply. Sadly, he rejoined his troops at the pope's order, sending his wife and her sisters back to the clutches of her illicit benefactor. Giulia took a long detour to get to Rome. The pope let it go. It was as if Father was resigned to losing the fidelity of his mistress so long as she did not trade his affection for her husband's.

This said, I remained in Pesaro with my husband. My father beckoned for his lover Giulia more than me. I was content in Giovanni's arms. Our abode was on the mountain of San Bartolo, overlooking the city. It was my dream come true. Life was easy. The French were moving toward Rome, but we were out of danger. I had a momentary rebellious reflection, "Father had chosen this lot. Let him work his way out of the mess."

Father combined mastery of persuasion with organization. He built an alliance which he called the Holy League, comprised of Milan, Venice, and the papal forces. At first, they fled the Vatican with the French King Charles VIII in hot pursuit. The French soon found themselves vulnerable in a nation which could fall upon them in an instant. The king quickly retreated realizing his goals could not be accomplished. Father with Cesare by his side succeeded in creating a greater fear of the papacy among the nations because of the pope's military, not divine, capabilities.

Another man who gained renown during the French invasion was Francesco Gonzaga who led the League's forces at the Taro River. King Charles was routed, leaving a scattered treasury along his path of escape. Gonzaga, the former brother-in-law of my husband, the brother of his deceased wife, was a true warrior, a military genius. He added to this, his magnetic personality. He was able to draw men to himself, to convince them they could do anything they wished with little effort. His military prowess became legendary among the Italians and those who dared threaten them or their pope. For his efforts, Father awarded him the Golden Rose papal commendation. He also obtained cardinal positions for his friends.

In times of peace, Francesco Gonzaga turned that magnetism upon the female population. He was not a handsome man, but his reputation among the men was a draw to their women. He could do, without looks, what Father did with looks and personality. He was married to a prominent lady — Isabella, of the powerful d'Este family. She was beautiful, intelligent, and gifted. Gonzaga carried her as a trophy upon his arm. Her intrigues were solely of the political nature. As a result, she cared little that he womanized any female who caught his eye. He even paraded mistresses to events with his wife. She gave it no mind. He was also said to have enjoyed young boys. He was in Father's inner circle. Efficacy not morality mattered. I would be repulsed by his reputation and dazzled by his presence. I was young but found myself keenly interested in the man. Again, he was like Father. Out of his range, he had no influence upon me.

My husband was soon sent to Naples to drive out the remaining French battalions. I returned to Rome and settled in for more than a year while my husband carried out his duties. Once again, I found myself entranced by my father, unwilling to leave his side. My husband wrote asking that I join him back in Pesaro. I was torn. My Father was adamant. I was not to leave his side. If I chose to be with Giovanni there, it was an affront to Father, a treacherous act of ingratitude. He said Giovanni could join me in my palace of Santa Maria in Portico. I believe during this time, my husband realized we would never be out from under Father's will. I disobeyed the Lord's admonition that a man leaves his father and mother and cleaves to his wife, as the wife should leave her father and mother and live under her husband's household.

In his absence, there was much activity at the Vatican. My brother Joffre came to Rome to see our father with his beautiful wife Sancha on his arm. Father arranged the marriage but often resented my brother's wife. She was five years older than her child groom and felt a dominance at the age difference. While in Rome, Father accused his daughter-in-law of having many men visiting her quarters. (Two of which were my brothers Cesare and Juan, though my father never singled them out.) The pope piously said such behavior was not worthy of the position she held. What a farce for one so carnal to charge another to be holy. Sancha's majordomo challenged the pope publicly intimating the only man in Sancha's bedroom other than her husband was a man past his sixties. The inference being my own father had sought to taste his daughter-in-law's delicacies for himself. The majordomo was quickly replaced.

I look back at the grand procession of my brother entering the city. My brother Cesare, who a few weeks before had daringly escaped King Charles' clutches, dispatched over two hundred men-at-arms, cardinals, ambassadors, and extended family. Joffre's entrance was made a spectacle for all the city to see. I met them at the basilica of Saint John's Lateran where we joined to pray before the high altar per our tradition, an empty one for us Borgias. The parade passed the Church of Saint Mark. I was riding on a donkey with black satin. Sancha rode a horse with velvet and black satin. Father waited, watching out the window of the Vatican with his hand raised to pass on his blessing. I think of Mark and how he suffered for our Lord. He won many converts to Christ in Egypt before being martyred there. Later his body was returned to Rome. Such a spiritual contradiction had never crossed my mind as I welcomed home my brother Joffre.

The grand entrance crossed the Tiber on the Ponte Sant' Angelo bridge toward the Vatican. Seated on a high chair was His Holiness, Pope Alexander VI waiting to receive his children as Il Papa. As each of us approached, we kissed his foot and his hand. Father than held our heads in his hands, bowing to acknowledge us. We then went through the line of cardinals, kissing each of their hands. I noticed how a few sought to kiss beautiful, green-eyed Sancha with her dark hair on the lips, but restrained themselves realizing all were watching. I then sat at Father's feet on one side, Sancha on the other. Crouching at his feet as we were, the pope seemed to draw a sordid pleasure.

The next Sunday, the day observed for Pentecost, we gathered with the pope at Saint Peter's for mass. Rather than sit with the rest of the congregants, youthful Sancha suggested we stand on the marble staircase where the canonics sang the epistle and Evangile. In a place of reverence for the Lord and our Dear Lady, we broke the boredom by mocking the speaker. We had a hilarious time. We could see the disapproving expressions on all the faces before us. We found that even more entertaining. At the time, our thought was, "What are they going to do? We are with the pope. These people are actually here for his approval, not us for theirs."

Sancha was the daughter of a king. She reveled in her royal position. While she was with us, my palace was the daily center of activity with dances, live music, parties, and masquerades. Dukes, cardinals, priests, and Father all frequented our abode. We made grand processions through the streets of Rome going from one place of interest to another. I think Sancha was surprised seeing religious men reveling in the same paganism as the men of Aragon. She was exhilarated by the removal of all restraints.

I am horrified as I think back at how I acted in the places set apart for worshipping God, how I contributed to Sancha's delinquency. One day, while riding through the streets, we heard a man preaching on the street corner near the Vatican. We stopped to hear his booming voice. The crowds gathered around this man giving him their undistracted attention. His name was Savonarola. He was from the pulpit of Saint Marco in Florence. I suppose he arrived for some elder meeting. I can hear him even today. He called for Rome to repent. He called out Father saying:

The Pope must repent. Look at his daughter and daughter-in-law parade their lewdness in public, daring the great God of Heaven to do anything about it. I declare God sees. He hears. He will act. He cannot destroy Sodom and let Rome continue to stand in its idolatry, duplicity, hypocrisy, and heresy. I declare Rome the new Sodom!

The preacher was correct. What he said made me angry, but it bore down into my soul. I remember full well. I was sick at my stomach and demanded our procession return to my palace. Today, I realize more and more the absence of God in these places so revered. Yes, these were historic places. Yes, from the brutality of the ancient Roman emperors, rose the Power of Christ. He ascended, and the Roman Empire was transformed into the Holy Roman Empire. Our first pope, recognized posthumously, held his office in the greatest humility. He did without. He made mistakes. He repented. He felt himself unworthy to be compared to Christ. He refused reverence for himself. The earliest popes Saint Linus and Saint Clement were devout followers of Jesus. Clement even was martyred for his refusal to compromise at the hands of Emperor Trajan. They were servants of Christ, seeking to please Him. They believed that He must increase, and they must decrease. My father felt he must increase. And if he increased, the Lord and His Will must decrease.

It is easy to place the blame at my father's feet where I sat that eventful day. The confessions are not for him, but for me. Everything we did was for appearances. We were to pray, so we prayed. We were to attend mass, so we attended mass. We were to reference God in our correspondence, so we mentioned His Name. If the appearances were not required, we would never have done any of these things. Our lives would have been no different than the emperors of old. We knowingly used religion to gain our power. Father used his position in the Church to wield an eternal fear if his bidding was not carried out. The quest was for an ever-growing monarchy with land, armies, wealth, and power. Alexander the Great's kingdom was the goal of Father. The division of it after his death was the inheritance, we his children expected. Religion was simply the additive to make our aspirations more palatable.

There we were assembled, the pope and his children. Soon after Joffre arrived, our brother Juan entered the city. As I have stated before, in times past, the offspring of popes were called nephews and nieces to keep with the sacerdotal celibacy expected. Father exempted himself from this upon his rise. He pulled back the covers daring any to question his right. Juan brought with him a Spanish girl as a gift to His Holiness, a new addition to his chamber of courtesans. The majority of cardinals celebrated, seeking to add to their own collections. To build the kingdom, he would need reliable subjects. None would be more than his children, so why not have many? He expected the kingdom to recognize each of us for his legacy to last. They did. God's Word on marriage and adultery were discarded. The pope took the authority to add to and subtract from what God had spoken.

Annulment

The Orsini rebels in concert with the French continued to challenge the hold Alexander VI had on his growing empire. Father appointed each of his male children to take part in eliminating any threats to the papacy. This included his call to my husband to return to Rome with as many men as possible. Giovanni refused at a great financial cost. I was not surprised. But I knew his fidelity to his family would cost him my hand sooner or later. I would go to him, but faced with the pressure, I did as he. I chose my family though righteousness was not on our side. How often do we choose family over what is right and true? I grieve this is our nature. We worship the gifts of God rather than the Giver God. We all find in time that He will not countenance any gods before Him — not even family.

When my father, through a papal brief dated January 5, 1497, issued an ultimatum that my husband returns to Rome or never sees me again, my husband showed his love for me. He came with his hat in hand, not apologizing for taking a stand, but showing deference to my father. Father immediately incorporated Giovanni in Father's public religious activities parading him side by side with my brother Juan on Palm Sunday at the Sistine Chapel. It was the pope's theater displaying his graciousness toward those who had evaded his will.

Giovanni witnessed the pope's hypocrisy day after day throughout Easter week. On Good Friday, he woke me with tears in his eyes. He let me know how much he loved me, but that he would love God above all. He said he understood if I needed to be by my father's side, but God would not allow him to play along with the charade of holiness any longer.

As we were visiting, a knock came to my door. Giovanni's chamberlain informed us both that my father and my brother Cesare plotted to poison my husband. We thanked our faithful friend and asked him to leave us alone for a time. After he left, Giovanni asked if I minded him riding to Sant' Onofrio on the Janiculum hill to make confession. He would then ride on to Pesaro for he feared for his life. I held my husband close. Together we wept. I assured him of my love and devotion. Once he arrived in Pesaro, I asked that he send for me publicly. My hopes were that Father would concede to my wishes, plus allow for the submission required of every wife.

I grieved for my husband. I could not leave my room to look at Father. Even then, I remember the passing notion of how evil my father was. This representative of Christ on earth was nothing of the sort. Anger overflowed, even at age sixteen. How could I tolerate this? Why wouldn't I leave? But for some reason, I could not leave the one who was behind so much evil.

On April 1, Father sent a messenger to Giovanni demanding his return to Rome. I was aware of Father's edict, but knew as did my husband, his return would mean certain death. Giovanni returned the demand with one of his own, "Send my wife to me here in Pesaro Your Holiness." Giovanni's two cardinal cousins would be no help. They refused to express their displeasure with the pope for fear they would lose their power and pay.

On May 26, Father signed two writs of divorce, both equated more formally to annulments. He sent them to Giovanni to choose which one to sign. Pope Alexander VI determined my marriage was over, but he would have it annulled so that he could shop me to someone more beneficial to his dynastic goals. The two writs offered — one blamed me for not breaking off my father's previous arranged engagement with Don Gasparo. The pope called the Gasparo engagement off, not me. The other writ blamed Giovanni saying he was impotent. In the eyes of God, the first one was a lie, but, if true, would be a reasonable out. The second one was a lie, and in the eyes of God was no reason for divorce. I should have stood up to my father. I should have run immediately to my husband's waiting arms. But I did neither. I expressed my displeasure. He shut me down in anger. I fled to the San Sisto convent instead.

There were many convents which had the air of holiness, but inside were bordellos of women who had not the means to marry, so they found a place to copulate freely. Men would make their journey to the convent for "prayer", but instead preyed upon the unmarriable. San Sisto was not that kind of convent. Here were nuns who sought the Lord. They gave everything up for Him including the lust of the flesh. Their marriage was to God alone. They had a peace like no other women I had ever met. When I was being brought up, and my mother had cast me aside, it was San Sisto where I was nurtured and loved. It was here where I had my taste of what it really meant to serve God. In this convent, I felt true, unselfish love not just from the women but from the Lord Himself.

While I was there, Father continued to push for Giovanni to sign a writ of divorce. Giovanni would not lie and say I had done something worthy of annulment. He also refused the fabrication which said we had never consummated our love on the account of his inability. My husband denied vehemently such claims. Giovanni was then commanded to prove his virility by taking a prostitute and copulating with her in the presence of the papal legate. He refused on the grounds such an act was a sin and an act of infidelity. He and I knew the truth. We had consummated our love an infinite number of times to my pleasure. Father knew we had as he released the dowry to Giovanni once he knew we made love. But in our world, a bride loved physically by another is a bride of lesser value with which to barter. Father was unbending.

I received news at the convent through a messenger Father's lawyer sent, stating that Giovanni had agreed to the annulment citing his own impotence. I had no idea what coercion was used upon my husband. But to protect him, I quickly wrote a letter saying the same. It was a few years later, I realized my husband had never signed. His cousins did it in his name. And like that, the love, the commitment, the devotion, the ring, the vows were all wiped away. A part of me died that day. I realized true love for me would never materialize in an earthly marriage. The religious vicar of our world had predetermined this. My role was to submit to my father, the most powerful Church leader on the planet.

But I would not submit for months. Father even sent a sheriff to escort me back to Rome. The prioress of our convent refused to let him in. The pope figured sooner or later, I would get bored and return, which I did. The Holy Father of all Christendom gave me no other option.

San Sisto

A terrible thing happened while I was in exile at San Sisto. My brother Juan, the apple of Father's eye, was murdered. He was found in the Tiber River by fishermen. His clothes were covered in river mud. His throat had been slashed. He had been stabbed multiple times. The keepers of the Castel Sant' Angelo employed by the pope washed, cleaned, and dressed my brother.

We were told that after a supper with my mother at her country villa, Cesare, Juan, and Cardinal Borgia were riding back to the Vatican when Juan said he had to go meet someone. Cardinal Borgia supposedly warned him not to leave as the streets of Rome were not safe for a man of his wealth and influence. Juan shook off the warning but did send one of his men to gather his light night armor. As the man did so, he was attacked but fought off the assailants. He rushed to meet Juan at the Piazza Judea. But Juan never showed. The last sighting of my brother was by a shopkeeper near the Piazza. He said he saw Juan ride off with a masked man in a black cloak.

The next day, when Juan had still not returned, Father issued an edict for an all-out search for his beloved. Spaniard allies of my father questioned many in the vicinity with swords drawn. There was great fear throughout the city of the culprits, but also of my father's men. Giorgio Schiavi, a timber dealer, recounted seeing the disposal of a body on the riverbank near his barge. He was lying down after loading his barge when he heard some horses approach. He rose from his slumber unseen behind some of his logs. Two men rode up, leading a third horse with a body draped over it. They looked around. When they saw no one, they dismounted and dumped the body into the river. They quickly rode off.

With the pope's call for the search, Schiavi reported to the Vatican what he had seen. When asked why he had not come forth sooner, he replied, "I have seen hundreds of bodies dumped at that spot. There just never has been anyone troubled by the missing until now." Those engaged in the fishing industry were informed of the account. They began their search. Several bodies were discovered in varying stages of decomposition. But a man named Battistino da Taglia brought up in his net the body of my brother.

When Father heard of my brother's death, he was wrought with grief. Juan was buried in our family chapel with a grand procession of mourners. Father was not in attendance. He had locked himself in his apartment at the Vatican and wept for all to hear for four days. When he finally came out, he had not eaten and was dehydrated. Many feared for his life. His first words were, "I have never loved anyone as much as I loved my son, the Duke of Gandia." My father was telling the truth. Cesare and I knew, next to the pope himself, Father loved this son above all others.

There were many suspects in the murder of my brother. There should have been more. He was a gambler who owed many people money. He was a womanizer who was threatened by many angry husbands. He was a married man who, on the night of his murder, spent the night of sexual pleasure with the courtesan Madonna Dalmatia. He flaunted his immorality so much so that King Ferdinand and Queen Isabella refused to address him by name but called him "the illegitimate one."

The Orsini family topped the list of main suspects. Father had one of their leaders, Virginio Orsini imprisoned for acts disapproving to His Holiness. Don Orsini died while in prison. Many believed it was from the torture ordered by the pope. Father then assigned the lead in ridding Italy of this family to Juan who was ill-equipped and had no intention to do anything responsible.

My brother Cesare was a key suspect as he benefited the most from Juan's death. My husband Giovanni was listed as a person of interest as he had reason to seek payback for my loss. There was no way he would have murdered my brother. This was not his nature. Besides, he was in Pesaro and had no influence in Rome. Two resentful cardinals of the pope were suspected. The region of Benevento resented the pope's appointment of such an important fief to be given to one such as my brother Juan. Some of their leaders were also considered guilty.

When all was said and done, the case dropped. Most likely because my brother Cesare became captain-general of the Church in the place of my deceased brother Juan. There was no desire to re-engage the war with the French and the Orsini's. Besides, Juan was not loved enough by even his own duchy for anyone to pursue.

The most remarkable thing happened which made me hopeful for my family. A report reached me at the convent that my father ended the blame game. From his lips, he said, "We have been punished for our sins. God is punishing me for how I have led His Church. We will begin to reform ourselves today and proceed to do the same throughout the Church." Never had I heard such a sincere repentance from my father in all the years of my life.

That evening Father sent for the preacher from Florence, Savonarola, who had ridiculed the pope for his godless lifestyle. When the preacher arrived, Father wept on his shoulder pleading with him for direction on how to turn his life around. I was told my father actually began to pray. He started taking the rituals and traditions of the Church earnestly. Father displayed a reverence for God. I wanted to be in Rome for my family. All anger toward my father had dissipated. If I could receive forgiveness from God in that convent, how could I not forgive?

When I returned to Rome, Father's devotion began to subside at the first sight of me. He sent the preacher of Saint Marco away. He pressed the matter of divorce from my husband on the false grounds he had created. He had me stand before the divorce commission to admit my virginity was still intact. All was carried on as if Juan had never died. Pope Alexander VI was back in all his chicanery.

I lied before the commission declaring my husband was impotent. I hated myself for the moment. Before long, I resolved this was how things were for women and for children of the pope. There was no need to pout or sulk. The best thing I could do for me in the situation I was born into, was to please myself. The best way to do that was to please the pope, knowing the benefices would follow.

A month after my forced annulment, another tragedy hit close to the pope. His favorite chamberlain Perotto, the one who managed his court of young women, was found dead in the Tiber along with one of Father's favorite mistresses Penthisilea. The Tiber had a habit of swallowing up enemies. No one seemed exempted. Father was considered the culprit as was my brother Cesare. The thought was perhaps Father had Perotto killed for partaking in Penthisilea's confections. He was never one to share what he claimed as his. The death could also have been a warning directed at the pope to show not even the ones closest to him were safe.

There was one rumor I knew was not true. Some believed Perotto had impregnated me in a lurid affair behind my father's back and that Cesare killed him to protect my honor. This above all was ludicrous in so many ways. Was Father the culprit or the target? Did Cesare have some insult for which he demanded revenge? Or were their deaths unrelated? The question of their murder was never settled.

My Second Marriage

Within two months of my annulment, Father was already shopping me for the next beneficial merger to his kingdom. Whispers and mockery followed my every step during this time. All knew it was impossible for me to have been a virgin. Most considered me a woman of ill-repute. Some said my father missed me in his bed. Others said Cesare had sought a dispensation to take me as his own bride. I was steeled through all this. Or perhaps, I became numbed by it. The pope paid no mind to the criticisms. He was the lord of the religious realm. Most acquiesced to his claim.

Father considered the prince of Salerno for my next husband. This one fell through. Father then met with the Orsini family leaders hoping a marriage to one of their male offspring would solidify a lasting peace for the papacy. The Orsini's demanded more than Father would concede. Finally, because Naples was the key point of contention, he worked a contract with King Fredric of Naples for his nephew Alfonso of Aragon.

Alfonso was given the principality of Salerno making him the prince of Salerno. Father desired a son-in-law with more property to his name, so in the negotiation, King Fredric gave Alfonso the territories of Quadrata and Bisceglie. He would be both a duke and a prince. Father in return, gave my hand along with 40,000 ducats as a dowry. The pope gave one last nonnegotiable to approve the merger. I was to remain in Rome. My husband was to stay at least a year with me there. Father had experienced his lack of control with me at a distance. He would not suffer such again.

I loved Giovanni. I missed him. Because my first husband and his family were no longer politically useful to Father, Giovanni was discarded. The family of my second husband offered much to Father's ambitions. This marriage could last so long as there were advantages to be gained and worked. The key reason for this betrothal? Father, as well as Cesare, wanted a marriage bond with King Ferdinand. This would place Cesare in direct line to royalty. Our father's quest was not for a spiritual kingdom alone, he sought a temporal one as well. Cesare, true to his given name, aspired to be the next Julius Caesar. Juan had had no ambitions at all. Cesare did, which was all the more reason why our beloved brother had to be removed.

As I gazed upon Alfonso, he was gentle, kind, well-educated, humble, and handsome. He had a sincerity which was similar to Giovanni. Beyond this, he was the brother of my friend, of Joffre's wife, Sancha. I was so happy. I was blessed by God that in all the thrashing out of details, I was held by another good man. I never saw it at the time. Women were chattel to be gained and discarded, to be abused and mastered. Yes, Father held a strong position, but he was marrying me to men with power and possessions of their own. Father also had enemies which could be ready allies should the need present itself. I had seen how other women of position had been mistreated. Yet, the lot was never mine. God, in His wrath, remembered mercy toward me.

Later, Alfonso told me of a caution he was sent prior to our wedding. A humanist named Fausto Evangelista sent him a note reminding him before entering this union, that he would be wise to deliberate with his two predecessors — Gasparo and Giovani. Alfonso paid him no mind.

At the age of eighteen, I was happily married to Alfonso, Duke of Bisceglie, Prince of Salerno about seven months after my annulment from my first husband. I saw my marriages as a teen would view the courtship of youth. Boys calling on a girl come and go. Seldom are any paid much mind. Never are any of them seen as a lifetime family member. When one leaves, another comes. This is the life of the immature. This was my life into adulthood. Marriages were no more than youthful romances to test and discard. I was an adult when it came to cardinals and ambassadors. I could play hostess over affairs of the papacy and the state. But in marriage, I functioned as a child at the whim of my father.

My wedding robes were splendid. They were comprised of silk, enhanced with jewels of every kind. The long robe was fashioned like a golden French brocade. More jewels and pearls adorned my neck. I dare to think what this gown cost the Church. What mattered was wealth and power were on full display to show the importance of the pope and his children. I grieve as I think back to these days again. Material wealth comes and goes. I have no idea whatever happened to those robes or those jewels. The Lord Jesus said our treasures should not be gathered here where they can rust, wilt, decay, or be stolen. True wealth which carries itself for eternity for our usage is in how we follow Christ, what we do in His Name.

Later in life, after tragedy struck my life in the worst way, I began to lay up treasures in Heaven. I wish I had not waited so long.

Our wedding celebration should have been seen as an omen of things to come. The event was semi-private due to the rumors moving throughout Rome about me, the pope, Juan, and Sancha. At the meal, a fight broke out between Sancha's servants and Cesare's. Men unsheathed their swords to kill. Father's attendants fled, while Father jumped in between hoping to broker a peace by his authority. He demanded order. He was pushed around like an old man between strong men of fighting age. Thankfully, wisdom dictated, and cooler heads prevailed. I looked over at Alfonso. He did not know me well enough to say anything, but his look appeared to say, "Is this the norm at the Vatican?"

Following the meal, Alfonso and I were led to our quarters for a time to consummate our marriage. I believe this was an undisclosed term from the King of Naples. He would not have this marriage annulled on a lie. Rising from our quarters, sweat-drenched and happy, all celebrated with dancing. Father pleaded for me and Sancha to do a dance together. He always enjoyed watching young women dance. We then saw a play in which Cardinal Cesare, my brother, played a unicorn. He could never play the eunuch.

My brother Cesare doted upon my latest husband. He invited him to his apartment. He threw feasts in his honor the following week. I had never seen such affection given to anyone as Cesare gave to Alfonso. I was delighted if the acts were sincere. My fear was these were superficial acts to ingratiate himself with the new duke, prince, and my consort.

At one of the feasts held in our honor. Cesare had sugar statues crafted for himself, me, Alfonso, Joffre, Sancha, and Father. The ones for me and my husband were kind and flattering. The master of sugar-craft made a shapely statuette of a beautiful woman for me. He said it embodied all that I am. He made a handsome cupid statue for Alfonso. The sugar confection Cesare had ordered for himself was of a mighty warrior connected to a goddess of war. It was sinister and it was sacrilegious — everything that Cesare represented.

The other statuettes made were mockeries of their recipients. For Joffre, his sugar statue was of a man sleeping. Cesare was signaling that our younger brother was a lazy sloth with no ambition. For Joffre's wife, Sancha, he had a statuette made of a unicorn, symbolizing chastity. His subtle scorn declared she was the antithesis of her model. The statuette made for Father pleased the pope. It should not have. For all those in attendance, there should have been a conviction, but there was none. He had a sugar model made of a woman holding an apple in her hand. The depiction was clear. Our vicar of Christ was the unashamed Adam of our generation, gladly taking the apple of sexual temptation along with whatever woman held it.

We lived in my palace, the Palazzo Santa Maria in Portico. To be in another man's bed did not seem to bother Alfonso. Though he hardly knew me, I believe he loved me. He sought to please my every whim. I loved poetry, so he encouraged me to pursue my passion. He even invited poets to visit our palace. Men like his former tutor, Raphael Brandolinus Lippus, as well as others like Aquilano, Accolti, Arention, and Vincenzo Calameta. Often these men would write about a forbidden target of their affection. They wrote as if they had shared the bed with the unobtainable human goddess. Arentino made love with me in his poems. Alfonso would blush as the poet read aloud his fantasy. I was relieved my husband had no jealousies. He was contented with the belief I was his and would always be. This was my determination as well.

The consummation of our love produced a child. I was pregnant. And I was young. My ladies-in-waiting were the only sisters I ever really had. They were also my constant companions, my friends, my confidants. They celebrated my pregnancy almost as much as Alfonso and my father. At this age, I felt invincible. One day on a picnic, my ladies and I decided to have a race to see who was the fastest. I told them, pregnant, I was as fast as any of them. Tragedy struck during the race. I tripped. One of my sisters fell on top of me. I miscarried that evening. I was heartbroken, but hopeful. Two months later, I was pregnant again.

Germany and Spain threatened to withdraw their support of the Holy See. Many of the papal states were in anarchy. The King of Naples, who married his nephew to me, was encouraging the uprising to dethrone the current pope. Father, Alexander VI, felt things were unraveling, but he would not be passive in the argument. Opportunity fell into Father's lap. King Louis XII, who was married to a woman he did not love, sought to marry his predecessor's widow to further his influence. He needed the pope's dispensation for divorce to do so. In exchange the king promised to give Cesare the duchy of Valence.

Cesare jumped at the chance. He hated being a religious leader. Before the College of Cardinals, he stated truthfully that his life was not suited for such an office as cardinal, and that he never had a desire to be a priest. Father issued a dispensation for my brother. In a matter of minutes, my brother became the duke of Valentinois, a French possession. He entered his kingdom in bright red and yellow garments sporting much gold and silver. Not long after, to complete his agreement with the pope, the king procured a wife for Cesare who would succeed in providing him money and more territory. Her name was Charlotte d'Albret. My syphilis-ridden brother consummated the marriage that evening with many witnesses to prove his virility. Father was pleased. His son was as virile as he. The French ties were cemented.

King Louis sent Cesare 1,800 cavalry and 4,000 infantry to bring the papal states into submission. Romagna fell allowing Cesare to expand his dukedom — this one in Italy. The French alliance alienated King Fredric of Naples because King Louis XII claimed Naples as part of his kingdom along with Jerusalem and the two Sicilies. A number of cardinals, sympathetic to King Fredric and the people of Naples, left Rome in protest. Alfonso decided he must leave as well to show support for his uncle, King Fredric. He asked for my consent, which I freely gave though I cried for days after his departure. My father had once again damaged the nest he had feathered for me. Pope Alexander VI sent troopers to drag my husband back, but they were unsuccessful. I heard nothing from him. I feared he had changed his mind about me. Later I was to learn Alfonso did write for me to join him, but Father's men intercepted his letter, giving it to Father not me.

I was six months pregnant at the time of my husband's parting. There was a war raging outside of me, another being waged inside for my life and the baby's. Stress overwhelmed me. My fear was I would lose this baby too. Some women have an easy time childbearing. There were times in history when women's survival rate was only about half once pregnant. As I recite my confessions at this moment, I realize this recurring nightmare was to be my portion.

Father in his anger at Alfonso, ordered his sister, Joffre's wife out of the city. My father never could see allegiances beyond those to himself. Jesus said a person must leave father and mother, sister and brother allegiances if need be, to follow Him. Father, who was nothing like the Savior, required the same thing. Jesus' requirement was for everyone's good. To follow Him meant to love our loved ones even better. He washed people's feet and expected His followers to do the same.

My Father expected his feet to be washed by all, period. His requirement to leave all other loyalties was loss for everyone but him. The pope saw himself as a god to be served by all as such.

Sancha left against her will. I was soon sent off as well though six months pregnant and struggling. I suppose it was to get my mind off the potential loss of another husband. I was escorted by noblemen to the papal castle in Spoleto. I was to be the keeper of the castle, and the regent or governess of the cities of Spoleto and Foligno as well as the district which encompassed them. I was nineteen years old. I was thrust into being the administrator of a region. I had learned watching Father govern. He discussed the things he did and quizzed my brothers and me with similar scenarios. It wasn't until I reached Spoleto, that I realized Father's intentions of a dynastic rule were slowly being put in the real.

Father sent Joffre with me. I suppose to remove him from Neapolitan influence. But he was given no training, nor position. It was clear Joffre was never a favorite, again because I believe the pope did not think Joffre was his biological son. This was apparent when Joffre was wounded in a scrape a few months before our dispatch. Sancha demanded punishment for his assailants. Father's reply was, "He got what he deserved."

Alfonso's escape followed by Sancha's dismissal reinforced Father's disdain for my brother. Far be it from our father's contemplations, he was the one who arranged both of our unions. He made the mess. He punished others when the mess matured. Other than his initial reaction to Juan's murder, he never ever blamed himself.

When the pope sent Joffre and me off, he did equip me with a cushioned, canopied litter for my comfort. He sent my ladies-in-waiting with me, along with a large company of noblemen and attendants. He provided supplies for us as well — over forty-three carts worth. All this was paid for by the worshippers in the parishes across the world. If only they could see where their money went. I dictate this, but I fear most would have no complaint so long as they gain Heaven for their financial sacrifices. If only they could see, what I see now. Their sacrifices cannot gain Heaven. Only a person's acceptance of the sacrifice of Jesus on the Cross gains both forgiveness and Heaven. Nothing more, nothing less. Yes, they were to tithe. Yes, they are to still tithe. And, in truth, God commends their gifts to Him. The guilt of how those offerings were used fell to us.

Near Spoleto, we were met by four hundred infantrymen to escort their new governess into their fair city. As we entered the city, the citizens lined the streets. The bells of their great cathedral rang at my entrance. There were fireworks and music throughout the city at every turn. The view from my castle was beautiful. It overlooked the old city and the valleys of Clitunno and the Tiber. The Umbrian plain was the fertile breadbasket for the region.

All were enthralled to see the daughter of the pope, albeit the illegitimate daughter, pregnant by her second husband. I was one who should be judged, but I was elevated to be the judge of this people. As Father, I gave one day per week to hear complaints, suggestions, and render verdicts. I had no contacts in this city, so I had no reason to show preference to one person or another. They were all strangers to me. I was very busy, but each night, going to my bed, I missed Alfonso. I wondered what he was facing, if he was alright, if he perhaps missed me too.

My questions were answered six weeks later. My husband rode into Spoleto. When he arrived, at first, I was not sure if the man on the horse was Alfonso or Giovanni. I honestly would have been contented with either. I could never reconcile how Jacob could love both Rachel and Leah as recorded in the Bible book of Genesis. But the day Alfonso rode into the city, I understood Jacob's ability to love both. I felt my blonde hair stand on the back of my neck. Goosebumps covered my arms. I was in the judgment seat, but all I wanted to do was throw myself into his arms — which ever man those arms belonged to.

Alfonso was cordial until we retired to my quarters. With an affectionate embrace, he expressed his love for me and his sorrow in our separation. He shared with me how Father had arranged for his return to me. His uncle, King Fredric, approved knowing how important this marriage was to my husband. He let me know Father was meeting us in Nepi with a special gift. We rode out for that city four days later.

When Alfonso and I arrived in Nepi, Father was there with his papal army, attendants, four cardinals, and several priests. The town clamored for his attention as their pope. While there, he bestowed his gift upon me, the city of Nepi under my authority. Seven days later, Father left us assuring us both of his love and commitment to our marriage. Ten days later, I was governess of two domains — Spoleto and Nepi. Because of my marriage, I was the Duchess of Bisceglie and the

Princess of Salerno. All of which increased my income as Father empowered me to remit a new tax upon the populace in payment for my oversight.

Once things were in order, Alfonso and I carried out Father's wishes, we returned to Rome to be near him. Of course, governing the districts was difficult being so far removed. I quickly arranged for couriers to bring me matters to settle. I made occasional trips when His Holiness allowed, but direct governing in my stead was the Archbishop of Valencia, Ludovico Borgia.

A mysterious murder occurred not long after we arrived back in Rome. One of Cesare's closest accomplices was found dead in the Tiber. His hands had been tied. His throat was violently slashed. He was then weighed down by some stones in a sack tied around his feet in the river, but it was not to hide his body. Two ropes were tied around his neck, each connecting to a post on the riverbank with a sign and his armor attached to one of the posts. It was an apparent warning to Father and to Cesare. Their acts would have repercussions. Neither seemed bothered by the threat, but I was. They saw every villainy toward them as an act of the hated Orsini's or of Giovanni Sforza. By publicly attributing retribution to one of two parties, they were able to carry on the charade that their acts were blessed and accepted by the masses.

A Child is Born

On November 1, 1499, my evasive dream was captured. I became a mother of a baby boy we named Rodrigo in honor of my father's given name. Though my father used me for every selfish whim, I still loved him. He treated me extremely well as long as I did what he said. When I did not, I believed he could never quit loving me, nor Cesare. He would chastise us. He would discipline us. He would punish us. And he would use us. But next to himself, he loved the two of us above all others with Juan removed from the chess board.

On November 11, 1499, my son was baptized in the Sistine Chapel at the pope's direction. The Governor of Rome was there, who also represented our emperor Maximillian. All the cardinals attended as well as ambassadors from Florence, Naples, Venice, England, and France. The Spanish captain, Don Juan Cervillon carried little Rodrigo. Two bishops were chosen by Father to serve as godfathers — the Bishop of Caputaqua and the Bishop of Modena.

I look back and am still shocked that the illegitimate daughter of the supposed-to-be celibate pope and another man's wife would be so celebrated by the religious circles of the Church. All knew His Holiness had many mistresses, that he had fathered many children out of wedlock. Yet, they were there to pay homage, to go through the religious, empty motions of setting the pope's grandson apart for God. I rejoice it was done. I feel the ritual was very important then and now. What I cannot comprehend is how evil acts were seen as good, and the evil doer was encouraged to do more.

Not only did the leaders know Father was immoral at home, but he was also thirsty for others' homes. Soon after the baptism, Father gave my husband a command in the papal forces. He sent Cesare with the troops of King Louis XII to seize Romagna. The pope sent his armies to take possession of Gaetani. The Vicar of Christ had armies, still does. Christ never had an army. Why? He never needed one. He came to love. He came to forgive. He came to bring change. Jesus challenged people to walk as He walked, to live for the Kingdom to come, not establish one here. My father was not the antichrist per se. In my studies of the Apostle

John's writings, he said the spirit of the antichrist was already in our midst. In my weakened state, from my bed, I make this confession: I saw everything opposite of Christ, against Christ in my father's dealings, along with many popes before and after.

I did not care at that time what my father did. I benefited from his work. Sometimes we faced hardships, but we seemed to be on a constant trend of more wealth and more power. Father reminded me that sometimes things must be broken to be fixed, defeated to be gained. He was resolved to increase the properties and provinces of the Church. Every cardinal benefited from the expansion. As a result, evil enriched the leaders, so evil was tolerated.

My familial Beatitude signed over to me eight cities from the Gaetani domain — Sermoneta, Bassiano, Ninfa, Norma, Tivera, Cisterna, San Felice, and San Donato after their ruler died conveniently from poison. I became ruler of the whole Sermoneta region, adding to my authority. In exchange, Father paid eighty thousand ducats to the apostolic chamber to close the arrangement. My income and influence continued to soar. This statement was true legally. Practically, it was Father's domain and income which grew substantially. He was establishing his legacy, building his dynasty to succeed him.

Unlike my father or brothers, I had a sense of God. I knew I needed His blessings. I knew I needed His intercession. I believed He punishes as well as protects. With my son four weeks old, I entered Saint Peter's to give God thanks for my son. My earthly father had given me many material things, but my Heavenly Father had given me the things most dear. While I was praying, I heard a celebration going on throughout the streets of Rome.

As I walked out, I saw my brother Cesare riding in. The horses of his company were shod with fine silver. The men upon those horses were dressed in jewels and gold. Cesare even had a privy covered with gold which he carried on all his conquests for his private usage. Everything he needed to show wealth and power was provided by the poor worshippers around the world who gave their alms to honor Christ. Those offerings were used to enrich my brother, a ruthless, vengeful murderer. I never connected the two until later. My family was using the Lord's Treasury to gain the things for which we coveted. Contrary to the saints who will wear white, Cesare chose to wear black from this time on as a human angel of death.

The Roman citizens had heard the news of Cesare's victory over Romagna as well as over Imola and Forli. The news had spread of his victories days before, but

I had been too busy caring for my baby while recovering from a tough delivery. People were lined seven deep on the streets. Trumpets blasted. Celebratory fireworks were set off ahead of his procession. People were shouting his name, "Cesare! Cesare! Cesare!" the bell towers rang. I pictured what it was like when King David would return victorious from war. The Holy City was welcoming its conqueror, its new Julius Caesar. This was the desire of Cesare — king, emperor, and perhaps pope rolled into one. Father wanted the same.

I made my way up to Father's apartment. He was elated. He would laugh and he would cry, both at the same time. He was overjoyed. Cesare had earned the position Juan had abdicated. He was truly the captain-general of the Holy Roman Church. His daring feats drew praise from every corner. He always tried to outdo his last conquest. Later, he would have six wild bulls released in the Piazza San Pietro. He rode in with a lance and killed five of them. He then dismounted. He threw away his lance, and picked up two swords approaching the remaining bull as the crowd chanted his name. He beheaded the bull in the presence of the masses. They roared with approval, "Who is like our Cesare! Who is like our Captain?"

Such was a good question to ask. Rumors of my brother's heinous acts were well-known, but no one seemed to care. As long as the papal kingdom grew, no one worried about the tactics he employed to remove all opposition. Cesare would later kill the man who held my baby at his baptism — Captain Juan Cervillon. He poisoned some. He ambushed others.

My brother was brave with the bulls, but when it came to his enemies, he always sought the upper hand before executing his hostile acts. This explained why he never ventured to take the state of Ferrara. This provincial jewel sought by king after king and pope after pope had an advantage like no other. The d'Este's who ruled it were benevolent to their people. They never lorded over them but served them as any governing body should. In return, the people loved the d'Este's and would fight to the death to protect them. Ferrara had invested in its own defenses to the point that any attempt to take it would come at an insurmountable cost. This mighty state which my brother avoided would one day be my destiny.

Cesare cloaked his violence so no one could make a clear charge against him. His henchmen, like Don Miguel de Corella, were happy to carry out his orders. Where Cesare killed for advantage, the men in his close circle killed for sport. But my older brother loved me. He protected his sister. And like Father, he would have no rivals for his affections, including me.

The End for My Second Husband

Father's war machine grew stronger and richer. In 1500, he declared the year of jubilee Pilgrims flocked by the thousands to Saint Peter's to gain indulgences. They brought offerings in gratitude for the release of deserved punishments. The Church coffers were overflowing. The money these brought for their peace before God bought men and weapons for Father's war to gain more territory for the Church, to steal from others what had rightfully belonged to them.

God seemed to have something to say of this practice of Pope Alexander VI. While he was seated on his throne at the Hall of Popes waiting to address the worshippers before him, a strong gust of wind tore a large portion of the roof above him. A wealthy banker before my pope was killed instantly as were three others. My father received a serious head wound. Rumors spread throughout the city that he had been killed. The city of Rome was in a state of mourning. To their surprise, it was later learned Father survived the incident. He attributed his escape to the Virgin Mary. The nearly seventy-year-old recovered rather quickly. He had many maladies in his life, but he seemed to live through each one.

I thought of what the Apostle John wrote concerning the antichrist in Revelation, chapter thirteen, "The dragon gave the beast his power and his throne and great authority. One of the heads of the beast seemed to have had a fatal wound, but the fatal wound had been healed. The whole world was astonished and followed the beast."

As I recited earlier, Father acted in a way contrary to Christ. It was not long, he received a head wound similar to Christ's contrarian, the minister of Satan himself. To this regard, many letters were circulating calling Pope Alexander VI a beast, a monster, a son of debauchery, and a subverter of everything Divine. At the time, I gave no mind to the chatter. In hindsight, I have grave concerns.

Not long after this, on July 15, my husband received an even more serious head wound. I knew for certain, there was nothing of his life anti-Christ. He was passing by Saint Peter's after attending a banquet held shortly after my father's accident.

Three men attacked him as he crossed the piazza. They stabbed Alfonso in the head multiple times, as well as in the shoulder, thigh, and arm.

Alfonso's gentleman-in-waiting came to his rescue, but the damage had been done. He carried my husband to the Vatican, bleeding and unconscious. They brought him to where Father and I were still visiting. When I saw him, I was aghast. I did not remember anything afterward.

When I awoke in the Borgia tower, my ladies-in-waiting surrounded my bed. I rose and asked about my dear husband. They told me he was near death. The pope had ordered last rights for my precious consort. Sancha, who had returned upon Father's forgiveness after the Naples uprising, was tending to Alfonso. Sixteen soldiers stood outside his room. In the short time of a week, I almost lost my father, and then was facing a life without my husband. Both were injured by head wounds. One I believe by God. The other by jealous malcontents as best I could tell.

Sancha and I had pallets brought in by his bedside. We feared someone might try to poison him, so we made his meals ourselves. We watched over him in shifts. I am not sure what we thought two women could do, but these two were determined to do whatever we could. I was encouraged to see on the ceiling in his room, frescoes of the Old Testament prophets who predicted the coming of our Savior, the Lord Jesus. I was struck by the peace of the depiction. Into chaos, sin, sickness, and death, the Lord Jesus came to save, to forgive, to heal, and to raise. I did not think the choice of this room was an accident. God had me where He wanted me, completely dependent upon Him, calling on Him. My father could not do a thing for Alfonso. Jesus could.

Doctors were sent from every corner to care for my husband. King Fredric sent his surgeon and his personal physician. Father sent his own. The Colonna sent a physician too. The immediate matter was to get Alfonso's fever down. The longer task was for his head wound to begin to heal. I prayed for the Lord Jesus to do both. He was the Great Physician overseeing it all. Funny, I had not ever given Him my life, but I did call upon Him in times of trouble. He often came to my aid, though my walk was far from His. I wanted His Help. I did not want Him.

On August 6, my husband was doing better. He could sit up in bed. He ate a good portion of what we brought to him. He was in good spirits. I asked if he could identify who attacked, or why. He said he had no idea. He and I both felt more attacks would follow, so I requested his uncle, King Frederic to escort him out of the city when safe for him to be transported.

On August 18, 1500, Alfonso was improving rapidly. We had a meal together in his room with his sister Sancha, his uncle King Frederic, along with his royal envoy. We were laughing as the king and his sister were exchanging stories with my husband. Suddenly, my brother's gentleman-in-waiting, Michelotto burst into the room with several armed men. They bound the king and his envoy and ordered them to the prison. When Sancha and I objected, they said we could go to the pope to obtain their release. With guards outside to protect Alfonso, Sancha and I hastened to Father to demand an explanation as well as their release. Father was bewildered by what had occurred. He immediately gave the order for their freedom.

When I returned with Sancha to my husband, the guards at the door refused to let us in. They said Alfonso had succumbed to his injuries. He was dead. I soon found he had been strangled to death. Why? Many were suspected — the Orsini's, the King of France's operatives, Giovanni Sforza's family, even Giovanni himself. Over the next few months, I was able to piece together the plot of that day. My brother's hand was behind the assassination. Cesare never would let a slight or an offense go unpunished. Since my husband supported what was right and good against my brother's ambitions, death was the sentence to be carried out. My son was left without a father just as my father's consort left me without a mother.

Cesare would also not countenance any contest for my affection. Joffre, Sancha, Alfonso, and I were growing closer. We were beginning to resist what my father and elder brother were doing. Cesare saw my attachment to him loosening. As a result, he found a second motivation to act. I lost my first husband because he no longer benefited my father. My second husband was taken because he no longer benefited my brother's ambitions and affections. It was a murder not ordained by His Holiness, but one he had few qualms with. My father had created this environment. He had enabled his son Cesare. But to his dismay, I noticed Father fearful of the son he had nurtured. This progeny was becoming a monster greater than the pope. The creation was threatening its creator. Wearing black with syphilis scarring, Cesare's presence left shivers for all who were nearby.

My husband was unceremoniously interred as one guilty of some criminal offense. I compared the disposing of his body to what happened to the thieves' bodies after their crucifixion with our Lord. I was greatly offended as were the Aragonese. To further my horror, brother Cesare showed up at my quarters the next evening. I was grieving in my bed. When I saw him, I cried out, "How could you? I loved him."

My brother began to weep. He was not regretful of his actions. He was only moved by seeing me in pain. He fell at my feet pleading for my love. Cesare acted as a jilted lover trying to reunite with his spouse. I should have ordered him out, but I could not. I loved him more than Alfonso, more than Giovanni, sometimes more than Father. We had been together through tumultuous childhoods. We had vowed to stay together regardless of any offense. I melted into his arms. He did his best to explain why such a deed was warranted. He promised to always protect me, to always do what was best for me. Even at age thirty-nine, I still believe he thought that. I did not realize Scripture was being played out before me. Cesare had rejected God entirely, so God gave him over to a reprobate mind. He could reason everything he did as warranted.

When my brother left my room, I was comforted for the moment. I would cry over the coming weeks, but that night, all my tears were suddenly gone. I thought nothing of Alfonso. Love for Cesare filled my heart. Even in treachery, he loved me. The one woman he could not lose, the only female he would ever regard was me. I cannot explain why, but I always separated him from the offenses he committed.

The next morning, after my brother left, I was consumed again with grief over Alfonso. I complained to my father for his lack of protection. The Vatican should be the safest place on earth. Instead, God's Hand had struck my father. My brother's hand had killed my husband, the one he had fawned over at the event of our wedding a few years before. I hated it all. Father ordered me out of the house, sick of my complaints. He had men escort me out of the city hoping fresh air would restore my spirit.

As we rode out, I saw the small houses with peasants wearing ragged clothes. They stopped whatever they were doing to smile and wave at me. They held their kids. Husbands stood by their wives, placing their arms around their waists to marvel at the site of religious royalty. They had none of the things that I had. Yet, they had something I needed. They were content to be loved, to have a roof, some covering called clothes, and a scant substance called food. They were devout. They were not perfect, but they tried to be. They worshiped the Lord in spirit and in truth. They were satisfied for now, awaiting the great consolation of Heaven.

I wanted to stop our caravan. I wished to discard my costly gowns, to grab a hoe, to stay the night laying on a pallet inside their home. I longed for them to teach me what they had learned. Life for me would have been better if I would have followed my instincts that day, but I did not. I am not sure I would have had the courage. I think even had I done what my heart longed for, Father's armies would have accosted me, taking me back to the palace prison he maintained in splendor.

No sooner had I dwelt on this thought, I saw Cesare ride out with thousands of men, weapons, and horses for his next campaign. He was bent on conquest and destruction. He cared not what damage was left in his wake. Lives lost were unimportant to him as long as his and mine continued. I felt conflicted. Part of me was proud of him. Another portion was cheering him on. Deep down, there was a silent fraction of my life which believed his defeat would be best for all.

My Third Merger

Because my weeping continued to grate at my father, he planned to send me away from him to Nepi. When I caught wind that he was sending me, I left with my nine-month-old son Rodrigo at first light. I gave no notice to the pope. If he wished me gone, we would gladly oblige. I left so quickly that I made no provision for my son's clothing. Thankfully, my servant Vincenzo Giordano was gracious to respond to my requests by letter, always in an expeditious manner. I also asked Vincenzo to take some of my benefices and hold an honorable service for my husband with his family, on my behalf. He also sent, for me, letters to all the monasteries to pray for me during this time of grief.

As always in trial, I drew near to God. When things were good, I looked to Father. When things were bad, I looked to the Heavenly Father. Until later in life, after the greatest tragedy with my son, I never comprehended the relation between how I lived and what I faced. My whole life, God's Spirit had called to me. He had warned me gently. He had beckoned me to leave the life of sin and selfishness and live for Him. I never realized in serving Him there would be bound together true joy uncontested with an unmatched love Divine.

Every step of the way, every moment of my life, God was calling me to Himself. He created me for joy. He made me for good. His plans for me were to bless me. I simply followed the way of man's mechanizations over God's declarations. He never left me. Even when I was at my worst, He called to me. God never sought to use me. He never would hurt someone to get for me what He desired. He desires all glory and blesses us with His glory. Only good succeeds when God is enthroned. All evil is trounced if we dwell in the shadow of His Wings. I know this now. Like most who turn to the Lord, there is the echo of regret, "If only I would have followed Him sooner."

My baby and I found refuge in Nepi. I was in grief. He was fatherless. But God was nearby. The people of Nepi treated us well. They were sensitive to our loss. I wore the black clothes of mourning. My covers were in black. My drapes were too.

These were displayed not just to communicate sadness outwardly. it was the grieving of my soul. There was no joy those first few months.

Many men of the city sought to fill the void by helping. Romance did not spur their attention. Power and financial reward induced none of them. Out of the goodness of their hearts, they helped us, rejecting anything in return. I remembered a sermon I heard at the Vatican by one of the guest preachers. Doing good for others who cannot give benefit in exchange is noble. Doing good for others motivated only to honor God is sublime.

The women of Nepi shared their food with us from the little they had. We were housed in the castle set aside for me, yet these poor women provided for me as if I had nothing but the street on which to live. They, like the peasants in Rome, had a piety and a walk with God which I needed. I had a grief many of them had experienced, some by the pope's own hand, though none would dare admit as much. They could commiserate. They had empathy. These ladies had the ability to come along side to grieve while I grieved. I will never forget those few months which were a respite for my soul.

As I gained strength, I began to make plans to return to Rome, if possible, but on my terms. Father and Cesare had robbed me of much. For me to be brought back into their workings, I needed some assurances. I began to lighten my Nepi castle, moving from the black tapestries. With every step out of grief, I took an equal step away from God back toward my old life.

I found a friend in the Vatican with whom I could confide. I needed ducats and supplies but did not want to be beholden to the pope for the time in exile. My good friend, and lukewarm friend to my father, was Cardinal Cosenza who could provide what was needed. Because Father controlled communication within the Vatican, often intercepting correspondence as he did with Giovanni and Alfonso's letters, I chose to write in cipher to Caterina Gonzaga. She was a consort of Cardinal Cosenza who was also shared with the pope for his own sensual pleasure. She resented the Cardinal's generosity of her services. As a result, she was one in whom I could confide. She and I had much in common. Though she was a courtesan, and I was the pope's daughter, we both were females who served for the religious leading men's pleasure.

While in grief, Caterina let me know my father was working on my next marriage to Alfonso d'Este of Ferrara. As dictated before, the Este state of Ferrara was on the top of every sovereign's wish list. Father chose to make the state for his own, if not directly, then indirectly.

The Este family had a long, successful history. They built a fiefdom over the last two centuries rivaling the influence of the popes and the kings of our day. Duke Ercole d'Este was the sovereign of the vast territory identified simply as Ferrara. It included Moderna, Reggio, and Rovigo. Through strategic marriages, he strengthened his state's position of independence. One of Duke Ercole's daughters married the Marquis of Mantua, Francesco Gonzaga, the highly sought after military leader. He was revered and feared by France, Spain, and Italy. Ercole's other daughter was married to the Duke of Milan. His twenty-four-year-old son Alfonso d'Este was heir to the Ferrara rule.

The benefits of such a marriage fell to Cesare as well. His conquest had built a great kingdom for himself. Having the state of Ferrara in his favor would form a buffer for him from the powerful kingdom of Venice. I was not opposed. Of all the papal states, Ferrara was the one most regarded. To be the duchess of such a noble state would be regarded as the highest position a female could obtain short of marrying the King of France or the King of Spani.

I learned later; the Duke of Ferrara was against my father's proposition of marriage. The women of Ferrara shared with me, after Ercole's death, how he felt I was not worthy of his son. I was the illegitimate daughter of a sin-loving pope. More so, I had been married twice before. All the dukes knew how Father had connived to annul the first and how my brother had killed the second. The duke wondered if his son Alfonso would fare any better. Ercole chose not to respond to the pope's request of a union. Instead, the Duke solicited a bride for his son from the King of France.

The King of France did not want my father's power to extend to Ferrara, but he did not wish to lose the pope's blessing, nor bring Cesare at odds with France. Ercole did not want to lose the support of France nor the blessing of the Church. He also knew Cesare could be vindictive to the point of threatening the lives of his family. Father coveted Ferrara for influence and Cesare for a buffer. All three had something to lose. Any fissure between the three could bring catastrophe to the outlier. The only answer Ercole could come up with was for the King of France to provide a bride, any bride, for Alfonso. In so doing, the pope would have little to protest as Cesare's military success depended upon the French support. The King refused to oblige Erocle, leaving the duke with no other option. As a result, I became the pledged bride of the most significant state in all of Italy.

The union was purchased with a dowry of 100,000 ducats of Church money, a reduction of taxes paid to the Church for Ferrara from 4,500 ducats to 100 ducats annually, plus some castles and land which the pope would soon acquire from Cesare's conquests. Duke Ercole wrote a sweet letter not revealing any of the negotiations nor his reluctance for the forced arrangement. I still hold this letter among my most precious keepsakes. He said he rejoiced in my marriage to his son because of my virtue. He also believed our union honored our Lord. The duke said he would regard me as his own daughter. He truly did.

Duke Ercole made a slight reference in the cherished letter, that in hindsight I see as a big reason for his conceding to the deal. He said his joy was also because of his regard for my illustrious brother Cesare, the Duke of Romagna. Romagna was my brother's latest conquest, having been the Duke of Valentinois first. I believe the fear of my brother's unhinged butchery brought fear to all three parties — the pope, the king, and the duke.

I returned to Rome after knowing my fate was sealed on August 26, 1501. I found it easier to return knowing I would soon be leaving the clutches of my father. He would benefit from this marriage as long as I remained in Ferrara. I was the item bartered off for his and my brother's goals.

At the death of my second husband, I made a decision in Nepi. I would no longer look for love in any marriage union, nor would I get attached to whomever they betrothed me to. I would find love outside of marriage. I would make my commitments to my lovers outside the bonds I took. This was selfish conduct. It was self-preserving at the time. I could love, have intimacy, find companionship at my choosing while playing the role my family assigned to me.

My faithfulness and virtue would be external only. I would live as my father had modeled before he gained power as a cardinal. After he gained power, he flaunted his indiscretions. As a man of power, he could afford to. As a woman in this era, I would dare not exhibit my passions. Such behavior could cost me and my family all that the schemes had acquired. I recite this for my faithful secretary. What followed for years hereafter was a path to degradation in the semblance of a Borgia.

When my betrothal was publicly announced, all Rome broke out in celebration. I am not sure if the joy was authentic or ordered by my father. I do believe the people blindly followed my father, and thus unequivocally endorsed anything I did. They may have also done so knowing of the tragic death of my dear Alfonso. Believing my first marriage was annulled due to non-consummation because of impotence, they may have felt a pity for me too. This would be an optimistic viewpoint considering rumors were rampant of villainy on my part.

The Church bells rang throughout the countryside. Fires and beacons were lit in every corner. Cesare arrived from his latest victory in Naples for the celebration. Parties were given. My brother and I danced as if the Alfonso murder had never happened. There was no rift to hide. We loved each other, always would. Father constantly had me, his twenty-one-year-old daughter, dance for his dignitary friends to see. He enjoyed watching me and thought others would too. I suppose he wanted all to see the prize Alfonso d'Este had won.

Father made a couple of trips away from the Vatican before I left for Ferrara. I remember clearly how relieved I was every time Father left Rome. I enjoyed being my own person in his absence. I also enjoyed the rest when he was away. Yes, my responsibilities were greater, but Father had energy with no limit. He would party, hold dances, play, and hunt into the early morning hours. Even Cesare could not keep up with the man three times our years. It was unexplainable. Why did he, unlike other humans, not need rest?

While he traveled, the pope put the entire papacy under my control. He had taught me how to administrate. I had exercised it in Spoleto. I would need this skill more in Ferrara in the future. He trusted me to do as he did. Again, I was assuming the role of a Borgia. Hearing of this vast responsibility given to my care endeared me to Duke Ercole.

When Father returned from one of his trips, he made it clear the Ferrarese desired their duchess to be a woman of responsibility, but also one of virtue, a virgin from all outward appearances. My two-year-old son Rodrigo was not wanted in Ferrara. I had to have the appearance of never having been intimate much less an unattached mother. I loved my son Rodrigo, but he would be an obstacle to my goals of a peaceful transition to power. I decided to leave him behind in Rome to be raised by Cardinal Cosenza. To have my son in Ferrara would remind the Ferrarese of my past not to mention the murder of my second husband which would pose a dark cloud of fear over my third. I gave over custody of my little boy three weeks after the marriage arrangement was made. I would spend the next three months in Rome without seeing him once.

Alfonso d'Este had already experienced grief in his young life. His first marriage was to a woman named Anna whom the Ferrarese loved. She died tragically during childbirth to the grief of the entire state. Their son lived but a few days afterward. Alfonso was traumatized. He poured himself into military and leadership training. He wanted to repay his people for the love they showered upon him with a resolve to always keep them safe and prosperous. He was not looking for a spouse, but his father wanted to fill the void as well as provide an heir to follow his beloved son.

I had little grief over the separation from my son at the time. My whole life convinced me of a reality — there are masters and there are pawns. I had been a pawn. My two previous husbands were pawns. My brothers, Juan and Joffre were pawns. Giulia was a pawn. Vannozza, my mother, was a willing pawn. My brother Cesare graduated from pawn to master. I would follow the same path. As a result, my son little Rodrigo was a pawn too. Whether he sought promotion to be a master was his choice. My outlook on family was opposite of what the Este's envisioned.

For four months total, three months after the dispatch of my son, I toiled in Rome. I wanted out. I wished to start a new life on my own. I was in my twenties but had already lived through many traumatic and less than ideal circumstances. Delegations from the leaders of Ferrara visited me often at the Vatican and at my Palazzo Santa Maria in Portico. They were excited about their new duchess and princess. They loved my husband-to-be with all their hearts. They expressed their sole desire was for his happiness. I communicated my desire for the same, though the desire failed to compare to my longing for my own. I was very upfront about my desire to get to Ferrara as soon as possible. The delay was helpful for the state as they were preparing a lavish reception upon my arrival.

We had never seen so many people from Ferrara in my father's papacy. I realized in the visits from the dignitaries of Ferrara, they desired to take advantage of the new relationship with the pope to gain every advantage possible for their state and their industry. In truth, we were using each other. It almost seemed their favorite son, Alfonso was merely a means to an end for all of us. He was the pawn. We were the masters. Such a realization removed any guilt for my ascendance.

Once the pope was back, he made ready to send me to Ferrara. Another delegation arrived which he thought would escort me to my new home. Surprisingly, they delayed. They said they knew how much the pope needed me, and desired to wait a little longer to assure all the affairs of Rome were in order. They expressed a priority of the papacy over everything else.

I knew the longer we waited, the more in jeopardy my future would be. Many were waiting on the pope to die so that a new supreme regent could be chosen to the liking of the parties out of power. Cesare and I both knew any gains we desired needed to occur quickly. Once our father was gathered with those before him, neither my brother nor I would have leverage to attain our goals. Time became of the essence. Yet, there was pushback from the family who had purchased me. Even the man whom I would marry was silent. I received no letter from him. I had not seen him personally since my first marriage to Giovanni. Our exposure to each other was so little, I could not recall even a faint recollection of his appearance. Delegation after delegation came which assured me of his Excellency's desire for me, but this was at best second-hand speculation.

Another issue arose regarding my dowry. Father ordered I sell my jewelry to pay for the promises the pope had made to the Este family. The avarice of my father was always before me, often affected me, but now it was being shown as a requirement upon me. He did not want to take from his wealth to gain wealth and power. He wished to use what I had. Granted, he had given me all that I had, but what good was it, if I was not allowed to keep it. Of course, his thirst for power had already cost me two husbands. His Holiness acted as if my multiple marriages were a fault of mine, not a working of his. I refused to sell my jewelry. If he wanted this marriage, he would find the money. Alfonso's father was to accept the pope's daughter with the promise of reward which he had yet to receive. The Este's were not the only ones holding up the merger.

Duke Ercole was a faithful correspondent. He longed to know me better. He assured me of his love. The duke wanted me to arrive in Ferrara, not as a stranger, but as a reunited family member. I began to realize firsthand why the state of Ferrara had this strong fidelity to their duke which could not be broken. His illustrious lordship acted toward me as a kindly father. I had never known such selfless love before from a person of authority.

In preparation for my introduction to his state, he asked for a genealogy of the Borgia family to be sent so the Ferrarese could see what a prize they were getting in their new duchess. When I approached Father for this, he had a secretary under his employment fabricate one showing a noble ancestry. None of which was true.

His Holiness was not holy at all. His nobility was a mirage. He would use this fictional family line years afterward thinking it befitting the man he pretended to be. I sent the created piece to my future father-in-law who was very pleased to see what fine blood ran in my veins. It was a facade. At the time, I claimed it as quickly as Father.

The more we corresponded, the more I realized there was a common interest I shared with Ercole. We both cherished nuns. At every crisis in my life, I retreated to a convent to be with the nuns who truly sought the Lord. I held them in the highest esteem. They would challenge me to chastity, to service, to reverence, to modesty, and to humility. I took on their lifestyle while with them. Once the storms passed however, I reverted to what caused me problems. I had a yearning for what they had. I could come close to it. I could feel what they had. I wanted it, but I was unable to surrender my life to receive it. My piety was as good as my ancestry claims. The difference? I could change my life. I could not change my ancestry. But later it would dawn on me, almost too late, that by changing my life, I could set a new path for the subsequent entrants on the family tree.

Ercole collected nuns like Father collected lands and lovers. His passion was for those who had the sign of the stigmata. These bore the mark of the Divine, a proof of the Savior's suffering. There was no explanation for the true marks. There were three such nuns known at the time. One was in Mantua where Ercole's daughter, Isabella, held authority with her husband Francesco Gonzaga. Ercole asked her to send the nun to him. She refused. In truth, the respective convents and authorities where the three nuns resided all resisted. They feared they would lose God's favor the nuns brought to their territories.

Saint Lucia of Narni from the convent of Viterbo was willing to move to Ferrara provided she could have some of her sisters from the convent join her. In return, Ercole promised her a new convent for her to lead. The Dominican order refused to let Saint Lucia go, so Ercole sent in a secret military party to smuggle her to Ferrara.

The pope never liked the nuns from this convent. Their role model was a nun named Saint Catherine of Siena who lived one hundred years before. Saint Catherine made her mark in Italy when she continually demanded the popes in her day to either seek a temporal kingdom or to work to save souls. She said they could not have both. She hated the corruption of the papacy feeling it completely repudiated what the Lord Jesus modeled. Naturally Father resented this. Even when the stigmata was received by Saint Lucia, His Holiness sent doctors to analyze the marks in hopes to discredit them. The pope's physicians were unable.

Where Father doubted anything supernatural, Duke Ercole truly believed. He gave Saint Lucia everything she requested but had trouble getting her requested nuns transferred to her. He requested my help as the pope's daughter and his future daughter-in-law. I gladly intervened on Ercole's behalf. Within three days, the nuns were on their way to Ferrara with the pope's papal bull. There were other things the duke needed from the pope. He would inquire of me. I saw that every wish of my father-in-law was granted. Though they were not ready for me to come to them, I readily showed my loyalty as a matter of good faith.

The Duke of Ferrara was a man who sought to do what was right. He had faults. He had two illegitimate children before marrying his wife, Eleonora. He strove to be faithful to her though he had one fall from this resolve in 1478. He sought a virgin or at least one publicly viewed for his son. I was willing to give up my son for him, but I had tried purity. My father overrode the effort, inviting me into his dark designs. In late October of 1501, on a Sunday evening after Mass in Saint Peter's square, Father and Cesare, having returned from one of their inspection tours, celebrated their return home. They threw a party and invited fifty prostitutes to join them and their guests. The orgy was promised to all attendees. Caligula and ancient Pompeii would have been pleased.

I attended the orgy from beginning to end though I did not personally join in all the festivities. We danced throughout the night. As the imbibing increased, the clothing decreased. Before long, we were all dancing naked, the pope included. He was never happier. I, too, was having the time of my life. All inhibitions were gone. It gave me a break from the front I had tediously presented for the Ferrarese crowd.

Father created a few new games for all to play. The first involved walnuts and the holy candelabras. He placed around the ballroom floor the girandoles flickering. He scattered the walnuts forming a course of obstacles. He then had the fifty naked women crawl around the floor picking up walnuts along the way. The top three courtesans received rich rewards, compliments of the Church. Afterwards, His Holiness, our illustrious pope, gave prizes to the men for their devilish exploits. Prizes were given to those who had sex with the most women and to those who had sex the most times in the three-hour period. Cesare, two cardinals, two ambassadors, and a priest won the male prizes.

The following week, I was going to confession with the delegation of Ferrarese, taking communion, and praying to our Blessed Virgin Mary. I felt no hypocrisy in any of this. I lived the way I wanted. I followed the traditions of our faith. Indulgences were freely bestowed. The envoys of Duke Ercole read to me a letter they had written relaying what a fine, devout Christian lady his family was soon to receive. I was gratified by their sentiment.

Guiseppe Takes a Break

After reading almost half of Lucrezia's confessional, Guiseppe gently turned the book over and laid it on the chest of Pope Leo X. He rubbed his tired eyes. He had completely forgotten that he was stuck in a hole beneath the high altar of Santa Maria sopra Minerva with no one having any idea he was stuck there. He wondered how much time had passed. The archaeologist was a slow reader. As best he could figure, he had been still for almost two hours. There was no noise above. No light but from his flashlight. The batteries still strong. He turned it off for a moment to rest.

Sitting on the floor of the secret room next to the remains of a Renaissance pope, Guiseppe was even more convinced all of this was preordained by God. He began to pray, "Father, I never dreamed I would be here. I never thought coming to a church I had never heard of, to do a task many would dream of, would fall so far off what man designed. I am not afraid. I know You are with me. I thank You for this discovery. My heart is churning. I sense Miss Borgia knew the life of regret without You. I read she also realized the emptiness that came. I cannot help but read into her writing, something happened along the way. She found You and her life changed. Father, I found You in Magdala. My life has changed. I praise Your Holy Name. Please help me be found by someone today. Please don't let me be stuck here long, but I do pray that the batteries in my flashlight last. I do pray You will let me finish this historic read before I am found. Please let this be the discovery You ordained. In Jesus' Name, I pray. Amen."

In the dark, with his eyes resting, Guiseppe was amazed to be in this place. He was shocked how in this church, so many of Lucrezia Borgia's roads intersect. Pope Alexander VI sought to be the next Alexander the Great. Here is the archaeologist in this church looking for Alexander the Great's body just to find Pope Alexander VI's daughter's confessional diary. In that very diary, he reads of the pope's hatred for Saint Catherine of Siena because of her call for the popes to live as Christ. Guiseppe shakes as he sits in awe to read this mysterious find beneath the very remains of the very same historic Saint Catherine. Cesare sought to be a Caesar. A

Caesar brought in the idols buried all around this location. Lucrezia's lover Bembo is buried above. Pope Leo X, the recipient of Lucrezia's diary, is entombed two meters away from where he sat. The enemies of Pope Alexander VI, the Orsini's, have a room in this church. There are no accidents with God.

Guiseppe Campise could not contain himself. He began to shout as loud as he could in the bottom of this dark, covered hole, praising God. He had no shame. He was overwhelmed with gratitude to the Living God who is with him. God has guided his life every step of the way. Just then, he remembered a psalm of David:

Where can I go from your Spirit? Where can I flee from your presence? If I go up to the heavens, you are there; if I make my bed in the depths, you are there. If I rise on the wings of the dawn, if I settle on the far side of the sea, even there your hand will guide me, your right hand will hold me fast. If I say, "Surely the darkness will hide me and the light become night around me," even the darkness will not be dark to you; the night will shine like the day, for darkness is as light to you.

The blessed man of God gave another shout of exultation. He then moved the ladder back to the marble ledger on top of the hidden room. He climbed, turned his head, pressing his left shoulder against the lid. With a mighty shove, he pushed, but nothing moved. A strange relief came over him. His prayer was answered. He had more time to read. He turned the flashlight back on. He walked to Pope Leo's tomb, pulling the book the pope seemed to have cherished from his chest. Guiseppe gave a slight giggle as he thought, "I'm reading the pope's mail!" He moved the ladder back to the corner. He positioned it on the rung above with the light shining on the book. With delight, he gently turned the page to continue reading.

The Departure for Ferrara

In early December 1501, Ercole sent a wedding escort to bring me to his duchy. Cardinal Ippolito, Alfonso's brother, was leading the procession. Two more of my future brothers-in-law accompanied him — Ferrante and Sigismondo. When they reached the outskirts of Rome, my brother Cesare met them in an intimidating fashion. He was accompanied by four thousand armed men on horseback and on foot. Cesare rode the most beautiful steed covered in gold, silver, and priceless jewels. He knew Ippolito well after serving with him as a cardinal for many years. Their exchange was festive. Other cardinals joined the procession from the bridge to the Vatican. Trumpets and cannons blasted as they neared. I was with Father. We watched from his window with great joy as they entered to enjoy the formalities of the season and ceremony.

For Christmas, I attended Mass at Saint Peter's with the Este brothers. My wardrobe was of the greatest value. Homes could be purchased for what just one ensemble of my robes, underdresses, and accompanying jewels cost. The following week we had carnival. Dignitaries wore costumes, attended balls, participated in races of all sorts — of horses, of boars, of prostitutes, of young men, of old men to name a few. The pope even arranged for a fighting tournament between sixteen of the papacy's best warriors. The tournament was more of an organized battle using swords and lances. Several of the men were killed for our entertainment. The Estes had a great time. None of the excesses bothered Ippolito. He had been in Rome many times. He knew what went on in the world's capital city of religion.

I began to direct the gathering of my belongings and comforts for the journey. I ordered my diverse collection of books to be prepared for transport along with my preferred furnishings for the estate. Clothes and jewels were packed with the utmost care.

While my servants packed, on December 30, I attended the seminal event before leaving — the ring ceremony. Alfonso's brother Ferrante stood as proxy. The Bishop of Adria officiated the event before Father's throne. The bishop was a serious gentleman, well respected for his unwavering adherence to the Word of God.

He spoke of the need to be faithful to each other and to be devoted to God. The bishop began to read from the Book of Deuteronomy, "And thou shalt love the Lord thy God with all thine heart, and with all thy soul, and with…"

I will not forget, Father cut him off before he could finish. With a wave of the pope's hand and a disparaging, "That's enough. We get it. Moving on." His Holiness called for the gifts to be exchanged. The Ferrarese gave him his first to his delight. They showered me with gifts as well. This was what mattered to my father — what he could receive. Happy with his lucre, we retired to the dining room for our celebratory meal. Before and after the Bishop of Adria's address, God was nowhere to be found in the event. Even the prayers which preceded the event, the prayers to bless the rings, the benedictory blessing for the meal — all were empty exercises of routine read by rote.

Father issued two papal bulls and an edict to cover for his moral lapses. The first papal bull was to legitimize Giovanni Borgia whom the pope claimed was the offspring of Cesare and an unnamed woman. In reality, the son was the pope's whom he acknowledged as his to his close confidants. The second papal bull was to make my two-year-old son Rodrigo a duke over Sermoneta guaranteeing him 15,000 ducats to go toward his care. His edict was to command Giovanni Sforza to stay out of Ferrara. He had banished my first husband from my bed through annulment. He would not risk Giovanni sharing his side of what happened in the State of my third husband.

On the day of my departure, January 6, 1502, I was called to sit at Father's feet at the Sala del Pappagallo. He dismissed his servants. It was just him, me, and the parrot caged in the corner from which the room derived its name. He expressed his love for me. But he also impressed upon me the responsibilities that were mine as the new duchess of Ferrara. I was to be the pope's eyes and ears in that State. I was to look after the welfare of Cesare. I was to be sure the census wealth was gathered and sent to the Vatican in a timely manner. As the revenue of the State increased, I was to ensure the proceeds to Rome were increased accordingly.

The pope, the Church father, wished me the best. He did not pray for me. He did not pray with me. There was a sense of farewell we both felt, yet no supplication for the Lord's or the Holy Mother's favor. Everything was horizontal in our lives privately. The pope acted and lived as if there was no God or as if he were the only god. I felt a longing for prayer. Even in my prodigal state, I wanted the Heavenly Father's blessing, but I had learned to live life without it, without Him. So, I left Father to go to Ferrara. I said no goodbyes to my son Rodrigo. I felt none were necessary to my mother Vannozza who was living a block away. Only Cesare saw me on my way.

I rose from my father's presence alone. Outside, I entered my own personal kingdom. I was somewhat surprised at the number in my contingent. All total, there were approximately 753 people going with me along with 660 horses and mules. My three closest ladies traveled with me — my cousin Angela Borgia, Geromina Borgia, and my caregiver and house manager since childhood, Adriana. Father's doctor accompanied me for the journey in case I had any issues. My majordomo was with us, as were the keeper of my stables, my master of ceremonies to oversee my formal events, my cupbearer, my under-cupbearer, my two cooks, my doorkeeper, my candlemaker, the keeper of my chapel, my tailor, my locksmith, my goldsmith, my saddler, my courier, two chaplains, and my choir to name a few.

The value of my clothes and household goods carried for my personal use was in excess of 200,000 ducats. The amount could have provided for at least ten average Italian families for a year. The extravagance was provided from the coffers of the Church. Isabella, my future sister-in-law, would do all she could to outdo me in clothing and luxuries in the years ahead. We were adults playing as selfish children. Our reality was material one-up-man-ship. When all needs were paid for by the Church or the State, when there was no struggle nor grasp of the struggle for the basic needs, it was easy to place our priorities on things — things which did not matter for the eternal. Such worldliness only led to leas contentment.

Cesare and his men rode with us as far as Pont Milvio. There, my brother rode up, caught the reigns of my white mule, and pulled him to a stop. I knew he would go no farther. I had left my father at the Vatican. Then, I would leave my brother. The two men who influenced my life the most, the two who had dictated my every move willingly fell back. The only reason they could do so was because they knew I would see after their interests in Ferrara. I was fulfilling their purpose for my life. I dismounted. He bent down. I reached up to give him a hug and a farewell kiss on his left cheek below the mask he wore to cover his pustules from the French disease called syphilis. I was honored he rode with me this far. Normally, he would still be in bed. His sleeping habits were opposite of most. He went to bed around 4 or 5 AM each morning. He would rise after 3 PM. He preferred to do his work in the dark of night. He made the effort for me. My love for him had not faded. This good-bye perhaps inflamed them more.

It was a snowy, cold morning when we left Rome. The weather continued inclement. I was told by Cardinal Ippolito that his brother, my husband-to-be, would be riding out to meet us. As to when, he was not sure. I did not want to look anything but my best, so we made several stops along the way to rest, to change wardrobes, and to wash my hair. I reflect on the Savior's return to this earth. Jesus compared it to a bridal party awaiting the bridegroom. He said the bride and the bridesmaids are to be ready. He declared the Church to be His unblemished bride. Just as I had no idea of when Alfonso would appear, we have no idea when the Lord Jesus will appear. Even in this bed, fighting for my life, I am dictating these confessions so that I may be found ready. I have not lived a spotless life, far from it, but I have been given the provision to be washed, to be pure through the precious blood He shed over a millennium and a half before. In Revelation, Saint John intimated we are to continually wash our robes. I am doing all I can as I know my hour is near to stand before the Groom of all grooms.

My goal back then was to make as many stops as necessary to be ready. The towns along our journey made this both easy and difficult. Yes, they provided whatever I needed. The townspeople poured out to see the pope's daughter, not to mention to see what commotion would require over 700 people in procession. They did make requirements in exchange. They desired an audience with me. They made their petitions known to me so I could pray for them and pass on their requests to my father. If only they knew, my father didn't really pray. The life I had chosen made what prayers I lifted ineffectual. Regardless, I gave them hope. I suppose this was worth something. My wedding party, especially the Ferrarese did not appreciate so many delays. I was glad though for them to see whom they were taking into their bosom, a woman the people revered.

In Foligno, the people made two floats — one tying me to the ancient Lucrezia of Rome, the other of Paris giving the golden apple promised to the gods to me instead. They said my beauty surpassed the goddesses in the firmament. This was not unusual to combine the sacred religion of Christianity to the pagan deities of the past and present. God had said we should have no other gods, yet my culture has accepted other gods for centuries violating the Holy Writ. We lived as if there was no consequence to this pluralism as long as the adherer was earnest and above all, the pope was pleased. Saint Catherine was right as to how corruptible our religion had fallen. When Herod was worshiped as a god in the New Testament, he was eaten by worms for not discouraging them. I realize how God patiently withheld His Judgment upon me, gently calling to me through every idolatrous and sordid deed.

Reaching the duchy of Urbino, the duchess of Urbino, Elisabeta, met me. She was obese and awkward, but she was very influential and well respected. She had been married to her husband, the Duke of Urbino when they were both in their late teens. Though he was impotent, she never uttered a word of it. She could have left him, but she chose to honor her vows. I was convicted greatly as the next region we were to pass through was Pesaro, the home of Giovanni Sforza. My marriage to him was annulled on the false claim he was impotent. I felt very uncomfortable riding with a woman of such virtue.

Father had sent a cushioned sedan chair for my travel which was built to seat two in case I chose to pass the time with a guest for company. As we rode, I wondered how many realized the contradiction passing before them. Elisabeta was a woman who remained married to an impotent man while never speaking of his handicap. I was the woman riding next to her whose father annulled the marriage and made public fodder of my forlorn lover's incapabilities which were all fabricated.

No one in Pesaro ridiculed me. Giovanni and his family had been driven out of Pesaro, possibly at my father's insistence. Instead of ugly sentiments, one hundred children met me at the entrance of the city with palm branches. They chanted, "Duchess Lucrezia! Duchess Lucrezia!" It did not hurt that my brother Cesare had taken over this region. I found later, he required every town under his rule to treat me as royalty or to pay the price in blood. My brother's presence went with me. So did my father's.

My father had threatened to confiscate the lands of Urbino from Elisabeta's husband. She came to win my favor as well as the mercy of the pope. She spoke highly of His Holiness, but I could hear in her voice the regret and fear they had of what Father was able to do. At a young age, I was glad to know everyone either revered my father or feared him. Both worked to his children's advantage. I suppose this was why he no longer hid his indiscretions. He was a force with whom few would try to reckon.

Even so, while in Pesaro, I stayed in my room. I was unapologetically selfish, but the Spirit convicted me constantly of my crimes. Often, a lover will dispose of his or her consort to find another. The one who violated the vow tends to blame the other and continually ridicules as if the innocent party was the sole cause of the indiscretion. I had this heart in me, but God would not let me go unchecked. Moses met Pharaoh at the Nile River in the mornings, time and again, to call him to repentance. I would look at my reflection each morning, feeling as though the man of God was pointing back at me in the mirror demanding I change course.

At Bologna, the Duke Bentivoglio met me. He too was fearful of my father and my brother. There was a rumor spreading that my brother Cesare had his sights set on deposing the duke and his family to add this state to the Borgia's holdings. Bentivoglio would be able to steer clear of my brother's wrath. The Urbino State would not. I was beginning to see the wisdom to my placement in this region. I held the area as a proxy to my family's ambitions. My presence alone held opposition in check. I realized their cordiality toward me at the time lacked all sincerity. Their regard was for my competing benefactors. At some point along the journey, I decided I wanted these people to revere me for what I do, not for what could be done to them. I remember writing down after washing my hair some goals as the duchess. I would govern fairly. I would defend the people. I would support their prince and duke. I would be the model wife in the public eye. I whispered a prayer, not to anyone in particular, for me to have some consequential moment where I would stand worthy of the welcomes I was receiving.

The Groom and His Father Appear

No sooner had I written out my ambitions, a surprise knock on my door startled me. My groom had arrived unexpectantly. I was glad for one thing — my heart had taken on a noble resolve. I was not ready to welcome him, but I had paced myself to be as near ready as possible. Torches were lit. I thought of the ten virgins who had no oil in their lamps when the groom arrived. Gratefully, our torches were lit. My ladies-in-waiting quickly helped me put on a flowing damask crimson satin gown highlighted with beaten gold. Pearls were placed around my neck for accent. My blonde hair was held in place by a headdress of gold.

When the door was opened for my entrance, there stood before me a man of great physical beauty. He was tall. He was dark. His biceps pressed tightly against the fabric of his sleeves. His boots were shiny. His uniform crisp. He did not appear nervous in the least. I was, but I could not display my anxiety. I forced myself to appear confident, to express myself as a woman worthy of such a man and more. There were smiles everywhere. No one spoke. All watched the interaction between the two to be betrothed. I felt they were watching for a misstep or some omen to determine what future laid before us.

We spoke as two sovereigns rather than two excited candidates for marriage. There was no sizing each other up as mates. Rather, there was an educational theme to our visit. He shared with me the state of his domain. I visited with him about the pope and the state of the Church. We visited about Cesare. He congratulated me on my brother's success. My betrothed noted how skilled my brother was at administration over Romagna. The illustrious Alfonso d'Este commended the new duke of Romagna for how he had unified this duchy and restored it to order. Cesare was a skilled warrior with the organizational skills of our father. He could have gained a position of renowned respect like Duke Ercole of Ferrara. But instead, my brother sought to rule the world which after a little more climbing would lead to a great fall.

For two hours, Alfonso and I visited with our attendants present. He quickly addressed the welcome awaiting me in Ferrara, the exchange of vows, and the condition of our shared castle. He made no reference to my massive caravan. He acted as if this was a normal following for anyone of importance. He had no such train. Of course, his three brothers were with us along with their own escorts representing the best servants ready to do my new Majesty's bidding.

The next day, we reached the bank to catch the boat sent by Ercole to deliver me to Ferrara. Onboard was Alfonso's sister, Isabella. She gave me the biggest hug. It was the first and last formality of affection she ever showed me. On the boat, she visited with Alfonso and Elisabeta, at first, as if I was not present on the vessel. She finally turned to me. She asked no questions of my journey nor of my life. She filled my ears with stories of herself.

Isabella boasted how tired she got of being called the most beautiful woman of the region. She spoke of the numerous artists who painted portraits of her including Leonardo da Vinci. She hoped I could draw some of the attention away from her so she might enjoy some privacy. When she heard of the number of books I brought from my library, she spoke of how she had to have a separate building to house hers. When speaking of reading, she assured me, the pope's daughter, that she had hired a Jewish man to translate the Psalms from Hebrew to ensure the Text we read was correct and unchanged. Isabella told of how she cared for Elisabeta when she was sick. She extolled her copious reading of Herodotus. She spoke of art and sculptures which captured Alfonso's attention. He had the same passion. She gave scant reference to the Marchese of Matua, her husband Francesco Gonzaga, except to express how every sovereign sought his employment for their armies.

As our boat entered the harbor of Ferrara, I knew all about my betrothed's sister. She knew nothing of me, but I could tell, she knew many rumors. This explained her dismissive attitude when I offered tidbits to the conversation. I left the vessel thankful Alfonso presented none of the arrogant qualities of his sister. My hope was Duke Ercole would be more like his son, but also more cohesive to the three of us. Alfonso simply nodded when his sister spoke. He made no effort to include me or redirect the conversation toward me. Perhaps, it was a test to see if I would be submissive to him, let him take the lead when he chose to.

At the shore of Torre della Fossa, seventy-five crossbowmen met me in red and white uniforms. In a synchronized, practiced exhibit, they pulled back on their bows to release their fiery arrows simultaneously into the air. All ascended to the same height, falling directionally back into the water. As the flames hit the river, the fires were snuffed out at the same time with the sound a rock makes as it falls into the water. The flames of these arrows were extinguished when hitting the water with the sound of a snake's hiss. Little bands of smoke rose from the water where each entered. The scene was quite unique. We all applauded. As the crossbowmen stepped aside, a tall, gray-haired, seventy-one-year-old man limped out from amidst his courtiers. He had a tender face with penetrating blue eyes. Alfonso leaned forward to whisper in my ear, "That's my father, Duke Ercole."

I looked back at Alfonso, for the first time, he gave me a familial smile as if he was bringing me home to meet his father after years of courtship. It had only been hours. There was a feeling of acceptance between the father and son. I saw Isabella sleek off as if angry to have lost all the attention the voyage had afforded her. I later found Ercole's limp was from a battle injury he obtained in his youth. As he approached, I had never seen such a kind face. I knelt before him in my fabulous wardrobe onto the damp grass. I heard one of the women of the town give out a shriek for fear I would stain my luxurious attire. I did not mind. There was something right about bowing before this man, more than tradition would require.

I reached for his hand to kiss it. Instead, the duke clutched my hand and lifted me up before I could place my lips upon the back of his hand. He embraced me as a father. Never in my life had my own father prevented me from paying him homage. Each time, every person, in his presence, was required to abase themselves, kiss his ring. Only then were they allowed to address him. This included kings, bishops, dukes, cardinals, even consorts before they gave him service. He was to be the human on earth representing Christ.

Before the Savior, we will bow. But His life will deserve such worship. These things crossed my mind as Ercole wrapped me in his arms. I still remember. Here was the duke my father feared. Here was the man Cesare sought to keep in check. This Duke of Ferrara had gained the love and respect of his people. They would do anything for him. He adored the Savior, the nuns, and the practice of our faith. Ercole was not perfect. He never pretended to be but pursued to do better each day. My marriage was arranged out of selfish reasons. God worked it for my good. My regret is I did not honor the Lord in the marital bed as He deserved.

A feast was given in my honor at the Venetian galley in which the duke held State functions. I was seated between the ambassadors of France and Venice respectively. Isabella sat on the other side of me between the ambassador of Venice and the ambassador of Florence. My Spanish clowns, I brought along, introduced me to the crowd in glowing and humorous ways. All rejoiced to see the tensions of formalities broken. I was more than the daughter of the powerful pope, I was submissive to my new family, and had a sense of humor to go with what they considered beauty.

My betrothed and his father presented me with several gifts. First, I was introduced to Madonna Teodorina who would serve as my chief lady-in-waiting along with twelve young Ferrarese women who would be at my service. They were dressed immaculately, in matching flack velvet dresses. Then five carriages were presented to me. Each were pulled by four horses matching the colors of the carriage. Each carriage and its team of horses differed from the others. They were exquisite. Once the two new men in my life were pleased with my response, they led me to the duke's brother's country home where I would stay the night.

Ercole and his party were to escort us the next morning to Ferrara. I had the privilege to visit at the country home with Alfonso. I wished to know more of him personally. What I learned was very impressive. He appreciated the simple things of life: the beauty of nature, the base joys of swimming, boating, hunting, and riding horses. He developed great skills for war. He was a man of initiative, teaching himself how to play musical instruments and how to work with metals and clay to make all kinds of useful things. He valued the arts — music, sculptures, poetry, and architecture. He was the most well-rounded man I had ever known. Where Cesare moved men by threat of violence, Alfonso swayed them with his novel qualities. He was a natural born leader. I should have loved him fully. I wish I would have been faithful to him. Neither of us was. I suppose because we knew our marriage was a treaty between two parties. Our own happiness and sensual pleasure would be derived separately. Our mutual success depended on our cooperation — two parties tied together.

The Entrance into Ferrara

Early the next morning, our procession crossed the river Po into the fabulous city of Ferrara. The whole city had been prepared for this moment, for me. The citizens were dressed in the finest attire. Never in my life had I been received so lavishly. I was honored in Rome as the daughter of the pope. In Ferrara, I was welcomed for being me. Yes, the pope's relationship played a role, but he was many days' distance away. He would not be their duchess. I would be. He would not be their governess. This position was mine alone. Isabella hated that. As the duchess of Ferrara, I outranked her to her chagrin. The city of Ferrara was sparkling. Even the children were dressed to meet me. They were as excited as their parents.

The city was filled with magnificent churches, stately buildings, lofty towers, awe-inspiring castles, sacred monasteries, and bridges marked by sturdiness and beauty. The roads were the best I had ever ridden upon. Tapestries and frescoes could be seen in every direction. The Este colors of red, green, and white were seen on flags, dresses, horses, and on uniforms. Trumpeters and woodwinds accompanied our entrance. I rode a mule after having been thrown from a horse. I was embarrassed, but the care the people showed, brought me laughter. I was being treated as the Blessed Virgin, but on the ground below the startled horse, I welcomed a sense of frail humanity. Yes, I could be thrown from a beast of burden. Alfonso lifted me up as a fine gentleman whose job it was to protect his wife. One of his groomsmen held the reigns of the mule the remainder of the parade to prevent a recurrence. His courtiers held a white canopy over me as we rode. I was being feted as the newly installed royal consort.

At the destination of our glorious procession, the piazza was so crowded, no one had the ability to turn around. If one lifted an arm to wave, they would seldom find a place to rest it when lowered. However, people respectfully made room as our party moved forward. When we stopped at the cathedral, acrobats descended from the towers. Gasps of surprise were heard across the mass of admirers. The acrobats gracefully opened the cathedral doors for my betrothed and me to enter.

I learned later that at our dismount, the prison doors of every prison in the town were opened. My advent had set every prisoner free. I found that interesting. Looking back, I regret the messianic perceptions. Our Savior Jesus Christ is the One who sets prisoners free. He is the One who remits sin. I do not believe they saw me as a savior. Rather, the act was most likely to bring joy for everyone under Ercole's rule. His son was getting married. Everyone should have good reason to celebrate. Those set free did as did their families.

Alfonso and I ascended the marble steps after a three-hour march to meet the Este family who were all smiling. Isabella forced a smile to match, for her brother's benefit. After the ceremony, Ercole escorted us, with the sound of trumpets, to our apartment in the Palazzo del Corte where we were left alone. Never in my previous marriages, had I seen such luxury as our bridal suite. My new husband was anxious to open the gift wrappings his bride wore. He made love to me three times during the first night. This news was passed on to the pope who anxiously awaited the reports from our wedding bed. My husband spent every night with me proving to all his devotion to his new bride. The duchy was filled with hope. It wasn't three days later, there was talk of the successor coming from our union. Alfonso's first wife died trying to provide one. My hope was to have greater success.

The next evening, practically the whole duchy joined in a wedding feast. Over three hundred head of cattle were served, fifteen thousand poultry, and preserves galore. Every sweet imaginable was served. All were welcomed to eat. Dignitaries came from far and wide to join us. There was so much food, a large amount was thrown into the river because everyone had their fill. I thought again of the wedding of the Lamb of God where His people come together eating freely to their souls' content. Such was the banquet Ercole and Alfonso set before me. Saint Lucia was presented to a few guests of honor to view her stigmata. She was gracious to all, willing to answer any questions they had. She even gave a rag she used to dab her wounds to the French ambassador which he cherished with all his might.

The week following our marriage consummation was filled with plays, jousts, dances, contests, and banquets. Poems were authored for us. Orations were given. Songs were even written in our honor. Ercole had an acrobat walk a rope across one of the town streets. The performer even did a dance upon the rope to everyone's amazement. Rounds of gifts were brought before us of great value. A nagging fear in the back of my mind was if I would be able to live up to their expectations.

We moved into the apartment in the Castello Estense which Alfonso once shared with his first wife. It was spacious. I had no qualms of being in my predecessor's bed. I carried more baggage than Alfonso. The duke provided for one hundred and forty-six servants to tend to my needs. Adriana returned to Rome, while Angela Borgia and Nicola stayed on to help me. I was thankful for Ercole's kindness acknowledging the difficulty of a young lady to be uprooted from her family and way of life. For my comfort, he welcomed my chaplain to stay as well as my master of wardrobe, my steward, my master of ceremonies, my tailor, my cook, and my doctor.

Ercole paid many visits to our abode while Alfonso carried on the business expected of his position. I saw him almost every day. My father-in-law was never forward nor romantic in his visits. He was unlike my father in so many ways. Only with Ercole did I gain a sense of what a healthy father-daughter relationship should be. He doted on me. He respected me. He made no suggestive remarks. His eyes always met mine. Sometimes, the duke would quickly scan my wardrobe, compliment it, then focus back on my face. He did the same with every woman.

One day, Ercole took me to see a hunt. On another, he took me on a tour of his favorite convent, the Corpus Domini. We traveled to San Vido for a mass on yet another day. Our most anticipated trip was when we went to see the famous nun Saint Lucia, with her sisters I helped relocate while I was in Rome. He and I visited the entire trip about our respect we held for the nuns. I shared with him how I often retreated to their convents in times of distress. I found my bearings in their midst. We agreed some were more bordellos then places of worship. We both criticized how a thing of God could be made so tawdry. I flinched every time we discussed such things as Father had made the Vatican a place of ill-repute upon his arrival. The pope had delighted in the worse kind of nuns. He cherished going to these convents under the guise of worshipping God like many would visit the temple prostitutes of Corinth.

My father-in-law taught me a lesson which I cherish to this day. I was accustomed to getting what I wanted at the Vatican. I was the pope's daughter. The expenses I incurred were covered by the offerings of the faithful Catholics around the world. There was no oversight. No accountability was required of me. I expected the same as the duchess of Ferrara and more. The duke would have none of that. He placed me on an allowance of 8,000 ducats. I wanted at least 12,000.

I complained gently to my husband. Alfonso said he was powerless to change anything of a financial nature. Ercole was always cautious to spend only where it benefited his fiefdom.

On many of our rides, I would softly address the issue any time he asked of my needs. He was tenderly adamant that I had plenty to live on. There were times I would get angry with him, I would not even ride with him at times, telling him he should better spend his time providing for his family. I wrote to Father often during this time concerning my allowance. If I could not force Ercole, perhaps the pope could. Father put pressure on Ercole, but my father-in-law was unmoved. In hindsight, I am glad. I learned to live with financial constraints. I learned to prioritize, to negotiate, and to get the best value for the expenditure. Over time, Ercole raised my provision to 10,000 ducats as a reward. This was a valuable lesson from a father-figure to his daughter.

Rumors of Alfonso's frequency with prostitutes were not substantiated the first months of our marriage. He stayed with me every evening. He never ventured far except during the day to conduct business. He took me to watch him hunt. He led me on tours of his duchy. We stayed in his favorite places. Like a young lad, he was excited to show me his favorite things. He decorated my quarters with my favorite colors. We dined together almost every evening.

My husband was not good at expressing his emotions. Some would describe him as cold. I had learned in my life, after being exposed to so many people living at the center of their pilgrimages, people are different. Just because one was cold did not mean they did not care. Shyness played a role as did a lack of confidence. Alfonso was aggressive in battle, timid in personal relationships. In public, he stood at a distance. In private, he vulnerably drew near. If I had not believed he could be removed at any second, I might have delved into a true love relationship. Instead, I kept my distance not wanting to be hurt again.

Regardless, intimacy was regular for the duration of our marriage. Within a few months, I was pregnant for the first of many times. Both Ercole and Alfonso celebrated the news. Nicola and Angela were my ready companions. I spent much time taking long hot baths to help ease my discomfort. The d'Estes had constructed a beautiful place for Alfonso's wife. The bath was constructed of marble and surrounded by marble columns which were surrounded by a beautiful garden and orchard. The whole scene was exquisite. During this time, I learned more of my father-in-law's character. His son Ferrante was interested in Nicola, one of my closest ladies-in-waiting. His other son, Giulio, was infatuated with Angela Borgia. Ercole forbid either from spending more than two afternoons in my quarters each week with the ladies to prevent them from the opportunity to sin. The atmosphere was refreshingly antithetical to that of the Vatican.

As my pregnancy progressed, I became very uncomfortable as in previous times. Being on the stage of Ferrara added to my strain. Ercole sent Alfonso and his brother Sigismondo to meet the king of France to receive the county of Cotignola. My husband suggested I retreat to his family's villa in Belriguardo. It was the most fabulous retreat. Once I arrived, I never wanted to leave. Alfonso's brother Ferrante accompanied me on my journey as did my cousin Angela. I found rest at Belriguardo. The palace glistened in the sunlight. There was a magnificent garden in the back consisting of almost twenty hectares with two beautiful ponds. Inside were many paintings celebrating Ercole and the people of Ferrara. It would become my favorite retreat.

While there, Sigismondo wrote to keep me updated on he and my husband's progress. Alfonso never liked to write, but he was considerate in being sure I was kept apprised of his ventures. I would often write back personally to my husband telling him of how the things under my watch were standing. Personal handwritten, rather than dictated letters, showed him of my commitment to our marriage. Again, there was very little affection shared because of my concerns regarding the longevity of this relationship. This worked fine for Alfonso who preferred to keep emotional distance with all people.

Cesare Strikes

I returned to Ferrara after my respite. Alfonso was still out. Ercole traveled to join him. I decided to visit the Palazzo Belfiore, a palace of my in-laws, northeast of Ferrara. I was delighted to explore all the Estes had built. While there, perplexing news reached the Palazzo. Cesare had invaded Urbino surprising Elisabetta's husband, Duke Guidobaldo. Elisabetta was in Mantua at the time. Guidobaldo escaped with his life.

Slowly Father was using his weapon of Cesare to bring the papal states into complete submission. The people of Urbino had been good to me. Elisabetta remained in Ferrara for as long as I needed her per my father's request. Father had given me every indication of his admiration for the duke of Urbino and his wife. He took extra measures to ensure my introduction to the intelligent and respected Elisabetta. Such considerations gave the duke and duchess of Urbino security through his courtesies. I should have felt a sense of guilt seeing this couple used for Father's pleasure to be later discarded, but I did not. Father and Cesare took precedence over everyone else.

In a matter of months afterward, my brother, the pope's sword, struck allies of the papacy. Suddenly, every friend of the pope's trembled, wondering who would be next. Isabella, my sister-in-law, feared for Matua. Many in Ferrara worried too. The thought was, I would be their protection from any aggressions. Urbino removed this misapprehension. Cesare fleeced the palaces and people of Urbino.

During this time, there was an eerie silence in my presence to the current events. I was feared. I was also highly regarded. There was a distance toward me, but there was also great appeasement poured upon my person. All knew of the regard my father and brother had for me. They wondered if I was a spy sent as in Hezekiah's day to ravage the prized region of Ferrara. I will admit I was conflicted. I wished for my brother's health and success. I also desired my father's increase. I grieved for Elisabetta. Her kindness had blessed me. I wanted what was right for the people, but I desired what was sinful for my family.

The vicious acts of my brother were communicated to me in fragments through my ladies-in-waiting. Ferrante also served as an informant regarding his overbearing sister Isabella. I believe she used her brother as a redoubt against any harm coming to her own well-being. Ferrante shared with me how Francesco Gonzaga, Isabella's husband, thus my brother-in-law, had made some incendiary comments toward my brother, whom they often referred to as "il Valentino." It wasn't long before Francesco met with Cesare to show his full support, as a safeguard for his own land of Mantua.

Soon after, Isabella asked my brother to send her the ancient statue of Venus and Michelangelo's most recent work, the statue of Cupid. Isabella had always wanted those two works, believing they were more worthy of her than the Urbino sovereigns. My brother gladly had them delivered to her. My sister-in-law feigned outrage over the vicious strike by my brother upon her sister-in-law Elisabetta. She then selfishly benefited from the Urbino massacre with a couple of statues she had coveted in jealousy. Obviously, duplicity was not restricted to Pope Alexander VI.

My brother had the duke of Camerino strangled in short order. When I heard, the memory of the death of my second husband brought me to tears. He was strangled in the same way on the orders of the same man — Cesare. Many leaders of the papal states, knowing their territories were in danger, joined together in a coalition called the League. They felt they had no chance if they waited. One by one, my brother was set to destroy them. But once my brother heard of their confederation, his actions became more heinous, more violent.

On Christmas day, Cesare moved further on Romagna where he had its former duke beheaded. He ordered the head displayed on a lance in the piazza. On New Year's Eve of the same year 1502, the day after, he called for the leaders of the League to meet. He led them to believe the goal was to settle for peace. When the leaders arrived, Cesare was adorned in his battle armor. They should have known this was a bad sign, but my brother's cordiality put them at ease. An hour later, they were all found dead, strangled by a cord.

On New Year's Day, my brother killed the leaders of the Orsini family, the pope's greatest rivals. The pope then had Cardinal Orsini arrested along with the religious leaders in Rome aligned with the cardinal. Father and brother were having their way while I held court in the duchy of Ferrara. Everything was going Borgia. The king of France aided the family's ascent with the promise of the kingdom of Naples for his support.

During all this, I had a silent elation. I reasoned that God was behind all of this. Now, I see all these diabolical acts were derived from an apostacy my family embraced. Even if I could have celebrated this in private, my life hung in the balance due to my troubled pregnancy. I experienced horrific seizures. I ran a high fever. Some strand of sickness was permeating Ferrara which increased the seriousness of my condition. Even one of my doctors died from the strand. Father began to send couriers back and forth to know of my condition. Ercole sent a doctor from where he was with the king of France. The king himself sent a doctor for my care. Cesare sent his personal physical too even while he was busy devastating the land.

I was surprised at one point to awake from my fever to see Alfonso and Cesare seated by my bedside. I did not recognize Cesare at first. He had dressed as a Jewish knight of Saint John. But when he spoke, I saw through his cover. My husband and my brother sat there before me. Their relationship was one in flux. They were allies, then they were enemies. They were trusted friends and doubting figures on opposing sides. They were held together by two adhesives — the king of France and their connection to me. I was overjoyed to see them both. If I had to order them, Cesare's visit meant more. As an invader with many enemies, he wore a target on his back. Yet, despite the danger, he chose to be by my side when I needed him most. He loved me. I loved him. Sadly, his love blinded me from all his transgressions. I felt sorry for Alfonso. My eyes saw his, but mine returned to focus on Cesare's.

As quickly as my brother il Valentino came, he was gone. Yet Alfonso stayed by my side. My sickness grew serious. I would burn with fever and then be chilled to the bone. I was in and out of consciousness. At one point, I could not speak due to the severity of the illness. My husband would wipe my brow. He oversaw my nutritional needs. He loved on me. Ercole was still out of the area, but he wrote to me avowing his love incessantly. Father was my overseer. With his attention from Rome, I felt I had God's full resources at my disposal. Again, the idolatry of my youth clouded my eyes to the Divine.

At seven months, I gave birth to a stillborn daughter. Alfonso was devastated. I was hardly aware of the loss as my life hung on by a string. Alfonso would not leave my side. My health did not improve as they had hoped after the delivery. My hands, feet, and face swelled. I was given communion and last rites. My stoic husband wetted my hand with his tears. The doctors decided they needed to bleed me.

When the procedure began, I was surprised to see Cesare at the foot of my bed again. My brother had ridden back to be with me in my time of duress. He held my foot while they did the painful procedure. He told me funny stories to distract me. This was the last thing I remembered. When I awoke, he was gone again, but Alfonso was still by my side. I received a letter from my father seeking to comfort me. He said he was saddened I had lost a daughter but to know it would have been worse had I lost a son. I agreed with his sentiment then. Now I am embarrassed at how easily I fell in with society, valuing a male child over a female.

At my bedside, Alfonso promised God that if He would spare my life, he would make the journey on foot to the shrine of Madonna di Loreto to give Him thanks. Once I recovered, Ercole asked the pope for a dispensation for my husband so he could ride to the shrine instead of walk. The pope granted the petition. My husband immediately set out according to his vow.

I learned an important verse in the following years from the thirtieth chapter of the book of Numbers: "If a man vows a vow unto the Lord or swears an oath to bind his soul with a bond; he shall not break his word, he shall do according to all that proceedeth out of his mouth." When a promise is made to God, it is to be kept in its entirety. It is funny how we cut deals with God to get what we want. When our request is granted, we often back away from the commitment made. I do not believe a pope, a cardinal, a bishop, or a priest has the capacity to release us from a promise to God. This was yet another abuse of the power God had given my father.

I too had promised the Lord that if I survived according to His Will, I would take time at Ercole's favorite convent, the convent of Corpus Domini. I also vowed I would wear gray to display my grief and gratitude to the Heavenly Father while there. When I was strong enough to travel, my attendants carried me there to fulfill my vows. Once again, I found solace in a convent. Corpus Domini became a favorite refuge in hard times. In this convent and its church, I felt God the nearest.

My Descent

By God's Grace, I recovered though slowly. Cesare continued his brutal campaign to the pleasure of our father. Yes, my brother's violence brought a hatred for my father, but it also garnered a fearful respect which kept the hordes at bay, fearful to do anything to upset him. Isabella was making inroads to appease my brother. She was negotiating a marriage between her two-year-old son to my brother's two-year-old daughter. Carnival was starting in Ferrara. My brother loved the event, so my sister-in-law sent him one hundred masks "to distract him from his worries." Ercole was back in Ferrara caring for me as a dear daughter. He even raised my allowance to the 12,000 ducats I had sought. Together, Alfonso and I enjoyed carnival which helped soothe our hurt at the loss of our first child.

I will admit, during this time, I became disagreeable with many. I had the pressure to bear an heir for the d'Estes. My predecessor had proven unsuccessful. My marriage to Alfonso was a forced one. I felt inside I would soon be abandoned if I did not produce. The Ferrarese were constantly watching to see if I was showing from a next attempt. Father continued to write, often asking for me to deliver any news of a pregnancy to him first. Every time I attended ceremonies by my husband's side, I felt as though I was failing the people for not bearing for their beloved Alfonso.

Beyond this personal struggle, I was courted constantly by those wishing favors from my father, primarily. Many sought after the lucrative hat of a cardinal. Once I made petitions to the pope, they would leave happily or angrily, but they left leaving room for the next supplicants. I grew frustrated by the ladies-in-waiting who were from Ferrara. They had their traditions. I had mine. Their service was to follow mine even if foreign or unfavorable to them.

I am bothered how high and mighty I regarded myself compared to others. Ercole did not act this way, nor did Alfonso. I am surprised I was not completely excluded with such behavior. During my illness after giving birth, many had whispered my husband or father-in-law had poisoned me because of my disposition. Thankfully, they loved me despite myself.

Alfonso's sister, Ercole's daughter, my sister-in-law Isabella was exactly as she was the first time, I met her. She always sought to outdo me in power, in money, in fashion, in popularity, and in favor with relationships we shared. Isabella counterintuitively sought the favor of my brother while seeking the demise of his sister whom he loved above all. She had spies watching me. I returned with spies to watch her.

Her favorite contest was in wardrobe. To hold my own, at one point, I petitioned Father to send me a year's worth of the bishopric of Ferrara's revenue so I could put Isabella to shame as she announced an upcoming visit. He did. When she arrived with her carts of clothing, I bested her with each passing day. My garments were more lavish, my jewelry more valuable. My chair was larger. My servants better uniformed. I did not care how "the people" were living, I resolved to put my chief rival to shame. And I did. It would not be long before I would take from her the affection of her own husband with relishing satisfaction.

During this time, my aged father-in-law had little energy to spend with me. My husband's duties increased to the point he was away more than home. To fill the void, I distracted myself with my favorite pastime of poetry and verse. One of my Ferrarese attendants introduced me to the son of a prominent banking official. His name was Ercole Strozzi.

Where one Ercole decreased in my company, the new one increased. Ercole Strozzi was a crippled man, a few years older. I should have known he would bring trouble into my life. His family had been expelled from Florence. Though his father was a judge at one point, he used his office to benefit his children. I guess in this way, we had a lot in common. But his family robbed, stole, and brought dissension. They were not skilled with the ability to move up in society through their chicanery. As a result, they moved from one province to another.

Strozzi loved poetry, running with a band of gifted bards. He lacked physical appeal, but he was wickedly entertaining. He flirted. He dared. He was amoral. As a result, he had many lovers. He propositioned me many times, but I had no interest. He was a close friend, a partner in mischief like Guilia had been in my youth.

Unable to seduce me, Strozzi made it his goal to push me into infidelity. He made no secret of his desire. I thought it was funny for him to try. He brought many of the arts into my company for that purpose. They were captivated by my youth, my sophistication, my mastery of languages, my energetic Spanish dancing, and the beautiful ladies who attended me. None of the men he brought could accomplish his goal.

Then the young Ercole introduced me to Pietro Bembo, the most gifted poet I had ever met. Unlike most poets who struggle and strive to get recognition, hardly ever gaining it, Bembo gained recognition with his very first writing. He was considered a prodigy with no peers. When Strozzi brought the man into my presence, he gave a wicked smile as he left the two of us alone. I grinned back willing to see if this man would have more success than his previous attempts.

Bembo was different. Where others saw me as a conquest, Bembo was captivated by me. He made no vulgar attempts to take me to bed. He admired me by letter as from a distance, though he stayed for the time with Strozzi not far from my castle. Strozzi would deliver his friend's sonnets to me frequently. Ercole Strozzi boasted of Bembo's admiration. He confided in me that he never thought I would have the effect on Bembo as Bembo would have on me. Strozzi encouraged me to form a close bond with his friend if nothing more.

When I read Bembo's couplets, he spoke of my beauty, of how he had dreamed of being a caged animal in the locks of my blonde hair. He wrote of how I intentionally lowered my hair in his dream to wrap and bind him and his heart captive. He wrote of the intimacy he imagined, with such vivid descriptions that my heart would flutter. I would find myself loosening my blouse, holding myself tight to imagine his embrace. The more I read, the more I was drawn into the full expression of love. I realized the most sensual organ on a woman was her ears. I was attracted to men by their appearance but never seduced. But, to hear words expressed, private descriptions, intimate longings entrusted to a page shattered the bands of moral behavior.

Before long, I was sneaking the man, ten years my senior, into my chambers. I would disguise myself to rendezvous at Strozzi's home by hiring a boat to navigate the distance between our abodes on the Comacchio River. Strozzi was my accomplice as was Angela who fully understood my need.

When Bembo spoke of my hair, I sent him a lock of it to keep. And he did. He later showed me the ribbon wrapped vellum where he had stored the strands of my blonde hair. When I spoke admiration for his scent, he sent an article of his clothing drenched in the fragrance. He cherished his dog Bembino so I would send delights from my table through Strozzi for my lover's four-legged companion.

The light of my life wrote of how he kept a ball of crystal in his bedroom. When he missed me, he would gaze into the ball imagining he could see my face to his delight. I obtained a ball of crystal for my bedroom and did the same. In one of our passionate nights there, unclothed we stood before the ball to see our reflection together. The picture was locked in my mind. The ball was our connection when apart.

I threw all concerns aside for my position. One day, I was almost caught as Alfonso returned home unannounced. Bembo scrambled from my chambers as I held Alfonso at bay with the plea to allow me to make myself presentable to my lord. From then on, our correspondence would need to be disguised. I would have Strozzi write the letters for me, address them to a pseudonym and sign mine with the letters "f.f.." I had used this signature when I was left to handle the affairs of the Vatican when Father was out with Cesare. The letters stood for "as acting in the place of another." I was the wife of Alfonso, but I was acting in the place of one single and in love. This was a subtle cover. Bembo gave the signature a more descript meaning "flame of the little fiery one." It was a term of endearment he and I shared. He had blown the spark of fire I had for him into a flame.

The secrecy, the passion was exhilarating. I could think of nothing all day but him. I read and reread his love sonnets. Each time, I felt the need to get alone. I wanted to be undressed by him. I wanted to be caressed by his hands. No man enflamed me like Bembo. I was unashamed. I felt no guilt. I had no compulsion to seek forgiveness. If indulgences were what I needed, I knew, in time, Father would provide at no expense.

Bembo was a man I could confide in entirely. We both had something to fear. There would be no benefit in either hurting the other. I opened my heart to him, exposing every fear, every dream, every hurt, and every aspiration. I finally had a confidant with whom I could both boast of and complain about my family. I could speak praises for the Estes and issue my gripes. He heard every one. He often responded to my confidence with beautiful, comforting prose. I shared with him my hesitancy to love Alfonso, and the reasons why I could never feel the way a wife should for him.

Pietro Bembo disclosed many of his secrets to me. Before me, he had been in a sordid affair with another married Venetian woman living in Ferrara. Her name was Maria Savorgnan. He explained how during the term of their relationship, he hoped to fill a void in his life. She was unable to do so. Then he met me. He expressed with flowing tears, with rhythm and rhyme, how I caused his cup to overflow. At one point, he even sang one of his poems to me. His voice was broken, a tad out of tune, but he moved my heart in his effort.

He confessed how he and Ercole Strozzi were driven by each other's conquests exchanging reviews the following day, seeking to accomplish more the next. Knowing Strozzi, I could not help by smile. He was even more wicked in private than in public. Bembo said things with me were different. He refused to share details of our lovemaking with his dear roommate. I do not think I would have minded, but the gesture drew me more in love with Pietro.

Our relationship was stoked to a fiery flame, but it also could be playful. At times, I would address a letter to Bembo in my own hand, but have the inside be a letter from our friend Strozzi instead. My poet said he was always aroused at the thought of reading something from me, but even more driven in his passions when there was nothing there but the assumption. I told him to imagine what I would write to help satisfy his longings. The longer our relationship lasted, the more he expressed his admiration. He said everything in this world had been reduced in significance because they failed in comparison to me. He expressed to "f.f." how he had never fallen in love at first sight until he saw me. Ever since, he said he panted for me constantly with an insatiable desire.

My love at the time would write of the robes I wore which were his favorites. He loved the way dark velvet caressed my body. He had a favorite head-dress that I wore and would speak of it often. When Alfonso would return home, I made sure to wear Bembo's favorite articles so Strozzi could report back to my admirer how I was thinking of him even when I could not be with him. He was gratified by the gesture. He said such acts of kindness made him love me more. He expressed his love beautifully with secret sonnets clandestinely placed in my hand when my husband was not nearby. Ours was a love which Father could never destroy. I suppose this is why I cherished it. State marriages could be broken, but affairs of the heart were untouchable.

When the summer came, so did the sicknesses. I fell ill. Pietro came to my side. Alfonso was out of town. Two days later, Pietro became ill at Ercole Strozzi's home. I gathered my strength, traveling by boat with Angela to see him. I stayed by his side for several hours. Knowing it was not wise to stay the night, I traveled back. I received a letter the next day telling me of how my celestial presence had healed his body.

The Beginning of the End for the Borgia Reign

They say a person does not really realize their own agency until they are left without the cover of a parent or guardian. In the year 1503, the Borgia influence decreased significantly. I had the choice but to leave the stage with my family, or to stand as my own person. It was a difficult decision, but Bembo encouraged me to stand. Though he would not be my lifetime partner, and even immoral one at that, he played an important role in my life at a time when I thought I needed human guidance as well as a touchable ally.

Cesare's power grew to the point, King Louis XII of France became fearful. Cesare had used the king's resources to have unmatched success. Louis XII equally used my brother to expand his own kingdom. The rule throughout my life came to play for Cesare. When my brother's successes no longer benefited the king, he was subsequently relieved of all support. Besides, the French were at odds with the Spanish. The Borgias were Spanish though my family's only true allegiance was Borgia. The King forbade Cesare from any other conquests northward, so he turned his sights to the south, specifically on Naples. My brother was trying his best to live up to his name. No limit would ever be accepted. Father joined in by creating new cardinal positions to be sold to the highest bidders in an effort to fund his joint enterprise with Cesare. The pope refused to ordain any French cardinals to make clear where he stood.

My husband's brother, Cardinal Ippolito kept me apprised of the activities in my father's enterprise. He passed on my father's blessing in the relationships I had formed with the Este family. Ippolito was closer to me than my own husband. He and I spent much of each day together when he was not in Rome fulfilling his duties.

On June 8, Ippolito let me know my brother was facing an uprising amongst his captains. Many took the side of the French over the Spanish. When Cesare feared his most active captain, Francesco Troche, had sold out to the French, sharing my brother's plans, my brother had him strangled to death by his henchman Don Michele. My sibling seldom gave reasoning with an enemy a chance. He gave orders. If they were not followed or if he was slighted in any way, the only remedy was strangulation or poison. The next day, he had a confidant of his lifelong enemies killed and hung from a bridge in Rome as a warning to all. Father gave his blessing through silence.

The pope never let a villainous act of Cesare go to waste. When a dissenting cardinal sought to hedge Father's indiscretions, he was mysteriously killed the next day. Most likely my brother had the act carried out. Father then had the cardinal's palace raided for everything of value. Enemies would be killed. Friends would take their place. Together, my family partnered to carry out unmentionable transgressions.

Ippolito saw a virtue in me which I had not seen in myself. He had his own weaknesses. He was carrying on a relationship with my sister-in-law Sancha. He let me know my brother Cesare was not fond of the relationship as he saw our sister-in-law as his property to enjoy. Knowing these things, the Estes treated me as a victim of circumstance. They never looked at me as the menace in their midst.

On August 1, Father's nephew Cardinal Juan Borgia succumbed to the fever which was rampant during the hot months of summer. Father viewed the funeral procession from his window. In a letter he wrote to me the day after, he expressed his sadness over the loss. My father was also concerned for my health as well as his and Cesare's. He wished me the best. I forwarded a letter to him praying the same for my favored family members. The most troubling element of his letter was a disturbing incident which he related to me as he watched the funeral march of his nephew. With Father's window opened, an owl flew into his room. The owl dropped at his feet and died. Father feared this was a bad omen, as did I. It was surreal.

In mid-August, Ippolito let me know both my father and brother were ill. Father usually left Rome in August because of the sicknesses which arose from the sweltering heat and the exposure brought by the incessant mosquito activity. He also liked to leave in August as many of the popes had died in August. Unfortunately, His Holiness was bound to his throne because of the conflicts with the French whose army was stationed a short distance from Rome. I used the papal couriers to keep me informed.

At first, Father seemed to rally, even playing cards after a bleeding administered by his physicians. Cesare grew more ill. No one was allowed into Father's chambers except for his doctors who informed my personal messengers. The Estes also had friends who kept them apprised of the pope's condition. We shared our respective information.

On August 18, 1503, my Beatitude died. I was devasted. I put on black clothing, locked my door, but my wailing was heard by all inside the palace and out. I had black curtains hung in my room. I would not allow a candle to be lit near me. All was dark outside to show what I endured inside.

What grieved me more, I was the only one really grieving over the loss of Pope Alexander VI. I remember in times past, people around the world grieved when a pope was lost. Throughout my life, I had seen or heard of moving tributes to popes gone by. They were lauded as shepherds, as models, as true vicars of Christ. None of that was spoken for my father in my lifetime. When Pope Julius II was elected pope after my father's successor, Pope Pius III, he closed off all Borgia rooms vowing to never step foot in any again. He said my father desecrated the Holy Church like no other before him. The bishop of Gallipoli said at my father's bedside, he took final communion. Afterward, my father made a personal confession of all his sins with a contrite heart.

Years later, my illustrious Marquis of Matua, Francesco Gonzaga answered my deepest fears concerning my father. He said that my father-in-law Duke Ercole felt no loss at the death of Pope Alexander VI. Ercole complained the pope had made many promises to the Estes in exchange for Alfonso's hand to me in marriage. He said Father would have to be coerced to keep any promise he ever made. The duke also said the pope treated the Estes as strangers though the pope's daughter was under their family's attentive care. I did not blame Ercole for this. He did treat me wonderful. I knew there were problems with my father and him, but he never treated me as anything but his precious daughter.

The next thing Gonzaga shared with me still sends chills through my spine. He said he had on good authority that Father actually spoke to the devil before he died, begging for more time. Many believed he made a deal with Satan to attain the papal chair in exchange for his soul. It is no wonder then that many of the doctors and surgeons who were present said they saw demons physically in his room the moment before his death, dwelling for a few minutes afterward with looks of satisfaction. The doctors said when my father died, there was a putrid expulsion from his mouth and nose. Foam was frothing out of his mouth. His body began a rapid decay before their eyes. His body swelled extending his width equal to his height. His body turned a light color of black with darker spots visible all over his body. Those to whose care he was given, were overwhelmed by their own vomiting. They had never seen a body like this before or since. His nose, mouth, and tongue were abnormally swollen beyond explanation.

There was an attempt to have a funeral, but few could stand the odor. He was laid out on a table for viewing but an old carpet had to be thrown over his body because the appearance was extremely sickening. With no one coming to pay their respects, the pope's body was wrapped in the tapestry, tied by rope, and drug off the table to the place of his coffin. The size of his decomposing body was too large for the largest coffin they could find. As a result, the porters dropped his body in an oversized one. With his corpse still wrapped, they punched it, cursing, until they could force the lid closed over him. He was then buried alone, with no service, to no one's regret as a vile murderer would be.

Time has allowed me a clearer head when it comes to the third greatest grief I have ever experienced. If my father was a good man, people would have mourned. If he was a vicar of Christ, women would have bore sackcloth, placing ashes on their foreheads as in days of Lent. But they did not. Even on his sickbed, my brother, Cesare, showed no sadness. Instead, he sent a host of armed men to our father's quarters to take all silver, gold, jewels, ducats, and anything else of value they could find. When they arrived, they saw only one cardinal at his bed paying respects. He was alarmed to see my brother's henchmen led by the evil Michelotto. They threw the cardinal to the ground, threatening to slit his throat if he did not give them the keys to the room where my father kept his most valued possessions. The cardinal quickly obeyed.

Once Cesare's men had gathered all they could carry and were gone, the papal servants stole whatever was left. When it was all over, I was told there was nothing left which belonged to the pope but the bed he died in (too nasty to handle), the throne he sat upon (too heavy to move), and a few hangings on the walls which were too high for the servants to reach.

My father died on the exact day, three years after my husband was killed by Cesare. Some felt he and Cesare were both poisoned at a banquet they had attended a few days before. Others speculated that they had planned to poison a dignitary to plunder but drank from the wrong glasses. Others say it was Father's time. His deal with the devil had reached its contractual conclusion.

I would like to think Father confessed his sins on his deathbed. If he did, I know our Heavenly Father would have forgiven him and allowed him into Heaven as He did the thief on the cross. What I fear is the bishop who spoke of Father's confession was giving a good spin on a terrible man for the good of the Church. No one in the Holy Catholic Church wants to think their pope was wicked, a vicar of Satan, ruling the Church.

Whose vicar was Pope Alexander VI? Clearly in action, he belonged to the dark forces of unseen principalities. All I can recall of my father is wickedness cloaked in papal garments. He never prayed for real. He never showed any repentance except for a few days when my brother Juan was murdered. Father never spoke of Heaven with us, nor of righteousness. The only debt he felt any of us owed was to him. In truth, Father was Father's own god.

I pray he repented. I pray he turned to Christ. In practice, he was bound for Hell, but with a simple surrender to God, every sin could be washed away. Worse leaders, such as Manasseh and Nebuchadnezzar, found God's forgiveness. God said through the prophet Isaiah, "Come now, and let us reason together, saith the Lord: though your sins be as scarlet, they shall be as white as snow; though they be red like crimson, they shall be as wool."

The Lord came to take away our sins. John the Baptist said of Jesus, "Behold the Lamb of God, which taketh away the sins of the world." The Apostle John, the one Jesus loved, said, "If we confess our sins, he is faithful and just to forgive us our sins, and to cleanse us from all unrighteousness." I am trusting in what God has said, not what a priest or Christian might say in addition or to this exclusion.

My father held the highest spiritual position on the earth. He believed he could grant forgiveness, sell indulgences, grant remissions at will. He had no right to any of this. Had he lived a better life, even a near-perfect life, he would not have the right. God gives forgiveness through Jesus alone. I find here, lying on my own deathbed, a great comfort. In fact, I am overwhelmed with a peace. The Apostle Paul declared to the Romans, "But where sin abounded, grace did much more abound." In Rome, sin has abounded. Sin has been promulgated. Indiscretions have been encouraged. People have been murdered time and time again. Children have been born out of wedlock. Pope John XII was even killed by a jealous husband for a torrid affair.

I took part in all the above. I mocked worship. I sat in the choir and laughed at the speaker. I was given money set aside for the Lord to increase my wardrobe. I would say my greatest comfort at this moment is where sin abounds, grace from God abounds all the more. God can forgive a sinner like me. God can forgive a sinner like my Father. Even Cesare could have found forgiveness if he repented. I pray he took the time before his time came. No one can know when. This is why I rejoice the Heavenly Father has given me this time to confess my sins, all of the ones I can recollect. I pray for mercy for the ones I cannot recall, praying God will bring those to mind as well.

With Bembo and Strozzi's encouragement, I rose from the ashes determined to continue to live. My husband arrived soon thereafter. He was affectionate, tender, and kind. I looked into his eyes feeling a strange guilt for the Bembo affair. I had to remind myself that our marriage was one of negotiation between two States. With Father's death and Cesare's future in jeopardy, I determined to not love him in truth. I could not bear another loss.

Angela shared with me the rumors in the castle of my soon disposal. I no longer had the pope to hold me in my position. The one unknown which she said prevented my ouster was Cesare's health. If he recovered, his forces were formidable, so much so the king of France readily feared him. Father, at his zenith, feared my brother as well. I was the one woman my brother loved. Everyone knew this. I knew his love was secure unless our sibling love interfered with the love which he had for himself. He loved me, but it did not keep him from killing my second husband. He loved Father, I suppose, but it did not keep him from complicating the papal relationships.

My brother's health was not the only thing which put his grip into question. The succeeding pope could remove Cesare from his position as Vicar-General of the Papal Army. Pope Pius III was selected as pope to succeed my father. He retained Cesare to our relief.

During the time of uncertainty, my father-in-law Ercole treaded lightly. My brother recovered to full health not to mention regaining a fearful respect by all. The king of France sought to heal the breach, offered his full support to my brother's endeavors. Cesare realigned with the French over the Spaniards. Knowing the precarious situation of my brother, I began to raise money and troops to support him fully aware of his villainy.

Nearly a year after leaving my son, Rodrigo in Rome, I received a letter from our friend Cardinal Consenza who recommended Rodrigo be sent to Spain for safety. To be transparent with my married family, I asked Ercole for his advice. No one else in Ferrara was to hear any reference to a son born before my marriage to Alfonso. Ercole agreed with sending Rodrigo to Spain. After further ponderance, I chose to have him sent to live with his father's family in Naples. Sancha, his aunt and my good friend, could render him the most steadfast care.

With my current husband Alfonso coming to my aid, a rapid departure occurred from the Strozzi quarters. My husband heard enough of the rumors concerning my affair with Bembo. Though he never confronted me, he did one better toward my lover. Unbeknownst to me, Strozzi overheard Alfonso's plans to deal a blow to Bembo permanently. He would not countenance disrespect in his duchy nor be made a laughingstock in the castle. Strozzi rushed ahead of my husband's men. Bembo fled to his father who had advised the exit months before. His father quickly worked to get him a paid position out of my husband's reach.

When I found my lover's letters had stopped, I inquired of Strozzi who said Bembo's father had called him away suddenly because of an illness. When Bembo finally wrote back, he explained as much. It was only through Angela that I found he had cowardly fled in the face of danger. I did not blame him for leaving. But if our love meant anything, I deserved a proper farewell. He had been bold in his love, even stating his willingness to give his life for mine. The least he could have done was give me a final kiss of farewell. I decided at that moment, not to be faithful but to find a man of such prominence that the threat of my husband would pose no threat to our continued love.

The annual plague was having its way in Ferrara. Alfonso sent me to Medellana, one of the Este country villas to stay. At one point over fifty of our servants were sick. Some died. I was helping Cesare from a distance with available support. In a very short time, Cesare's position as Vicar-General was lost. Pope Pius III died after serving as pope for less than a month. He had been chosen as a compromised candidate to begin with. The French wanted a French pope. The Spanish wanted a Spanish pope. An Italian pope was chosen who was old and sickly. The hope was, he would not live long, but long enough to give the papal conclave more time to select a better option for their future.

Cesare was in Rome at the time seeking to strengthen his position. The Orsinis along with the cardinals, bishops, and priests were turning on the leader of their papal army. They had had enough. The prevailing opinion was, though he was corralling Church regents and states into the fold, they were being melded into his own personal empire not to the will of the Church leaders. Twenty-six days after being selected, the new pope was dead, much sooner than expected.

With Pope Pius III's death, Cesare made an agreement with Cardinal Giuliano della Rovere whose life ambition was to be the pope. Rovere promised Cesare he would remain the head of the papal army as well as the duke of Romagna. Rovere went on to promise every cardinal their heart's desire for their vote. With my brother's help and Rovere's multiple promises, he was chosen as the next pope. He took on the name, Julius II. Where Father was a man of sex, lust, and power, Julius II was a man of hot temper, much wine, and war for war's sake. One would think this would make the new pope and my constant familial benefactor a nice pair. But, with two men bent on war and possession, it did not take long for them to want what the other had.

The new pope decided to do what our family had done many times before — use my brother until he was no longer a help but an obstacle. He wanted Cesare to be a determent to the Venetian forces. My brother was a successful arm of the new pope bringing many into submission. The papal contest against Venice brought division between my husband and my father-in-law. Ercole felt Cesare would keep the Venetians at bay protecting Ferrara. Alfonso had sentiments with the Venetians feeling they were less of a threat compared to my blood-thirsty, duplicitous brother.

I found myself in a similar position as Ercole but for personal reasons. Should I support my brother or my husband? I made the foolish choice which brought my husband hostility from the Venetians. They objected to the fact he was supporting them financially while I was supporting my brother's army. He did his best to pacify their complaint. Even through this, Alfonso never sanctioned my actions. He dealt with me tenderly as a couple with differences should. He respected my position. I respected his. His affection for me never changed. During this time, I became pregnant. He and I were both hopeful, but again, I lost our child. Even with the loss, the failure to produce a male heir, the Este family showed me love without reservation.

Alfonso and the Venetians got their wish. My brother and his cavalry, fighting for Pope Julius II, were captured. Per my friends at the Vatican, the pope was elated. A branch of his army and his Vicar-General were captured, and he was glad. Cesare offered a part of his own territories to compensate for his loss and to gain release. The pope accepted the territories. When he sent a man to formalize the agreement with Cesare's officials, the officers hung him on Cesare's castle wall for some unknown reason. This sealed my brother's fate. It did not help that the Spanish queen demanded the pope hand Cesare over for the suspected murder of her husband.

The pope negotiated my brother's release into his custody. He was then escorted to the Vatican to be imprisoned in the very room where Cesare had my second husband strangled. Pope Julius II had closed off all Borgia rooms for the sacrilegious actions of my Father. He made one exception by opening one room to confine my brother. I wondered then, I wonder now, was he reserving another room for me?

Things continued to get worse for my brother. Every possession of his was stolen. The things he took from the duke of Urbino, the things he had taken from various cardinals after their executions, the things he took after our father's death, every ill-gotten gain was summarily confiscated. My brother was without a ducat. Every territory under his rule was stripped from his hands. He was shipped off to Spain to answer for his crimes there.

I had no one to confide in with Cesare in prison far away. Bembo was out of my life except for an occasional letter exchange. Father was gone. I could not visit with Alfonso about my brother. I knew how he viewed my sibling. In addition, he was not in Ferrara. He went to tour some European countries which grew his reputation far and wide.

My husband is here with me now as I lay on my sickbed. All these years, I saw my husband as a pawn placed on my board by my family. I submitted to the pope and the duke of Valentinois as the true men of success and power. Yet, often by my bedside was the most honorable man I have ever had in my life. He is the man who held a State together, who fought valiantly, who dealt shrewdly but fairly, who grew in favor with every major leader, whose people revered him above all monarchs. I wish I would have realized it early in my marriage. I wish I would have committed my whole heart faithfully to him. I repent of this with great regret.

Back to my worries at my brother's fate, Ippolito was nowhere to be found. Pope Julius II had taken a portion of his cardinal territories which angered Ippolito greatly. He sent a scathing letter to the pope with all the disrespect he could muster. It was written in truth. When my father-in-law heard of the letter, he demanded his son show respect to the pope which Ippolito refused. Ercole then banished him away from Ferrara until he repented.

So, I had no one to console me, but then Ercole came to my side. He had little regard for my brother. I found later he was glad to be rid of him. Even so, like a loving father, he empathized with my hurt. He assured me of his love. He offered to do anything he could to ease my anxieties. He knew what it was like to be separated from a loved one — for him Ippolito, for me Cesare.

The Marquis of Matua Rises

Not long after, I was made more acquainted with the insidious Francesco Gonzaga, the Marquis of Matua. He had sailed down the river Po on a mission. His wife was the arrogant Isabella, Ercole's daughter, Alfonso's sister, my sister-in-law. She was also Ippolito's sister who loved her little brother very much. She assigned her husband, Francesco Gonzaga, the task of bringing peace between her father and her brother. He had a commanding presence. He was a man of war, victoriously so. On his barge was the repentant Ippolito. Ercole quickly took him back into his embrace.

I first met Gonzaga at the Vatican after his massive victory at Fornovo. He received wide acclaim for that victory. The pope, my father, gave him the highest Church award for his achievement. He was not a handsome man, but he was powerful. He was inside and outside, completely of the male species, almost animal to a degree.

His passions were women, hunting, falcons, boys, sex, war, and politics in any order. He was married to Isabella, the duke of Ferrara's daughter, but he kept a mistress in addition. He carried on with his extramarital consort openly taking her on his arm to State functions where his wife was presiding. Francesco was a frequent visitor to his wife's ladies-in-waiting. On hearing one such consensual meeting, Isabella had her lady's hair cut completely from her head. She told her, this is what you get for playing the nymph to my Marchese. With his wife and with many others, Francesco had many children, too many for which to account.

Gonzaga loved sex with boys always keeping one with him when in battle for his sensual pleasure, feeling the battlefront was no place for a lady. He had a servant whose sole job was to solicit and mine subjects for his insatiable sexual deviance. Gonzaga's reprobate exploits were known by friend and enemy alike. Boys would be sent to him as gifts to gain his favor or to congratulate him for some heroic effort.

Francesco was known to defile nuns in convents, delighting in sodomizing the sisters. He fantasized, and I dare consider, actualized sexual exploits upon his daughters. He was a carrier of what we called the French disease, syphilis. The disease brought him much pain. He did not care. My brother-in-law by marriage also did not care with whom he would infect.

One would think such a man would repulse me. His effect upon me was quite the opposite. He was like my father and brother to a degree. They were men who had no consideration for a woman. I do not understand why I was willing to engage with him, but his charm and sexual magnetism were more than one could resist.

There were so many elements which flamed my passion for this man. For sheer competition, he gave me a chance to show my superiority over the hubris of my sister-in-law Isabella. He gave me the opportunity to distance myself from Alfonso by doing something which would be utterly unforgivable if found. Alfonso despised his brother-in-law, Isabella's husband. In his vile, wicked way, Strozzi pushed me to the Marquis as a medicine to Bembo hurt. I think more than anything, I wanted to see if I could tame such a man, if I could capture a heart so averse to being restricted. More powerfully, I believe the evil darkness willed my relationship with such a recalcitrant. As some would say, the stars were aligned. The Marquis of Matua took his place amongst my worst misdeeds for which forgiveness is necessitated. I want to regret these acts. I pray God will help me to do so in earnest.

I began to write coded letters to my new love, Francesco. Our metaphor for his sexual organ was to refer to it as his falcon of which he was very fond. Gonzaga was a lover of falcons, collecting them at will. But he had one he had entrusted to my care before he left Ferrara. Every time I referred to his falcon, and how much I loved it, he would smile with great pride. We had a secret sensual language which set me a flame for his caress. My courier Strozzi, ever thrilled by the profane, carried messages between my lover-in-law and myself. I was serving Francesco, the husband of my husband's sister, yet we were a pair of which no one but my trusted accomplices knew.

I wrote in every letter that I would do anything he asked of me. He knew what this meant. He took advantage of my willingness, asking that my damsels join our bed on occasion to enjoy his falcon. The ladies-in-waiting were happy to obey. We took turns trying to arouse him. There were times our correspondence was so alluring, he would leave his men in the field, showing up to obtain what was flirted. It became a running joke amongst us.

Francesco made no promises of exclusivity. My only request was no boys be allowed in our love making. He wrote me sonnets on occasion. They were not as well written as Bembo's, but Francesco was one hundred times the man Bembo was. When I would ask for more, he would mock me. He let me know he would write them when he felt the desire, otherwise, I should be grateful for the ones I had. And I was.

My relationship with Francesco became beneficial to me during this time in a way Bembo's could never benefit me. My father-in-law, Ercole, was very sick. He was unable to conduct the affairs of the State. Alfonso was in Britain at the time. As his first wife carried on the business of Ferrara when Ercole and Alfonso were out, I carried on as her replacement.

Petitions from our people poured in daily. I did my best to meet each one. Matua was the place many offenders were exiled. Because Francesco was the Marquis of Matua, I made use of our relationship to gain special favors for the people of Ferrara. One mother came requesting her son, a murderer, be released from the prison in Matua. He was a wicked man, taking joy in killing. I thought he could be useful if Ercole died while my husband was traveling. The Marquis granted my request. The mother was pleased. I had a henchman of my own as my brother Cesare had found useful.

Ercole grew sicker. Many ventured to guess he would not live much longer. My husband's brother, Ferrante, was at the Vatican with Pope Julius II, his godfather. Many thought the pope would install Ferrante as the new Duke in Alfonso's absence, in fact to spite my husband. Alfonso had leanings toward Venice in the scrape between that State and the papacy. Ferrante's allegiance was to the pope. Ippolito was ostracized by Julius II at the request of his brother Ferrante. Things did not look good.

As the storm clouds gathered, I chose to protect my husband's right to the dukedom. I knew this was Ercole's wish. My desire to uphold Alfonso's right, I must admit, was to defend my own right to the highest position a woman could obtain in Italy — to be the sole duchess of Ferrara. I wrote Francesco to move his army closer to Ferrara for I might need his intervention to prevent Ferrante from succeeding Ercole.

The people of Ferrara loved Ferrante. He was affable. He was attentive. He was handsome. Alfonso was the warrior. His absence caused the populace some reason to doubt his affections. I was fortunate to be in position to handle petitions from the people for a time to ingratiate me to them.

To solidify Marguis Gonzaga's support, I made a few day trips to satisfy his bestial desires. I needed him beholden to me as much as he could be to anyone. Francesco was temperamental in nature. He never did what he did not want to do. He was famous for giving excuses for his failures in keeping his commitments. As long as I could bring him pleasure, he would suffer my requests. I am not sure if he would have delivered, but his presence nearby posed a threat to those who sought to dethrone me from my husband's seat.

Alfonso kept close tabs by letter. I believe someone informed him of a deeper relationship shared by his brother-in-law and his wife. Francesco and I planned to meet at a hunting palace of the Estes. My lover wrote to Alfonso for permission, under the guise of innocence. Alfonso granted him the right, with the caveat my husband would cut his trip short, gather me himself, so the three of us could meet at our palace. This prevented me from leaving to meet Francesco. My husband made it clear we would go there together for some rest. Our plans were deterred. I do not believe my husband ever fully trusted me. He knew our relationship was arranged, but for him to hold me from another signaled he would not be disrespected, or that he truly loved me. As he is my frequent companion during this illness of mine, I believe he loved me then as he loves me now.

The Duchess of Ferrara

My father-in-law died peacefully on January 23, 1505, while his hands kept time as his harpsichordist played. He was surrounded by his sons and their families at his death. There was grieving throughout Ferrara. The whole populace turned out for his funeral procession. The buildings, palaces, and bridges were draped in black. The Church and convent bells tolled. As I followed the casket, I remember several thoughts. My first was, how honorable this man is treated at his death. He was pious, religious, caring for the things of God and the people under his care. He encouraged righteousness in his children. The news of his death spread throughout Italy, hardly a bad thought was conceived, just admiration.

My own father's death was nothing like this. He was the pope, the leader of our religion but he cared for things of secular and civil, not for things of God. He was given no procession. No one mourned but me as far as I know. Perhaps those who benefited from him, his harem, the men who joined him in play grieved things would change, but this is probably the only sympathy extended. Ercole received the honor he deserved. I am saddened to write so did my father.

The second thought which came to my mind was all that Ercole had built. He doubled the size of his State. He was ahead of his time in renovations, buildings, and the lay-out of a thriving city. He built churches and convents. He looked after the duty of worship. He had broad streets built, architecturally admired bridges. He was a man of the arts with the largest collection of musicians, singers, artists, and poets in all of Italy. The duke made Ferrara the place to visit, the model to emulate. Businesses thrived. Theaters were built. There was a realm of safety for all who entered as his army was the one feared. His empire was coveted by kings and popes, yet none could take his fiefdom from his grip. He ruled in love, but he also administered justice.

When Father died, what were the improvements he brought to Rome or to the Church or to the papacy? He brought corruption. He brought greed. He brought dominance through fear and treachery. Who benefitted from his reign? He did first and foremost. Cesare and I did as well so long as it extended his power. Nothing was better because of my father. Ercole was so loved. The people of Ferrara wanted more of the same, so they chose his eldest son to continue his work.

Father was so hated, no one sought to continue anything he started. There would be no dynasty for him. This is not entirely true. Pope Julius II condemned everything of Father but continued on his road with greater harshness. I thought of how Solomon had worked the people of Israel. He was the wisest man of all, but he fell to lust, to greed, and to idolatry. He was a fraction of the man he was at the start. When he died, people grieved from memory of his earlier days, and those of his father King David. Solomon's son, Rehoboam, followed taking his father's sinful excesses and multiplying them. Julius II was not my father's son. At least, I do not believe so but who would be surprised. Pope Julius II's penchant for sin was different from my father's, but the outcome was not much different. Evil will continue regardless of the familial connections. Evil shares the father of lies as its forebearer, bloodline not necessary.

Right before the funeral for my father-in-law, my husband was installed as the new duke of Ferrara. Alfonso's brother, the cardinal Ippolito, offered the oath by which my husband accepted to the city's delight. A crown was placed upon his head. He was given the baton and the sword of the dukedom by the elders of the State. The rulership was invested upon the eldest son of Ercole without contest, though the vying would begin soon thereafter. At the moment of his investiture, he sat on a throne clothed in white with a fur collar around his long, muscular neck. He wore a crown of sorts with jewels. A speaker adored him, followed by prayer for his reign at the chapel service. My husband ascended to his rightful place.

The parade rounded the streets until they reached our palace. I watched through the window with excitement. When they were a few feet away, I made my way down to honor my husband. I stepped out on the piazza, bowed, and reached for his hand to kiss it. I was surprised when he took my face in his hands, lifted me up, refusing to let me kiss his hand. He embraced me with such tenderness. He then kissed me in front of the crowd. All roared in adoration. I was amazed that as Ercole had done this when I first met him on the outskirts of Ferrara, my husband followed suit. He would carry himself as humble as his father, as caring as the former duke.

I was blessed to be Alfonso's duchess. The leading gentlewomen of the State held a reception for me. They pledged their prayerful support. My dreams were coming true. Though the arrangement was made by my father, to still be here, to have reached this position was nothing more than the Grace of God. I see this now. Back then, I felt the position was earned by my efforts. I was a self-made woman at the pinnacle of my aspirations. I had one sad thought, I wanted Cesare to be there to share in the moment. He, instead, was languishing in a prison. My thoughts turned to getting him released. I had already obtained the release of one murderer, I decided to make it two at the first possible opportunity.

The First Year as Duke and Duchess of Ferrara

I was honored to serve by Alfonso's side. Hastening back to the days of Rehoboam following his father Solomon as king of Israel, Rehoboam increased the kingdom's burden upon the people. His greed cost him more than half his kingdom. In fact, ten of the twelve tribes left him. Alfonso looked at his father's reckless expenditures and the debt he had accumulated. My husband, the new duke, immediately went to work. He lessened the tax burden on the people. He cut the State's expenditures. He also relieved many officials who added nothing to the good of Ferrara. The duke sought the best for his people. There was nothing more on his mind in the early days of his rule.

The famine was raging. With the famine came the plague. It was said the best way to prevent the famine is to fill the pot with food. The converse was being played out. Families had no food, so the plague thrived. People poured into the city from all over the State begging for food. Other than our castle, there was no food to be had. Families were eating acorns, grass, and bark to survive. Women begged for their children. One man killed his two sons because he could no longer bear their cries for sustenance. He was arrested before he was to take his own life. A huge epidemic hit the children. Panic was rampant. Mass graves were being dug to handle the victims.

As a result, Alfonso traveled to Venice to purchase grain for our State. He worked every deal imaginable, even at exorbitant prices. The new duke would do whatever it took to save his people. While he was foraging for Ferrara, he put all petitions under my care. He placed two men under my authority to assist. To make communication with me more readily available, he built a passageway between our rooms. Many felt he did so to keep a watch over my affairs, not business but sexual. I do not argue as to his concerns. He was not fond of Strozzi who seemed to always be whispering in my ear every time Alfonso entered my quarters. Ultimately, Strozzi was removed. I missed him, but his dismissal was understood.

My husband had good instincts about people. He also had a special sensitivity or perception to what was going on around him, even when no one made him privy. I did not share this gift, but I was aware of his fetish for female prostitutes. I believe he rationalized it as right, the more he realized I would not give him my wholehearted fealty.

During this time of transition, the duke dismissed many of my attendants. Some because they had no love for Ferrara, or their devotion was to another State or another country like Spain. He replaced one out of every three with the Ferrarese. Among other reductions implemented by the duke, he took away my chapel choir. He believed his choir could be shared. There was no need for the citizens to foot the bill for excessive entertainment for its officials. I joined in the reduction. I sent Polissena Malvezzi away due to her desire to monopolize Francesco Gonzaga's affections. I, as the duchess would not countenance or pay competition within my household. I kept an eye on my ladies. Alfonso kept the same eye out for me.

The more the duke depended upon me, the more I pressured him to help me get Cesare out of prison. This goal became a relentless pursuit. In hindsight, I am embarrassed by how much I loved him, thinking everyone loved him as I did. I wrote cardinals, kings, Francesco, the pope, and everyone of influence I could think of. I felt he was wrongly imprisoned, that he did no wrong. I felt he was a treasure for Italy, the papacy, and the world. How blind was I!

Cesare took my second husband. His acts of violence were infamous, leaving blood stains across all of Italy. He cost me much. He dishonored the Lord. He posed a threat to anyone who got in his way. As comfortable as I was in the State of Ferrara within the Este family, he would unapologetically disrupt my serenity if it helped him attain his dictatorial ambitions. He would combine the Church and the State under his rule if possible. He had worn a cardinal's vestiture and sought it again. He wore the crown of a duke wishing to exchange it for that of a king. As I read Scripture from my sickbed, I realize, if given the opportunity, he would rebuild the Temple in Jerusalem, make it his throne, and declare himself God. Yet I continued to beg every person of notoriety to help set him free.

Cesare was imprisoned in Chinchilla for a while. He sent envoys out constantly to work for his release. When this failed, he tried to escape, but was caught. He was then sent to the Torre de Homenaje in Medina. This fortress was considered inescapable. Knowing his nature, Alfonso loved me enough to try to help gain his release for one reason — I asked. Gonzaga did the same. My brother-in-law Ippolito did the same. The Este family loved me as their own — all but Isabella.

The Estes had trouble of their own. The brothers Ippolito and Giulio caused my husband, their eldest brother, much pain. They first vied for the service of the most talented musician named Rainaldo. He was in Ercole's stable of musicians. Upon my father-in-law's death, Ippolito claimed him for himself. Not long after, Giulio stole him with crossbowmen. Cardinal Ippolito complained to my husband who ordered Rainaldo returned, and banished Giulio from Ferrara. I tried to intercede, but my husband demanded I not meddle. Since he was assisting me with my own brother, I dared not dishonor his dictate. Their sister, Isabella, tried to intercede but her brother, Alfonso, would not listen. Giulio spent a few months in exile. Finally, Isabella petitioned her husband Francesco Gonzaga to help. With Gonzaga's request, Giulio was allowed back.

During this time, I was carrying on a torrid affair with Gonzaga. He came for Ercole's funeral. We found time together for intimacy. He came to deal with the Este brother feud, he and I slipped off for a morning of passion. I was pregnant so I feared no other repercussions. Later, during one of our nocturnal visits while Alfonso was acquiring grain for our people, I went into labor. Francesco left with one of my ladies to finish his carnal business. I understood. He had his needs. I subsequently gave birth to a son whom I named Alexander after my father. Alfonso hurried to see his first heir. Francesco left in the dark of night to be undetected by my husband, his brother-in-law.

I say there were no repercussions to my unfaithfulness, but my little boy died within a few weeks. So often, I prayed to God for help. I pleaded with Him for miracles. I was oblivious to the fact my actions deserved none of his blessings. Bembo, my former lover, sent me an astrological chart trying to explain the death of my son as something ordained by the stars, that his death was determined at his birth. I resented his letter. I wished to never receive another from this man. God determines all things, not some capricious superstition concerning His Creation.

For some reason, we believe we can live how we want, apart from God's Commands, but He is to be a good sport and grant our requests. It is funny how I would not allow that from Polissena Malvezzi who copulated with Francesco constantly without my permission. Alfonso would not allow disobedience from Strozzi or his brother Giulio, yet we have the audacity to expect God to bless our rebellion against Him?

As Alfonso and I grieved together over the loss of an heir, we distracted ourselves by renovating our apartments. My cousin Angela gathered suitors by the day. She was a vivacious, voluptuous eighteen-year-old with pedigree. She lived in the duke's household. She was from the legacy of two popes. She had wealth. She had my closest confidence. Angela shared my duties and in my affairs. People shared their needs with her to share with me, for me to share with Alfonso. And, for nice rewards, she carried their concerns to us. This connection was not a concern for her two greatest admirers. They were Alfonso's brothers Cardinal Ippolito and Giulio. Cardinal Ippolito told all the ladies with whom he desired sex, "I am your pastor. You are my sheep."

Angela was happy to serve as one of the cardinal's sheep. Her affair with Cardinal Ippolito was embraced by my beautiful cousin because it was considered forbidden in the public eye — a cardinal and a former pope's niece. It was also Angela's way of gaining standing in the Este household. Sadly, the young girl was flattered by the love of two brothers. She was inebriated by the reality that two so powerful would compete for her love. What surprised her was the viciousness by which they dueled for her affection.

Over time, Angela was coming to a decision as to which would receive her commitment. Ippolito pushed her, saying it was her duty to serve his needs. He demanded her reverence for his office. He extolled her saying God and the Church would be pleased. He was like my father in this way.

Angela's heart was falling quickly for the younger brother, Giulio. He was reckless. He had no regard for authority. He was fun. He was handsome. And he was adventurous in their lovemaking. Together, they took risks copulating near public areas, in his father's bed, on his elder brother's throne on which he ruled, and on the table in the cathedral where communion was served.

While on one of our ships, Angela gave birth, out of wedlock, to a son. She believed he was Giulio's. My cousin informed Cardinal Ippolito of her decision. She also told him that the child was his brother's. The cardinal was furious. With brutality and insult, he castigated her. She returned it by saying Giulio's eye had more value than Ippolito's whole being.

Angered, Ippolito, a cardinal of the Holy Catholic Church, ordered the death of his brother. Several of his henchmen assaulted Giulio who was coming from a time of leisure in a field south of Ferrara. The cardinal's order, "Take both his eyes and then kill him." A cardinal, an exalted man of our Church, had the audacity to do this to his own brother over an illicit affair with a woman.

The cruelty of someone in this sacred position never registered with me at the time. I had no expectation of Christ-like behavior from our religious leaders to my embarrassment. The men carried out his wishes, but not to the full measure. Giulio being young and athletic was able to fend off the four assailants. He was seriously wounded. He lost the majority of his vision in one eye. The other could see, but the muscles of the eyelid were severed. He had to physically lift the lid up with his hand to see through it.

The division in our Este family festered the whole year. I stayed out of the fray pleading instead for my brother Cesare. Ippolito may have been inspired by my brother's infamous acts. The cardinal was also like my father, seeking to get what he desired regardless of how sinful the tactics used.

On Christmas Eve, Alfonso arranged for a meeting between he, Ippolito, and Giulio. My husband was the peacemaker like our Lord spoke of in the Gospel of Matthew, chapter five. As I sat by his side, holding his hand, he spoke to both his brothers of the love he had for them. He referenced how much their father, Ercole, sought the Lord's righteousness in his land. Tears began to pour down my husband's face as he boasted of the attributes which he admired in each of his brothers. He pleaded with them to end the ungodly discourse.

I looked at the man who was my assigned mate. Of all the people who deserved honor, I believe Alfonso should have been the most regarded. The men I loved aspired for greatness. Alfonso was great. I grieve over my past. Three men I loved with all my heart — my father, my brother, and Francesco deserved little. The three men whom I loved least — my three husbands — Giovanni, Alfonso of Aragon, and Alfonso d'Este, deserved my complete devotion.

Of my three spouses, Alfonso d'Este proved most worthy of my love. The people of Ferrara saw it. Ercole realized in whom he could entrust his kingdom. The Este brothers even granted he was the better of them all. Every day with this man, I saw a different facet of his magnificence. I wish I had recognized this before my final days. How much better would life have been if I would have saved myself only for him?

Cardinal Ippolito expressed sorrow in his actions. In the dimly lit room, because of Giulio's light sensitivity, Ippolito made out the damage he had wrought upon his brother. His stoic eyes clearly moistened. In sincerity, he asked for forgiveness from Giulio and from Alfonso. He vowed to be the brother they deserved. He also told his younger brother he would spend the rest of his life trying to make up for his wrongs. I looked at Giulio who stood distinctly different from his two brothers. He was hunched over as in great pain. He lifted his head, turning his head slightly to the left so his opened right eye could make out images and movement. His left eye remained closed because of the disconnected eyelid muscles. He was a dreadful sight.

Giulio in turn expressed his sorrow. He had taken the musician by force. He purposedly stole the love of Angela from his brother. He bore the scars of his crimes. He intimated Ippolito's actions were not out of the realm of what he would have done if his love had been stolen. With this, he embraced Ippolito telling him he was forgiven. They kissed each other on the cheek pledging a lifetime of peace. My husband Alfonso placed his arms over both. They wept as I watched. This was a private moment. I excused myself from the room and ordered a feast to celebrate the reunion.

The annual plague was coming to an end in our city. The wealthy and powerful had left hoping to avoid it. The fever found its way into the rooms of the palace as well as into the shacks of the poor. All total, almost two thousand of our citizens died. A few of my servants died too. With the peace of the brothers, came a health in the streets. Food was returned on family tables across the State. When we do things God's Way, things tend to work out regardless of the outside forces. When we go against God, the most evil forces often attack from within.

The Brothers' Este Coup

Carnival began as usual with gaiety. Alfonso arranged for all kinds of entertainment. There were dances every night. There were tightrope walkers doing the incredible. Masks were everywhere. Food was available in excess. Alfonso instigated our first pig fights, an amusement he had witnessed in Venice. I arranged a play concerning the three kinds of love. Strozzi with his wicked disposition would have loved it, had he not been banished from my company by my husband.

I filled my time matchmaking. I recruited damsels under the age of twelve to refine. I had them taught the virtues of work, marriage, and religious living. As to a ceremony of completion, I married them to promising young men of the community. During Carnival, I held a daily marriage of these maidens, one at a time. As the duchess, men pledged made vows as to the care of my students. Sometimes, they would not fulfill their vows without pressure and punishment from the duke himself.

I was playing games with people's lives. Who was I to teach young ladies the virtue of work? I did work. I had administrative gifts. I filled in effectively for my father and for my husband here in Ferrara. But work? I worked when I saw fit. These young ladies would not have the advantages of birth and privilege. Teaching them about marriage? I was not an example of unconditional love. I loved what was wrong. I avoided what was right. I taught them the value of religion. I practiced the traditions of religion not the daily practice.

Jesus' condemnation of the Pharisees convicts me to this day. He said in Matthew chapter twenty-three, "Woe unto you, scribes and Pharisees, hypocrites! for ye compass sea and land to make one proselyte, and when he is made, ye make him twofold more the child of hell than yourselves." Angela Borgia was a perfect example. After giving birth to Giulia's son, I married her to a local lord named Alessandro Pio with Alfonso's approval. Her marriage was carried out quietly. Her child was kept highly secret. Alessandro's mother would have never permitted the marriage had she known about Angela's son. After the marriage had time to ferment, only then was his mother told. By then it was too late for her to object.

Angela would give Alessandro much grief over the years arguing for more ducats, more things, and more luxury. I trained her well to my shame.

As to an instructor of the sanctity of marriage, not only was I not faithful to my husband, I, often, plotted against his wishes. When there was a battle between two neighboring provinces, Alfonso took one side. Francesco took the other. I threw my support behind Francesco. My Marquis hated Alfonso. He would even gather information from me regarding my husband's movements. I shared some as long as it did not jeopardize my husband's life and holdings. My future was tied to his.

It was during this time, in 1506, Alfonso was brought to his knees in brokenness. He had overseen the peace treaty between his two brothers — Giulio and Ippolito. We did not see much of Giulio after this because he was self-conscious about his deformed face after the attack. In isolation, he grew in hostility. He was angry more at my husband then the man who disfigured him, Ippolito. He carried a grudge, an anger his elder brother and his lord would not demand justice for his injury. He was even more irate when he found his love, Angela, had been married off to another man.

To top it off, the sounds of celebration of carnival reached his dark dwelling place. His eyes were still too weak to get out in the light. His disfigurement stole any thought of joining the festivities. Ippolito had relegated his life to solitary misery. Giulio began to plot with their other brother Ferrante who sought the dukedom from Alfonso. I loved all the brothers. Ferrante was the one who stood in for Alfonso at my ceremony at the Vatican. Giulio was my constant dance partner. Suddenly both hated my husband. We later learned they plotted his assassination as well as Ippolito's.

Giulio and Ferrante hired two men to attack the duke during Carnival. During their trial, we learned they used poisoned darts, but at least twice they missed my husband. Alfonso, cautious seeing storm clouds coming from the pope, began wearing his chain armor under his clothing. On one occasion, the assassins believed they found their target. We believe the chain mail saved my duke. They also recruited my husband's favorite singer, Gian Cantore, who planned to poison my husband during one of his performances in our castle. Another of my husband's servants drank it by mistake. He died with convulsions moments later. Cantore fled through a side entrance.

When the plot was beginning to unravel, Giulio fled to Mantua under the protection of Francesco Gonzaga and the Este sister, Isabella. Some correspondence between he and Ferrante was captured and delivered to Alfonso. He had Ferrante arrested and placed in the dungeon. Under interrogation, Ferrante admitted to the plot citing Giulio as the driver to the crime. When my husband learned he was being protected by Francesco, Alfonso demanded he send him to Ferrara. Gonzaga refused. I could have supported my husband. I could have requested my lover release him to my consort duke, but I found the perfect opportunity to follow Alfonso's admonition to stay out of family altercations.

Ultimately, the co-conspirators were captured. They were beheaded. Their bodies were quartered. Their limbs and heads were displayed on three city gates upon staves. Cantore, the duke's favorite singer, was found hiding at a local farm. He was suspended in an iron cage above one of the city's major thoroughfares in nothing but a loin cloth. He shivered in the cold. He was fed only bread and wine. He was seen days later in the cage, hanging inside by a rope. No one ever knew for sure if he took his own life or if his life was taken from him.

Alfonso rode to Matua to take custody of Giulio. He rode with two hundred of his most fearsome fighters. When the Marquis saw my husband along with his reputed warriors, he chose to release Giulio. Why would Gonzaga not fight? I think he showed his character. He did what was most easy for himself. Any time he was called to do something which he did not want, he would often pretend ill to avoid anything dissatisfying to his taste. I thank God and the Holy Lady for never letting me remain in his arms. I deserved a man like Francesco. He used people. I would be discarded as any other. What kept his passion for me was his inability to freely have me.

Ferrante and Giulio were sentenced to death by the five most prominent men in Ferrara who served as judges. My husband pardoned his brothers from the death sentence choosing rather for them to serve life in the palace dungeon. This is where they are as I dictate my confessions. Life went on as if they never existed. I loved both, but I supported my husband. Once again, he did what was right. He also showed mercy when none was warranted. Alfonso stood up to the acclaimed warrior Gonzaga. My husband made the bedfellow of his wife blink when faced with a fight. Francesco would continue to use intrigue against my husband, to my enablement. I am filled with regret.

The city of Ferrara had a four-day time of thanksgiving to God for sparing their duke. Mass was held each morning which my husband and his men, me and my ladies attended without fail. Alfonso had all businesses closed for those four days so all could take part in giving God praise for His protection of our sovereign. I felt our city was drawing closer to being what God intended.

The Warring Pope

Pope Julius II was on a war-footing again, seeking to bring all the Papal States under submission to the Church. After crushing Perugia, he turned his army against Bologna. Cesare had sought this State for his own empire but accepted a bribe to drive past. The pope, seeking to make Bologna an island, offered indulgences for any Bolognese killed as well as ownership of any possessions of the person killed. Julius II ordered the cardinals to leave Bologna or to lose their benefices.

My husband knew this was an abuse of papal authority. He rode to the Venetian State to get its support of the Bolognese. In the process, the pope excommunicated my husband and the cardinal Ippolito. Pope Julius II did so as well because he had a special affinity for Alfonso and Ippolito's brother Ferrante whom my husband imprisoned for the previous coup.

Alfonso decided to meet the pope in Imola to gain his forgiveness. He had no intention of helping the pope. He also secretly offered refuge in Ferrara to many of the duke of Bologna's family. At the time, I was gladdened he had obtained the favor of the pope. Now, I look back angry that my husband, myself, and our State would pay homage to a corrupt man who had no influence with God. My husband did so because he needed to stay in the good graces of the Church so the State of Ferrara could conduct business with the other papal states as well as stay in their coalition for safety. A blatant disregard for the pope would make Ferrara vulnerable to attack by the papal armies which Francesco Gonzaga helped lead.

Again, my husband and my lover, brothers-in-law, were at odds. I straddled the line between the two. I wanted success for Francesco, but I realized if Alfonso fell, my position would be removed immediately. I had no other allies of which to speak. Cesare's presence once provided a hedge for me. But with him in prison, his royal supporters had no fear of his retribution. They moved on without him. My brother thus provided no succor.

Father was dead. Ercole had passed. The Este brothers were at odds with my two closest in-laws in prison for life. The Marquis, as infatuated as I was in him, would lose his care for me if I lost my authority in Ferrara. My situation was precarious at best. I needed Alfonso to be successful. I needed him to be strong. And I needed the pope to know we supported him in case my husband was removed. I had little hope, but I held to a prayer the pope would treat a former pope's daughter with some charity in the worst of outcomes.

I remember how frayed my nerves were over all this. In November of 1506, my prayer was answered. I received word Cesare had escaped prison. He was loved by many people for his previous feats which benefited the Church. His soldiers loved his aggressive nature. I later learned he had been greatly injured in the escape. He had obtained a rope to let him down the wall of the prison castle. As he was still a quarter of the way down, someone above cut the rope causing him to fall a great distance. He summoned the strength to mount a horse to gallop away, but his injuries were serious.

I wrote Francesco, who was with the Catholic army, to protect my brother. He never responded. The pope was leery of the trouble Cesare could bring. My brother still had support among the people and from several papal states if he could get an army reinstituted. King Louis XII refused to help him. He also refused to reinstate my brother to the dukedom of Valentinois. I could tell Alfonso was not excited about my brother's escape, nor was Francesco if I read his nonresponse correctly. To some extent, Cesare found himself as a man without a country. Without food or provision, I remember wondering if Cesare's escape was a blessing or a curse.

Heartbreak

The year of 1507 started so well. It would end as one of the worst in my life. I remember being so excited. My brother was free. I had no doubts, in a matter of time, he would be back leading his armies, finding success. I was pregnant. Carnival was beginning. Our State was at peace. And Francesco was coming to spend the festive time with us in Ferrara, more specifically with me. With the crowds as our cover, and so many people in the city, he and I had ample opportunities to slip away to rekindle our carnal love. Alfonso was busy with his duties as duke, so we were able to do so without detection.

What Alfonso did notice was the elevation of my mood. Some would say it was the glow of an expectant mother. He had seen me expectant before. He became dour knowing the change was due to his brother-in-law's presence not his baby I carried. I cast all cautions aside. I enthusiastically threw myself into the festivities. I ran. I danced. I drank. I feasted. I was loud. I laughed constantly. I noticed my eye in public was constantly glancing toward Francesco, seeking his favor, his attention. As much as I tried to avoid looking his way, my gaze was constantly fixed on the Marquis.

Suddenly, I felt a horrific pain. I knew something was wrong. I collapsed on the dance floor. My attendants carried me to my apartment where I lost the baby. The child was hardly formed. Alfonso checked on me but said not one word. I could tell he was angry and hurt. His eyes said it all.

Meanwhile, below our castle, my lover Francesco rode quickly out of Ferrara leaving only a cloud of dust and hoofprints of guilt. My husband knew his love was never my joy, my sadness was not over the loss of a child, but from absence of Francesco. I do not know why he stayed with me. He should have let me have the man I longed for so I would receive the just punishment for my infidelity. Sometimes getting what we want is the worst thing that could ever happen to us. God in His wrath remembered mercy.

The distance of my husband's affections weighed on us the rest of Carnival. There were cardinals, commanders, and kings in Ferrara. The State's reputation for the annual feast was Ercole's legacy to all of Italy. There were concerts and plays. The best musicians, singers, poets, and actors could be seen and heard each day. The food was the best. Ferrara's specialty was its sugary sweets, especially the much-sought-after lemon delicacies which were only found in our city. The future pope, Cardinal Giovanni de Medici, was our frequent guest. He would soon become Pope Leo X. Sadly, he would forget our kindness once he achieved his goal. My celebration ended on the dance floor the day I lost another heir for Alfonso.

Lent could not come soon enough. I knew in my heart, there was much that needed to be atoned for in my life. I felt if I went through the right motions, my sins could be absolved. I brought in the most serious of all preachers, Friar Raphaele of Varese. Under his direction, we implemented harsh restrictions. Not only would we abstain from meat, but we called on the State to put away the clothes of luxury as well as all cosmetics. Alfonso joined the piety by doubling the fines for blasphemy throughout our State.

I felt if I could treat myself poorly for the days leading to Holy Week, I could be in right standing with God and with Alfonso. I wanted Alfonso to see me repentant. I wanted to see his approval again. I wanted to restore his look he gave me which testified to his unconditional love. Such assurance of his love allowed me to continue to push the definition of unconditional. While practically wearing sackcloth, I continued to write Francesco thinking I was doing nothing wrong. In a time of confession, I would admit my sins to my personal priest with the understanding I could have dispensation to continue in them. I truly believed I could please God, honor Alfonso, have sex with Francesco, and please myself at the same time.

Cesare was making his move to be back on top. I knew it would not take him long. I was so proud. Once again, the Borgias were a force to fear. Many of my brother's warriors rallied to join him. His brother-in-law, the king of Navarre, gave him the main arm of his fighting force. in addition, Cesare had always been a mercenary of sort. But those who hired him always knew his ultimate goal was to grow his own power. The king of Navarre was desperate. A wealthy count had rallied a large opposition force to dethrone him. Desperate times required a desperate hire. The king believed, with Cesare leading the bulk of his army, the revolt could be quelled. Also, because my brother had lost all properties, the king felt his familial relationship would keep Cesare from challenging him when the war was over.

Pope Julius II kept a keen eye on the situation. He even pulled his forces away to prepare for Cesare's threat. My brother's motto in war was always, "Either Caesar or nothing." Father had given my brother his name with the hope he could build a legacy for himself. He chose the name Alexander as pope because he envisioned an empire like what Alexander the Great built in Greece. He named my brother Cesare with the dream of a Roman Empire being reinstituted through battlefield conquests. But neither my brother nor my father ever sustained durable alliances. They would burn any friend if this was required to take the next step up the rung of the ladder of greed and power. Father met a tragic end with no mourners.

On the morning of March 12, 1507, my brother was gathered to our father. In an ambush, Cesare was knocked from his horse and killed by seven merciless assailants. What he had exacted on others, he received seven-fold. He was stripped of all armor and clothing, paraded naked through the streets behind his own horse, mocked by all who clamored to see. Afterward, they placed his body before the altar of the Santa Maria de Viana as an offering to the Lord. He was killed just three days shy of the date of the assassination of his namesake, Julius Caesar. He had carried the mantra, "Caesar or nothing." He ended with nothing.

I remember on that very day; I was boasting of my brother's battlefield successes. I did not care who he killed or what it took for him to be successful. Having Alfonso still upset with me over the loss of our child and my Gonzaga affair, the thought crossed my mind of how I would be fine if he killed another husband if it fulfilled his desires. I was wearing plain clothes at the time, a few weeks before Easter. I felt a draw to God, but evil's call had my ear.

Fifteen days after Easter observance, my favorite preacher was still in Ferrara. The Friar Raphaele preached every day. He never veered from God's Word. He never countenanced acceptance of any sin. He saw me as the pious duchess of Ferrara. I wonder, even this day, did he not know of my activities? Had he not heard of the walnut supper in the Vatican with my father and a palace full of prostitutes? Surely, he knew of my reputation. I cannot imagine no one told him. If one was known by the company they kept, I would have thought he would not have spared a moment of his righteous time with a sinner like me. But then again, Jesus dined with sinners. Perhaps this was the friar's thought on the matter.

Regardless, he was scheduled to leave Ferrara on April 22, 1507, when the news reached my castle. Cesare's squire Juan Grasica arrived. I saw him through my apartment window. I quickly put on my new robe with all its jewels to welcome my brother. I waited for him in my quarters. The Ferrarese expected their duchess to be reserved and dignified on all occasions, that is except for Carnival. I suppose this was why we always wore masks during the celebrations. Everyone knew who I was, but I guess the disguises allowed levity to our persona. After a while, my brother had still not called upon me. I assumed he was meeting with Ippolito. They were both cardinals once upon a time. As a result, they were very close.

Hours passed. I waited. Then there was a knock on my door. I jumped with expectation. When I gave the command for the door to be opened, Cesare did not appear, nor did his squire Juan. Instead, it was Friar Raphaele. He had a sad look on his face. I knew bad news was moments away. The friar pulled a chair beside me. He took my hand in a gentle, fatherly way. He bowed his head. In a few sentences, he asked the Lord to give him the words to say. He prayed for my comfort. He lifted his head to catch my eyes with his. With remorse, he informed me of my dear brother's death.

Ferrarese expected a dignified lady. In secret, I fell far short. On April 22, all saw a sight opposite of dignity. I began to wail so loudly that I could hear all activity below the castle come to a complete and silent halt. I could not help myself. Like a sick person with uncontrollable seizures, I shook, trembled, and screamed out his name over and over, "Cesare! Cesare! Cesare! Oh, my sweet Cesare! Oh, I love you Cesare!"

The friar could not contain me. My ladies-in-waiting ran to my wailing they wept too, but not for my brother. They were moved by the grief I bore. After an hour of trying to console me, the friar left. The ladies soon followed with my orders to leave me alone.

All day and night, I bellowed. I would not eat. I would not drink. I was devastated. At one point, I considered leaping from my castle window impaling myself on the lances made ready below. I was distraught. I had lost three babies to miscarriages. My father had died a horrible death, given to an even worse reception. I grieved more for Cesare than all of them combined. I grieved for my brother who had my husband and brother Juan killed. I wept for the culprit. I was ready to end my life because of the death of a murderer. Part of me wondered if I should curse God and die, like Job's wife had advised in Scripture. But I would not. I ordered Masses to be held to pray for my brother's soul. I feared for my own.

In my grief, I made no call for Alfonso. He was out of the State at the time. He would have tried to comfort me, but he had no love for my brother. I could write Francesco, but I knew he would be glad to hear the news. Ultimately, I blamed God. I prayed to Him over and over, "I do all I can to please You, yet You continue to bring me pain."

I tremble at the reflection of those dark days of heartache. I honestly thought I was doing all I could to please God, while cheering for a murderous brother, while carrying on an affair with the consort of my husband's sister. Before him it was Bembo. Before him it was my father to whom I sought to please for his pleasure and mine. Never did I seek to please God in those days. If anything, I sought to please myself by using God. God knew all along, yet He never snuffed out my life. He continued to call to me. I could hear Him ask as He did through the prophet Isaiah in his first chapter:

Why must ye be stricken anymore? The whole head is sick, the whole heart faint, from the sole of the foot even unto the head, there is no soundness in it; but wounds, and bruises, and putrefying sores…To what purpose is the multitude of your sacrifices unto me? saith the Lord…When ye come to appear before me, who hath required this at your hand, to tread my courts? Bring no more vain oblations; incense is an abomination unto me; the new moons and sabbaths, the calling of assemblies, I cannot tolerate; it is iniquity, even the solemn meeting. Your new moons and your appointed feasts my soul hateth: they are a trouble unto me; I am weary to bear them. And when ye spread forth your hands, I will hide mine eyes from you: yea, when ye make many prayers, I will not hear: your hands are full of blood. Wash you, make you clean; put away the evil of your doings from before mine eyes; cease to do evil; Learn to do well; seek judgment, relieve the oppressed, judge the fatherless, plead for the widow. Come now, and let us reason together, saith the Lord: though your sins be as scarlet, they shall be as white as snow; though they be red like crimson, they shall be as wool.

The people of Ferrara were loving and kind. None grieved over my brother, but they did grieve for me. What I wanted was someone to come alongside me, to truly grieve as I grieved. I needed someone who actually loved my brother to sit by my side. Just then the Lord sent Cesare's principal secretary, Agapito. He visited my chamber and we visited for hours about my most illustrious brother. He shared delightful stories with me about Cesare. I told him some he did not know too. He assured me of my brother's love. Agapito said never did a day go past without my brother speaking of me. His hopes, his dreams, his future involved us being together. Agapito said he believed I was the only person Cesare truly loved. This was the genesis to my recovery.

Not long afterward, Alfonso came to Ferrara. He had left everything when he heard the news, to be by my side. His eyes of love returned as if the lost babies and the affair with Francesco was in the past. He stayed with me several days, sharing my bed. He then left to resume his work among the other dukes in the surrounding states. I wrote him daily and he wrote me. My cousin, Angela, came to stay with me for a few months along with her husband. She brought me a distraction. She was pregnant. It wasn't long after her arrival, I found I was pregnant again myself. In wrath, God was remembering mercy.

As soon as I was back on my feet, I began my correspondence with Francesco again. How horrific is our sinful nature. We cry out to God in the hard times. We plead with Him like Pharaoh in Egypt during the plagues, saying, "I have sinned, I have had enough. I will do right. Please just stop the pain." The minute God does, we, like Pharaoh, return to our rebellion. Isaiah's plea never registered with me, "Why must you be beaten anymore?" But I continued, asking God to bless me while I sinned.

The hurt in Alfonso's eyes did change my manner of flirtations. I began to have Strozzi write Francesco for me. The wicked fun Ercole Strozzi was never far from me when Alfonso was out. He continued to encourage my indiscretions, getting a thrill from my secret rendezvous. I took on the name, "Madonna Barbara." I addressed Francesco as "Guido." I let my "Guido" know I was pregnant again. He enjoyed me most when I was pregnant. He found a devilish pleasure in consorting with the pregnant wife of another man, particularly the pregnant duchess of a powerful duke. We had many clandestine candlelight encounters while Alfonso was gone. My quest to tame Francesco with my love was insatiable. I was risking everything for what was bad.

There were some lessons I learned from the past. Carnival came around again in 1508. The Marquis and I continued our trespasses. But he was called away from

Carnival, probably because Alfonso was back. With my lover gone, I took much better care of this pregnancy to Alfonso's gratitude. I did not dance. I did not drink. I delegated work to the ladies. After fulfilling his ceremonial duties, Alfonso was back out of the State to benefit the State in forming stronger alliances. The pope was seeking to destroy every papal state. Our best hope was to hold the states together deterring His Holiness from outright dominance. Ippolito remained in Ferrara to assist the duke's wife. Knowing the cardinal's penchant for violence, Francesco stayed away.

My husband's love for me was rewarded. I gave birth to a healthy child on April 4th. He was a beautiful baby boy. He was fair-skinned, dark eyes, and a snub nose. Admiring him, I caught a glimpse of what Alfonso looked like at his birth. There was no doubt, this was his son. I shed a few tears remembering my sweet father-in-law Ercole. He had longed for this day but did not live to see Alfonso's heir. Regardless of my failures to bear one in his life, he never resented me, nor treated me any differently. Ercole loved me as if I had given him ten heirs. As a result, I named the baby Ercole after his grandfather. I wrote to Alfonso to give him the news. Once again, he left everything to be with me, arriving even a day earlier than what we thought possible. Together, we cherished this eventful occurrence. The city of Ferrara lit bonfires for our newborn son. Celebrations broke out everywhere. An heir had been born.

For the first time, I felt I was truly married with a family of my own. I reached adulthood seeing families — husband, wife, children. I thought such a construction was simplistic, even primitive. They seemed so happy with very little. Even in poverty, they would lift their heads from the grind to find relief in the faces of a child or a spouse. I never really understood. But on May 9, 1508, when Alfonso came home to see his son, I realized the beauty of Holiness, of following God's Design. I vowed in our nest of a castle, that I would no longer venture outside the bounds of matrimony. My life was changed.

Then Alfonso left again, regrettably. He was never demonstrative, but his eyes filled with tears as he kissed me and our little one goodbye. He talked of how much easier life would be had he been a tailor or a cobbler. He could work a regular hour day, come home to his wife and son to relish the setting sun and the evening by candlelight. I kissed my lord goodbye with the full resolve, he would be my love. Little Ercole would have what my first son Rodrigo never experienced — a loving mother at home to raise him.

I had not thought of little Rodrigo until then. He was less than two years old when I left him for my third husband. He would have been nine years old at the time of little Ercole's birth. I kept up with him to a degree. I had clothes sent to him on occasion. I recite this, but the manager of my accounts did this often without my knowledge. My vow was fidelity to my husband. My commitment was to be a mother to this son.

As was my custom, Alfonso left. Strozzi entered. The embers of my love for Francesco were rekindled. "Madonna Barbara" began to write her lover "Guido." I was desperate for him to come to me. I wanted him to meet little Ercole. I had no fears. My household would protect me and little Ercole would not know enough to tell. Strozzi amused himself by saying I really named my son after him not my father-in-law. He teased the little boy looked a lot like Francesco and was more beautiful than any child his wife Isabella had bore the Marquis. The more he pushed, the more I wanted my bedfellow, but he would not come.

I would hear Francesco was at some camp with the pope's army. I would have my carriage brought to me. Strozzi would drive me to a village or house near Francesco. I left little Ercole with my ladies. We had a total of two nights together during this time. Other than that, the Marquis was unavailable. I never realized one of us got our wish. I wanted to put a bridle upon this wild stallion. He wanted to be put a leash on me as his adoring pet. He got his wish. I never received mine. Wherever he was. I sought to go. If he gave me a slight nod that he might be available, I left castle, child, and responsibilities to be with him. Petitions made by the Ferrarese were placed on hold, even neglected at his call. Francesco, my "Guido", would then change his plans leaving me alone waiting for his arrival which never came.

At one of our secret meeting places, I sat by my window waiting for the Marquis to show. He did but he had three of his commanders with him. He stopped on his fine steed looking through the window to see me waving with the bed behind me. He looked at his commanders and pointed toward me. They all laughed. He made a bowing gesture toward me and rode off. I was a mockery. I had abased myself to his amusement. It did not matter. I still wanted him. I loved him as much after the disrespect as I did before. I could not contrive even a pinch of anger. Strozzi continued to carry my correspondence begging Gonzaga to see me.

He assured the Marquis I wished nothing but to please him with my whole being. As I was submissive to my father, I was submissive to him.

I do believe my husband Alfonso knew yet he never once brought it up in our visits. He did work against Francesco at every opportunity. When our son was born, he made sure no one told the Marquis. When Franceso's servant escaped, Alfonso gave him refuge. When Isabella got tired of her husband's sexual dalliances with one of her ladies, she sent the young girl to Alfonso to give for my service. I did not want her, but Alfonso, as the man of our house, the duke of our State, insisted. I acquiesced. I did not realize it at the time, but I think Isabella, knowing my affair with her husband as well as her servant-girl's, thought the two of us deserved to fight for his illicit affection as she had their twenty-five years of marriage.

As Alfonso grew stronger, he never lost his integrity. He became a power in Italy to be reckoned with. Leaders across Italy, Spain, and France sought his favor. I believe during this time, Francesco decided he better be in good standing with the Estes if he hoped to survive and prosper. He wrote my husband to congratulate him on the birth of our son. He sought forgiveness for being upset about Alfonso's harboring the Marquis runaway slave. I was glad for the effort by Francesco, hopeful it would open him to more visits to Ferrara for me.

More heartache followed over the next few months. Both hit close to my weaknesses. The first was the murder of Martino, a captain of Cesare's force. Don Martino had helped my brother escape prison, had ridden with him in his newly formed army, and was not far away the day my brother was killed. Martino was stabbed numerous times in the face and the head. He was serving my court at the time. I feared an enemy of the Borgias had him killed. Martino's presence in Ferrara reminded many of the heinous acts of Cesare. His presence also may have been seen as threat toward the Estes. Some speculated he was the Judas who tipped off the assailants of my brother's whereabouts and had come to our State to uproot Alfonso. Perhaps this was so. My passion for my brother blinded me to any mischief which might ensue. No investigation to his death was undertaken possibly due to Ippolito's orders.

My second passion, my relationship with Francesco, was struck a blow. Ercole Strozzi was found brutally murdered, stabbed twenty-two times. His hair was all pulled from his head. He was left lying in the middle of the road. Strozzi was a womanizer. I was one of the few he had not bedded. Some figured an angry husband had exacted justice upon the man. What I lost was a go-between for me and Francesco. Strozzi was a man who appealed to my base depravities. He instigated my affair with Bembo, after making the attempt with others of his friends. He flamed the fire I had for Francesco, keeping him abreast of Alfonso's comings and goings. I quickly recruited his brother Lorenso to take his place as my liaison with my "Guido."

Who killed Strozzi? There was no investigation forthcoming though Strozzi's new bride pleaded for one. The method of his death reminded many of Masino del Forno who traditionally had the hair pulled from every one of his victims. He was a close confidant of Cardinal Ippolito. Pope Julius II accused Alfonso of the murder. My husband was in Ferrara at the time. He had ordered Strozzi out of the castle only to hear of his presence when the duke was out of town. In a way, I felt the walls closing in on me. My last contact with Cesare was cut off. Then the entrée to my affair was no more.

I began to wonder if my husband had done this. I bore him no resentment. I at times wished him dead for the sake of my brother. If my father and brother could kill people I loved without complaint, why could not my husband, the duke? It was within his right. He was the defender of peace for the State. Our home was part of his State.

I was undeterred in my affections for Francesco. The danger in continuing only made my efforts more invigorating. When the Marquis continued his cat and mouse game, I longed for him so badly, that my court jester did me a favor. He began to dress as Francesco for me. I had a set of his clothes from one of our nocturnal visits. I stored them away. At times, I would pull them out to smell his scent again. The jester adopted all my lover's mannerisms, rhythm of speech, walk, and tone. I made love with my jester on one occasion after I had him ride for a day into the country. He then came to me in Francesco's clothes with his odor from the outdoors. My yearning was temporarily pacified. With great risk, I even wrote to Francesco in my own hand, telling him of what my court jester did. I was determined to have him, to please him, to do anything to be with him again. Lorenzo Strozzi was successful in delivering my letter. Francesco sent a reply expressing his approval.

The War

A welcomed distraction snapped me to reality. The Italian wars had broken out. Pope Julius II was seeking, once again, to bring the papal states to our knees. Though he could present himself as a kind grandfather, many in Italy knew the truth. They called him Il Papa Terrible. This vicar of the Prince of Peace was unsuited like many before him for his position. Prayer was an imposition. God's Will was not what he sought, but his own. The pope's will changed continually. What he demanded was to be done immediately, then changed a week later as if he had nothing to do with the previous command. Regardless, he was pressing forward for full subjection.

My deceased brother, Cesare, posed no threat anymore. Thankfully, the work Alfonso had been doing over the last few years provided a check on the pope's conquests. I again was conflicted. Alfonso fought for the states. Francesco fought for the pope's forces. With activity in one region of the nation, the pope sent Francesco and his men to close proximity of the coveted Ferrara. I wrote several letters to my lover. I found he had some favor left for me in reserve.

I had no time to go beyond my request they not invade. I was the administrator for the State of Ferrara. I was the mother of the heir, the wife of the duke. I was also Alfonso's main source of information regarding his beloved duchy. Alfonso joined the Treaty of Cambrai. The goal was to join forces with the French and King Louis XII, the Italian army under Emperor Maximilian, and several of the papal states.

Surprisingly, the pope and his papal forces sought entrance into the treaty as the Venetians were threatening all sides. Spain also sought to join the alliance as did Hungary. In exchange for their admission, Alfonso was made captain of the papal forces over Francesco Gonzaga, the Marquis of Mantua.

My husband began to see some success on May 14, when a Venetian army of 50,000 mercenaries were summarily defeated by the Treaty forces. Ippolito, the cardinal brother, showed a skill for war by the side of his brother. Lands were regained and then lost over the years of the war. Of significant note, my lover was captured by the Venetians. We later heard the pope was not saddened by the Marquis' capture because of his hesitancy to fight. Instead, His Holiness cursed Saint Peter over the defeat endured by his men.

I wrote to Alfonso continually as he trusted the defense of Ferrara to my care. I served my most significant time as the duchess. I never dreamed so much would be required of me. I was not seen as a woman or as a mother or as the pope's daughter or as Cesare's cohort. I was the leader of Ferrara, ruling in the stead of my husband. We were made for that moment. The arrangement of our marriage had been for selfish gains, but in God's Master Plan, He allowed the merger for the good of the people of Ferrara who had a love for God and a love for the Estes. I made daily decisions — where troops should be placed, where arms should be delivered, what armies to allow in our State, and which ones to block. I fortified positions. I worked to build the trust of our French allies.

I also wrote Francesco while he was in prison. I used whatever contacts I had to make sure he was kept safe and comfortable. I sent frequent dispatches and gifts for his comfort. He relayed to me of his disappointment. I was the only one of all his friends and cohorts, to show any concern for his well-being. This grieved me, but I should not have been surprised. He gave no care for others. He used people as skillfully as Pope Alexander VI. I was also elated. I hoped the kindness I showed when all others abandoned him would win his heart to me. I could not get over his spell.

The French arrived in Ferrara for a respite. I treated them with dances, feasts, and receptions to show our appreciation. Meanwhile, the papal forces had offended one of the states with their ransacking of goods. Alfonso immediately sent a letter of apology, making restitution of all which had been lost. My husband and I were working in coordination like the right and left hands of a man.

Alfonso arrived in Ferrara to great celebration from the Ferrarese. He was feted as a hero which he was. I was a little embarrassed at his arrival. Though I had held down the affairs of the State, our castle had unexplainably caught fire. There was damage to a few rooms, but nothing which could not be repaired. He gave me a smile when he saw the aftermath explaining he hoped this was the worst of our casualties. He knew it would not be.

My husband left again. I was a few months pregnant. Where Father always sought a husband to do his physical duty for me as the wife, and where he condemned Giovanni falsely of not doing so, my husband Alfonso d'Este was always in my bed anytime he was home. After he left, many in our surrounding area were being threatened by the Venetian armies. I dispatched reinforcements upon request, but I always kept Ferrara well manned.

In August of 1509, I was overwhelmed by worry for our State, for Francesco in prison, and for my troubled pregnancy. I retreated to the Corpus Domini convent for prayer. I returned after two days, to give birth to my second son on August 25th. I named him Ippolito after his uncle. I sent word to my husband along with reports of the enemy's movements. He rode hard the next day to see his new little boy. Unfortunately, he could only stay a few hours. The Venetians were making a move on Ferrara. Alfonso rode to the Vatican to have more men dispatched to meet them. I did my part as well. The State's finances were in dire need of infusion. I sold my pearls, several pieces of jewelry, and other items to bolster our resources for war.

The Venetians continued their move. They seized our territory of Comacchio moving up the river Po to the outskirts of Ferrara. I was urged to flee with our children, but I would not. In less than a month, the huge fleet of the Venetians began an attempted siege. They sent an appeal to Ippolito to surrender the city. He refused. Ippolito arranged our artillery on the banks. The river Po at just the right time rose making the fleet easy targets. With rapid fire, all but two of the Venetian fleet were either destroyed or captured.

On December 27th, Alfonso and Ippolito sailed up to the city with the largest captured vessel. The flag of the captain of the papal army was proudly flown on its mast with the Venetian flag below it, displayed upside down. Again, my husband was a hero. The Ferrarese welcomed him as their beloved hero. The feeling was as long as Alfonso was their duke, nothing could threaten this State. Trying times lay ahead, but Alfonso was up to each one. He was surpassing his father Ercole's fame.

With the Venetians neutered, Pope Julius II made a, not-so-surprising, turn. He decided with his armies victorious, the time had come to bring the states under submission. He resented the alliance Alfonso made with the French. He revoked my husband's title as head of the papal forces, giving it to Francesco. The Marquis had recently been released by the Venetians at the insistence of Spain to whom Francesco repaid with a gift of some prize horses.

At the start of 1510, Pope Julius II had closed in on Ferrara spurring his lead warrior Francesco forward. Every time the army would stall, the aging pope would ride out to force his troops forward. The wicked pope excommunicated my husband. This pope was like my father and brother. He used people, then threw them away as unwanted trash. He deserved the same end. All states were warned to abstain from assisting the duke of Ferrara. Even the French pulled away from us thinking our defeat was certain. Julius offered rewards as his army snowballed in size rolling toward our State.

I wrote my "Guido" for help. If he loved me, I hoped he would do his best to slow the movement or go around our fair city. I shared with him that he was my only hope, the most trusted person in all the world to me. How weak was the one I leaned upon, but he did remember my care when in prison. According to my hope, my unwillingness to abandon him caused him to realize I was his only unfailing friend. I showed an unconditional love for him as my husband showed to me. Francesco did his best to help.

Many again tried to persuade me to leave the city with my sons, or to send one or both away, but I refused. How could I flee without bringing panic to the city. My departure would signify all was lost. I would like to say I prayed during all that time, but I reasoned I was too busy for prayer. God would have to help without my petitions.

It is funny to recite this. I petitioned everyone else for help except the One who could. Only in complete despair did I ever acknowledge my utter dependence upon Him. Thankfully, I found Him an ever-present help in times of trouble regardless of my actions. He causes the rain to fall on the just and the unjust.

Things went from bad to worse. The papal forces were taking territory after territory of our State. Many Ferrarese were falling. Desperation filled the State. The people of our State pledged their loyalty to our family vowing to shed every ounce of blood to save Ferrara and the Este family. I took a day's ride to a closer convent called San Bernardino. Finally, I sought the Lord's Help in my utter despair. The pope had taken Bologna again. He rallied his troops to take Ferrara at the ebb of our strength. Then the French arrived following Alfonso into Ferrara.

The pope sent an envoy to demand the keys to the city. Alfonso asked the man to follow him to a corner of one of our fortifications. There was a new gun he had designed. He called it the "devilchaser." He told the envoy that gun was the only key from which the pope should expect to receive anything. The pope could easily qualify as the devil to be chased. He was killing Christians for not following him, for not surrendering to his whims.

The Christ we served never used a gun. He never forced anyone to follow Him. He loved. He forgave. He exemplified what Holiness and God looked like. The true Christ was nothing like the parading vicar. Yes, one day every knee will bow. Yes, one day the forces of Heaven will cause every evil knee to kneel, but only after offering mercy after mercy. And that would only be when Satan himself takes control of the armies of the world. Pope Julius II, much like Pope Alexander VI, was more aligned with the vicar of the devil. It was said later that Julius II would curse his troops in such a way that even the most godless man could not repeat such words.

The papal forces took La Bastia, a fortress on the river Po. Alfonso rode out to lead the counterattack. He succeeded to the praise of the citizens there. Alfonso returned to Ferrara to another hero's welcome. We had cancelled Carnival for the year 1511, but we feted the French in gratitude as there was a lull in the fighting. It was so important for our allies to know we did not take them for granted.

In May, the former duke of the defeated Bologna was returned to his position. The Bolognese in celebration, tore down the statue of Julius II which Michelangelo had made out of bronze. The head was given to Alfonso for his conquests. Julius' bronze body was melted down and reforged into a cannon which was named after the wicked pope.

Another intermission of sorts allowed for a letter to be written to me from Francesco. His messenger relayed how the Marquis had beseeched the pope to spare me from harm in any papal victory. He said the pope had been very impressed with my presence of mind when all was falling around me. I was flattered, but only in a small way. The Marquis then sent a mule and a horse to bring me to his side. He redesigned his castle making rooms for my lodging. I, instead, went back to the convent of San Bernardino. I sent the animals back to the Marquis with a letter of gratitude. I needed rest.

Alfonso came to see me while in the convent. The rules there were strict. No man, not even the duke, could enter their quarters. My husband made no scene. He politely visited me at my window expressing his love and prayers for my restoration. Alfonso was a hero. He was highly regarded by friend and foe alike. Yet, he humbly came to my side to reassure me of his protection. He humbled himself before me as Christ humbled Himself to wash feet. I was and am amazed.

In 1512, the war resumed at a feverish pitch. The French came to Ferrara for a quick rest. We entertained them with the best we had to offer. On April 11, 1512, the costliest battle of the war occurred. It was Easter Sunday. Over ten thousand men were killed in total. The pope's army was crushed. Many Italian enemies were captured including Cardinal Medici who would soon become Pope Leo X. Alfonso treated him with great kindness and respect even though he had sided with Julius II against our state. I later learned my husband had saved numerous women and children from a purge the pope had ordered.

Once again, my husband entered the city of Ferrara to a State's welcome. He was victorious again. The drums beat, the trumpets blasted, the bells rung. His procession ended at the Cathedral, where he entered to give God thanks. He then joined me in my quarters loving on me and our sons. I, ashamedly, resumed my correspondence with Francesco. I do not think my husband minded a degree of kindness to the Marquis. His reluctance to invade Ferrara or his inactivity, perhaps saved our city. For this alone, Alfonso was grateful. But he would only countenance so much gratitude. I tried desperately to see Francesco, but there was always something blocking our encounter. I suppose in hindsight, God was protecting me from myself. I have needed this my whole life.

With the papal forces subdued, Alfonso again sought to return to the good graces of the Church and the pope. For us, this relationship was vital. We saw acceptance of the pope and the Vatican as acceptance by God. All the states did. Without the blessing of the Church, the people of Ferrara would suffer trade, grain, and standing. To be a continued antagonist of the Church also meant war would continually be a threat. We learned quickly, even making peace, war with the pope and the Church remained our most ardent danger.

Alfonso traveled to Rome to meet officially with Pope Julius II. When the pope heard he was coming, he ran through the Vatican shouting, "There is no one like Julius! There is no one like Julius!" I hate the thought that in the seat of Peter, of Clement, of Paul II, there were sinful men who ascended to the throne of the Lord's Church. Julius II condemned my father incessantly, yet he was no better.

After giving my husband absolution, the pope made demands on Alfonso which were untenable. My husband fled in the dark of night, taking a three-month detour to return to Ferrara knowing Julius had sent assassins to kill him. When he returned, artillery was repositioned. We prepared for the next assault.

Alfonso's journey back was tortuous. There were spies everywhere looking for him. Pope Julius II would be satisfied with only one thing, the death of the Duke of Ferrara. Julius continued his quest to gain control of Ferrara for himself. Alfonso stood in the way. More so, Julius could not get over the melting down of his statue during the war with the body being made into a cannon to mock him. His outrage grew the more he realized the head of his statue hung in our castle. I do believe, had he captured Alfonso, my husband's head would have hung in the Vatican.

When the duke returned to Ferrara, he came again with a hero's welcome. All of Ferrara turned out to see their victorious duke clad in plain clothes for disguise. Alfonso had fought so hard for the people of this State. He had replaced the pope in their hearts. The leader of the Church could give orders, but they would not be carried out without their glorious duke's approval. The righteousness of my husband clearly surpassed that of the current pope. Alfonso's first act every time he entered the city after battle was to enter the cathedral and give God thanks.

In 1512, upon his arrival, Alfonso sought to commemorate the victories by having silver plaques made to honor the patron saint of Ferrara, Saint Maurelius. I had to learn about this saint when I first became the duchess of this State. Legend has it, Maurelius was the eldest son of a king in Mesopotamia. When he reached the age of 30, he began to be drawn to the Lord. In his research, he was convinced Jesus was the Christ, the Son of the Living God. He realized he was a sinner, in need of a Savior. Because of his sinfulness and fear of Hell, he knelt by his palace bed and asked Jesus to come into his life and save him.

The archives record he rose from the foot of his bed, a changed man. He was consumed by peace. The things of the world no longer mattered. Knowing his father's quest for wealth and power was never satisfied, he shared with his reigning patriarch the joy he had found in Jesus. Hoping his father would kneel to ask Jesus to be his Lord too, he was crushed at the response. His father cursed the Lord. He then commanded Maurelius to never speak His Name again. A Christ-like life was forbidden. His son was to live as the pagans lived if he ever sought to follow as king.

Three days later, his father died. Maurelius was to be crowned king, but he declined the promotion. He handed the throne over to the brother next in line. With a smile on his face, Maurelius left the center of his father's kingdom to pursue a life of peace, joy, and righteousness. He grew in his Christian faith under the tutelage of Theophilus of Antioch who ordained him as a priest. Later, he was appointed a bishop of Voghenza by Pope John IV. After years of Godly service, he was called back to the kingdom of his father to settle a dispute with his brothers — one who was a Christian and the other who ordered him to recant. The Christian brother was killed. Marcelius was arrested upon his arrival. He was tortured but would not recant. He was then crucified.

If ever there was a man to honor in Ferrara and in all of Christendom, it would be Marcelius. What troubles me here on my sickbed as I have pondered my past, Ferrara had a patron saint. Mantua had a different patron saint. Urbino had a totally separate patron saint. Francesco Gonzaga, like my father, prayed to our Holy Mother to cover over their blatant sins.

We made silver plates to honor Saint Marcelius for protecting our city. Though he is in the Presence of the Lord, he did not save our city, nor did he ask God to do it for us. In the Apostle Paul's letter to Timothy, he says, "For there is one God and one mediator between God and men, the man Christ Jesus, who gave himself as a ransom for all men." We have one mediator, one intercessor to God for us. His Name is Jesus. I believe if Saint Marcelius relics could rise from our San Giorgio church here in Ferrara, he would say, "Don't thank me. Thank God for hearing your prayer. Thank Jesus for praying on your behalf to the Father."

This is my position now. But I am writing my confessions through my trustworthy secretary. We honored Saint Marcelius at our victory. Sadly, the most traumatic thing in my life followed. God works all things together for good. The turning point in my life began when I married Alfonso, though I did not realize the blessing at the time. Slowly, I was changing. Gradually, I was seeing what real love looked like from a father like Ercole, and a husband like Alfonso. The greatest change in my life followed my greatest loss.

The Time when Everything Changed

In August of 1512, my firstborn son, Rodrigo died at the tender age of twelve-years-old. I had not seen my son in ten years. I abandoned him to follow the mechanisms of my father in Ferrara. He was raised by the Isabella I respected, Isabella of Aragon. I was overwhelmed at the news. I immediately left my two sons to the care of my ladies and escaped to the safe confines of the convent at San Bernardino.

I was inconsolable for good reason. My son did not know me. He had no memory of me. He knew the nurturing of another who was not his mother. I had two opportunities to see him when he was near Ferrara, but I conveniently found something better to do. For all he knew, I was a mother who did not want him. When God compares His Love to that of a mother, He says, "Can a woman forget her suckling child, that she should not have compassion on the son of her womb? Yea, they may forget, yet will I not forget thee."

God does not forget those children of His. I did not forget Rodrigo, but there were many times in those ten years in which he did not cross my mind. But God was not speaking of simply remembering the child. His statement means He will not only not forget, He will look after and protect. I have not done that. I am the mother who has forgotten my suckling child. I did not have compassion on him when he needed me. He died at the age of twelve with me nowhere in sight.

I closed myself off in the convent for over a month. I wrote no letters. I received no visitors other than Cardinal Ippolito. As a member of the clergy, he was allowed into the convent. I named my second son after my dear brother-in-law. He was a warrior. He was a man of a hot temper. He had ordered the killing and the cutting out of the eyes of his brother Giulio. But he also was a devoted supporter of Alfonso. And he never failed me once. He was with me at the death of my father. He was with me at the death of Cesare whom he abhorred, but none-the-less he empathized with me. Ippolito had looked after my son Rodrigo when he was alive. He was with me for a time in the convent to grieve with me over Rodrigo when he died.

The cardinal understood the price I selfishly paid for my position. He expressed repeatedly our God forgives. But that forgiveness was hard for me to grasp. I had seen such displayed in Alfonso, though I seldom sought it. I had never felt I truly needed forgiveness until the moment of my son's death. They said my father felt the need on his deathbed. I hope this was the case. Pharaoh after many times of rejecting God's command to let His people go and worship him, felt the blows of hail destroying his nation. Pharaoh then pleaded with God, "This time I have sinned." This time? What about all the times before? In the convent, in my grief, I realized I had sinned against my son Rodrigo. As I recite my confessions, I realize this was not the first time I had sinned. I had sinned over and over before and after. I needed God's forgiveness then. I need God's forgiveness now as I am on the cusp of eternity.

My grief was unmatched. I grieved when father died. I was one of a few. He received what he deserved. I was an accomplice in many of his crimes. His death was a personal loss, but not a tragic one. When Cesare died, I may have been the only one to really grieve. Even his closest captains probably saw his death as an opportunity to move up, to take his place. I grieved over Cesare though I realized then that, perhaps, he was a brutal murderer. I joined in aiding his exploits. I welcomed him after he killed my second husband as I would have received a long-lost relative released from unlawful imprisonment or a loved one raised from a sickbed. I grieved for he was of my own blood, my own consort in all things immoral.

But Rodrigo? What crime had he ever committed. He was an orphan in the main. His father was killed. His mother abandoned him. Yes, he was left some provision. Thankfully, he was not left the name Borgia. I hear he loved to ride horses. He was humble. He was kind. He was selfless. Of all my relatives to live, he deserved to, above us all. Perhaps he could have changed the trajectory of our family line. I abandoned him. He knew me not.

I consoled myself with one thought. Perhaps Rodrigo was better to not have known me. If he had been in Ferrara, would he have been in danger? If he had been exposed to his uncle Cesare, would he have wanted to be like him? If he had been in this castle when Francesco visited, or Bembo called, would he have sought his own pleasures regardless of who they hurt? If he had been near enough to our circles, would he have seen popes vying for wealth and power with no connection to the Living God, believing this thing of religion is nothing but a fanciful façade?

I praise God, my son did not know me. But what does this say about me? What of my future? What of my eternal destiny?

I pried myself away from the convent to travel to Naples to settle my son's affairs. Shame covers my memory as I remember how I fought to get what I declared was mine. I told all who would listen, I was the rightful heir to my son's possessions. Isabella of Aragon gave all she had to raise her brother's son, and I stepped in to take what she had given him.

I hate myself for what I have done in the past. I hate I still have that bent in this sickbed. I achieved my covetous goal, but only as of last year, 1518. What good did it do me? By the time I received Rodrigo's possessions, I only wanted his favorite robe. Even now, the robe lies here on the foot of my bed. His scent no longer lingers, but I imagine his smell. I hold it near my bosom when I grieve over the loss of one true heart. My prayer is for Alfonso's sons to be like their father and my firstborn, nothing like me.

I attended my son's memorial service, then departed for Ferrara. When I returned to the castle, I did not enter. I could not. I excused myself for several more weeks at the convent to pray. In October of 1512, I rose from the ashes a new person. Old things were passed away, all things were new as the Apostle Paul wrote in his second letter to the Church in Corinth. I could no longer rest on my righteousness. I had blown such thoughts away. I could not do enough ritual to atone for my sins. I could not begin enough convents or recruit enough nuns to pay for my transgressions.

I learned an important lesson. God offered me forgiveness but not a cheap one. He is merciful, but He is also just. He said without the shedding of blood, there is no forgiveness of sins, that in the fullness of time, God sent His Son to be our propitiation so any who call upon His Name, shall be saved. I received God's Gift in that convent as Sister Gabrielle led me in what she called the "sinner's prayer." I no longer would trust in my efforts to go to Heaven, I would trust in what Jesus did on my behalf.

Everything was new. I wish I could end my confessional there. I wish I would have begun at that moment to live a sin-free life. I have found the Christian life is one of gradual transformation. The redeemed life makes steps forward and in flesh slides backward. God says the righteous will fall, but they get back up. I know this is true for I get back up, covered by the blood of the Savior who died, of the Lord who rose from the dead. The Mass took on a whole new meaning. Easter was embraced. Carnival no longer had any appeal to me. The revelry to sin knowing Lent was coming to atone was a carnal approach to God through ritual and tradition. I sought a life of daily repentance. I found no consolation in superficial Christianity. I was saved. I would seek to live righteously but not to earn forgiveness and Heaven. I would seek to live as Christ in gratitude for both had been freely given to me when I received Jesus as my Lord.

A new zeal came over me to start more convents and hospitals. I began to visit the sick in our city. I helped the fatherless. I cared for those who were homeless. I was faithful to pray for those hurting. I became an ear to counsel those bereaved. The more I gave of myself, the happier I became. I found Jesus' words completely true. If we lose our life, we will find it. I had gained the whole world practically and was dead within. But when I gave my life to Christ, losing the world and its riches brought me no fear. My life was changed.

Leonardo and Federico Wait

Guiseppe's assistants, Leonardo Accardi and Federico Bandoni were surprised to be leaving their respective hotel rooms at the exact same moment. They greeted each other with a smile. It was clear Leonardo had a restless night. He had traveled a long way a few days before. He never slept well the first few nights in a new bed. He acknowledged as much to his coworker when Federico pointed out that his buttons were misaligned. Leonardo looked down, and began to laugh, "I told you so!" He unbuttoned and then rebuttoned his shirt.

A few minutes before 7 AM, they were in the coffee shop waiting on Guiseppe. They waited for about ten minutes, and then went ahead to order. Leonardo ordered a cup of coffee and a sweet pastry for the late-arriving Guiseppe, hoping his tastes had not changed. Politely, the two waited a few minutes not wanting to start without their foreman. Not wanting their coffee to get cold, they agreed to start without him, assuming he would understand.

By 8 AM, Federico grew antsy. He asked Leonardo if Guiseppe was usually late for their appointments. His former colleague answered, "Guiseppe is a lot of things, but he is never, ever late. Perhaps he was called to meet with Father Ferrua. Let's give him a few more minutes."

By 8:30 AM, Leonardo shrugged his shoulders, "I suggest we head on to the Santa Maria sopra Minerva. We know what we are to do. I am sure Guiseppe will catch up. He will have a good explanation. I know you do not know him well, but he is diligent and dependable in all he does. He is the only foreman I ever worked with who needed no oversight."

The two assistants were pleased to see the basilica open. They were excited to continue their work. They were also pleased to have the opportunity to show their boss their initiative to start work with or without his presence. The basilica began its daily fill of tourists.

Guiseppe was distracted from his reading. He heard the faint echo of the huge basilica doors as they were pushed against the inside walls. He moved his ladder to bang his fist on the lid of the memorial slab. As heavy as it was, he assumed the priest opening the basilica would not hear the attempt. The trapped archaeologist was having no trouble breathing. He was also near the end of the discovered diary. He settled back down to read the final few pages. His hope was, by then, there would be tourists near the main altar who could hear him, if his assistants had not already discovered his open tool kit behind the barrier curtain. Plus, he was mesmerized by Lucrezia's story. He bowed his head to thank the Lord again for this find. He turned the page.

The Wars Outside and Inside

Pope Julius II resumed his attacks on the state of Ferrara. He soon took possession of every corner of our State except for Comacchio, Argenta, and the city of Ferrara. Alfonso fortified our city to the point every invader was dissuaded from the effort. Instead, the pope exercised intrigue, threats, and promises to any who could separate the duke from his dukedom.

Francesco separated permanently from Isabella. He even wrote her letters of accusation of being in an affair of her own, or worse, striking out as a woman in no need of a man. Rumors had it, she began to use men as he had used her. Such actions of a woman were intolerable for a man like the Marquis. Perhaps in payback or in loneliness, he tried to entice me to move in with him. He had gained permission from the pope for my transport as long as my sons and Alfonso did not accompany me. I was still grieving over leaving Rodrigo and then losing him. I would not repeat that mistake again. I still loved Francesco, but I determined to love him at a distance, though I continued to write him with furtive sentiment.

The year of 1513 was a fearful one. It seemed the Estes and Ferrara could not catch a break. Isabella wrote Alfonso to let him know, Pope Julius II had made his life's sole goal to extinguish the Este line. She ended her letter, which Alfonso shared with me, "I wish him dead." Many in his cardinal circle wished the same thing. Julius II had become unbearable. His murderous temper was being exacted throughout the papal states. The people resented him, turning their ire upon the cardinals in their region. If he lived much longer, the Church would be dead.

The pope's health continued to deteriorate but his evil spirit was still in full force. I find it interesting, though the body ages, the spirit in the man knows no age. Without mental decline, inside people feel they can still do the things they did when they were young. The spirit is willing, but the flesh is too weak to carry it out. Such was the state of the pope. When it appeared, he was in his last hours, the cardinals threw a carnival in Rome to celebrate while he was unable to leave his bed. When he found out, he vowed to have the papal army kill every cardinal and start afresh. But then the wicked pope died. It comes to all men, regardless of their power. It will come to me. It will come to His Holiness, Pope Leo X. No one is exempted.

Humanists summed his life as one which any secular ruler would admire. As far as the things of God, there was not a hint of anything Divine. The Venetians said he did more harm to Christianity than any pope before him. They wished he had died five years earlier. Alfonso and I could not agree more. We held celebrations throughout Ferrara. I went from church to church in the State to give God thanks for His Deliverance.

Cardinal Giovanni de Medici was chosen to succeed Julius. He took the name, Pope Leo X. Alfonso had taken him captive in his last victory over the papal army. We treated the young cardinal very kindly. As a thirty-eight-year-old pope, we prayed he would remember our kindness toward him. It appeared he did when he invited Alfonso to his coronation. My husband left immediately with twelve of his best men to pay homage to Leo X. The pope rewarded Alfonso with a private dinner before the event, and then suspended the interdict on Alfonso issued by Julius, giving the cardinals time to investigate the complaint. Alfonso left soon after the installation excited for a new day for our war-weary State.

Things continued to improve. Even the warring Venetians reached an agreement of peace with Alfonso, giving back some of the lands we lost in the war. Two months after his ascent to the papacy, Leo X made a treaty with Spain and England against France and the Venetians. War resumed with similar fury. Alfonso kept Ferrara to the side, but pledged his support to France and the Venetians should they need him. The pope soon came after the coveted State of Ferrara unrelated to his stated reasons for re-instigating the war.

Pope Leo X took from our State, Moderna and then Reggio. His plan was to give these and chiefly Ferrara to his brother. Alfonso strengthened the defenses of Ferrara, then left to retake Moderna and Reggio. I did the duties of the duchess but focused on the duties as a Christian. I was drawn to the radical reformers of the Church who demanded the leaders of our faith be men of obedience, love, and righteousness, rather than territorial expansionists. The Franciscan preacher, Bernardo, preached strict adherence to God's Commands. He did not believe any man had the capacity to change a jot or a tittle of God's Word, nor did any religious leader have the authority to allow for indulgences, or as he called them "papal permissions to sin."

My former mission to collect damsels of Ferrara in whom I had invested myself for their education and marriage was changed. The goal turned to teaching righteousness, chastity, and encouraging many to become nuns. For those set on marriage, I taught the beauty of virginity and faithfulness to one's vows. I wanted to follow the Lord's admonition to make disciples, seeing them observe all the Lord had commanded. I found joy in this redemptive venture. I felt a contentment. Fear also dissipated. Being in the Lord's Will gave me assurance that He would protect me and our State. I was trusting in the Lord with all my heart. I chose to not lean on my own understanding.

As the Lord held the enemy at bay, Alfonso was often called away. Regardless, when possible, he was a frequent visitor to my bed. I became pregnant three additional times. I lost a boy, but was blessed with a sweet daughter, and then a son whom I named Francesco. I could explain naming my first son in Ferrara after Ercole, my father-in-law. I named my second Ippolito as a reward for my brother-in-law's loyalty to my husband. But the name of the third was not easy to explain.

Alfonso had no Francesco's in his family. I had none in mine. I always liked the name, but deep down, it was a tribute to the first human passion of my life, the illicit, immoral, selfish lover Francesco. I explained the name to my husband by saying this was a reward to the man who kept the pope's armies at bay when they could have easily invaded Ferrara in his absence. My husband honored my request. He would love our third son as the first and second, but I knew this was a sensitive matter to him. I had become a Christian, but there was still some old self abiding. I regret not naming the third son after the one man who deserved my love, Alfonso.

To make amends, I began to defer all decisions concerning our children to my husband. Together we decided on their education. Together we chose their tutors. Together we decided when they should be moved out of danger, and when they should remain under our care. I did nothing without his approval. I prayed to love him as the Lord loves His Church. I also wished to be the spotless bride, washed by the blood of Jesus.

With Alfonso's approval, we built more convents throughout our State. We also established an academy of sorts for the training of intellectuals. If we wanted our own sons to be well-versed in all areas of knowledge, who were we to keep the privilege from the citizens of our State? Our desire was to make Ferrara the hotbed of education believing our State could build on what Ercole had dreamt. Our State continued to be a model for others to follow.

Inebriated by the finer things, I realized the value of a person is not in what they wear, or in how they look. Our true value rested in who we were on the inside. An ascetic lifestyle was to be desired. Virtue could adorn any human. We began to lay up treasures in Heaven where moth, rust, nor any army or ungodly pope could destroy.

During this time, my brother Joffre died. Sancha had left him years before. He had remarried at her death. We never corresponded after I arrived in Ferrara. Cesare had kept me abreast of events in Joffre's life. He was especially gladdened when Sancha left our brother. Cesare hoped he could take her as his own personal consort. Sancha had grown past both of them.

Joffre's second wife bore him four children. She was the one who wrote to me concerning his passing. I find it commendable my brother Joffre would not marry again, nor take on a consort until Sancha died in 1506. From all I can find, he remained faithful to the one who was unfaithful, much like Alfonso. With the fact Joffre was younger and there was question as to who sired him, I wonder if, he had chosen Christ as his Savior too. He had seen the multiple bad examples. Maybe, he decided to be a Borgia rebel and do right. This was my prayer.

France and the Venetians were having success against the papal forces. They defeated the pope's Swiss army regaining Milan. With their wins, Ferrara found itself in a momentary state of rest. Carnival time came. Alfonso was excited for our sons. He allowed masks throughout the city but set limits on what weapons could be carried to prevent any breakout of violence. Our two oldest sons had the time of their lives. People came to stay with us. The boys shared our quarters so the guests could lodge in theirs. Little Ercole and Ippolito were given responsibilities in the castle. They also began to assume some of the formal duties. When guests came, I sent them out with the servants to welcome our callers. They were obedient and respectful to all.

We had three nights of dances. We also served a feast in our castle for our guests and dignitaries who came. In the past, I would have been appalled at the lack of silver and gold flatware, but the war had caused all those things to be melted down for war implements. The pottery dishes which replaced the fine metals, were artfully made by none other than my husband.

There was a sense of joy celebrating with less extravagant means. The masses who came for Carnival gave Alfonso the opportunity to showcase his building projects to our castle, our new villa, and the city itself. Much was built with Carrara marble and Venice nutwood. He also built a studio to show his collection of fine sculptures, statues, and antiques. The duke took special interest in preserving the Este history. He was a man of abundant tastes.

Privately, Alfonso was like a little boy showing off his newly remodeled bedroom, which he oversaw with a desire to delight me. This room would be our room together. For our time alone, for sanity's sake, he had a bridge built to connect our apartments so he could come to me with ease, covered from the outside elements. My husband provided allowances for my tastes. He was into the secular and historical. I was into the spiritual. As a result, he provided money for a specially requested bust of the Lord Jesus' Head. We called it, "The Head of the Savior." It is my most precious piece of art.

Following my new pattern of life, I no longer wanted the monasteries or convents to exemplify the values of the world. These institutions were to be righteous examples for the world to see. Jesus said we are to be in the world, but not of the world. With this commitment, I called together the Dominican monks of Ferrara with the duke present to enforce my wishes. They were to conform to the tenets of the Holy Scripture or they were to leave our city. No volitional disobedience would be tolerated.

The word spread throughout our State. There was a holy fear more of the duke, than the Lord, but it achieved the same purpose. How dare popes, cardinals, bishops, priests, monks, or nuns exempt themselves from obedience to God? God said He would bless those who obey. He would curse those who disobey. I had lived under the curse for too long. I did not want them, nor my children, to ever face the tragedies which I brought upon myself through my carnal, selfish lifestyle. Every parent should want this for their children. Every leader should want this for their people if they really love them. Loving God, obeying Him, beseeching others to do the same is the best way to love others.

Friar Thomaso gave sermons throughout the month exhorting all to follow God because He has commanded it. Jesus said if you love Me, keep My Commandments. By doing what we wanted, we were showing a hatred for our dear

Christ. As we sought to be an example for the country in education, we sought even more to be the shining light of what a state can be if it follows after God wholeheartedly. I hoped all Christendom would follow suit.

The last year, 1518, was filled with sickness. I was in and out of bed. Alfonso, my dear husband, would constantly alter his plans to be near me. It was my practice to hold court with the people of the State, to render judgments upon their disputes. Alfonso filled in for me several times. He had never had time to do this in the past, always going to war, or working to form alliances. The people were thrilled to have him as their attendant. There was joy in all Ferrara. He was not keen on administration, but he loved the audiences. Everyone wants to be loved. The duke reveled in reassuming his role in a time of peace. He fell more in love with his citizens than ever before. They had pledged their lives to his and the Este defense. They were reaping their just reward.

Alfonso allowed for me to care for my half-brother, Giovanni Borgia, the son of my father by some woman. I am not sure who. The boy was always in trouble. He was never appreciative. He felt the world owed him a favor. At least my father worked thirty-two years as an underling to gain the papal chair. Giovanni felt no work should be required. Where his hands were idle, open and waiting for gifts, his life was in a constant state of trouble. He would rob people. He would harbor murderers. He would borrow but never repay.

My husband was sick of dealing with him, but for my sake, he continued to seek to assist him, with the hope he would one day mature. When Giovanni sought an audience with France, believing somehow, he had the talent to benefit the new king, Alfonso let him accompany him to a king's celebration. While there, Giovanni acted as a spoiled ingrate. Even so, Alfonso obtained the introduction requested, then promptly left my half-brother in Paris to sort things out for himself.

I was proud of my husband. While on this errand because of his love for me, the king of France, the king of England, the royal commanders, deferred to Alfonso. They gave him the best seats. They even honored him with a gift of a sweet mule which he brought back for young Ercole. Finally, my love for Alfonso surpassed my love for any other man — more than my father, my brother Cesare, my lover Francesco. He deserved to have my love all along. He earned it with every year that passed. He won it by his character and steadfastness unmatched.

My father's last son, Rodrigo, was born after I had left for Ferrara. I was not aware of who his mother was. Once Father died, he was pawned off to one relative and then the next. When I learned of his existence, I used the reputation Alfonso had gained, to find him. Together, my husband and I provided for his needs. We also hired a God-minded tutor for him in Naples. My only charge for my youngest half-brother, was that he be brought up in the way of the Lord, to love and obey Him alone. The tutor assured me he would.

While Alfonso was in France, I was back as the governess and judge of the State of Ferrara. There were some tough arrests during this time. Many of them required strict punishment on the face of the crime. There were a few which were truly violations, but harsh punishment was not warranted. One man was arrested at dark with no light. The duke had required all citizens to carry a light on their person when traveling the city. Anyone without a light was considered a robber. The man who came before me, was out at dark without a light. As I listened, I learned that after his workday ended, he met a lady in need. He chose to help her despite the late hour. Darkness fell upon him quickly. By the time he had finished assisting her, he was a long way from his home. He hurried but was caught without a light. I pardoned him against my husband's letter of the law. When I wrote to Alfonso to explain it, he fully agreed.

We had another man who was caught at dark with another man's robe. He had once worked for Ippolito. When he came before me, the order was for him to be tortured. I suspended his punishment when he presented papers from Cardinal Ippolito. Later, I found the letters were falsified. I had him rearrested and punished. As I made these decisions, I felt I should act as our forebear Solomon, seeking God's Wisdom. With our God, mercy and justice go hand in hand. My husband approved.

Another incident occurred in our city which was in keeping with the national sentiment, but not with our State's virtue. My father-in-law, Ercole, had always made Ferrara an inviting home to any of Jewish descent. Long ago, miscreants, under the false banner of the Church, sought to kill Jews in our city claiming they were killing babies and using their blood for their sacrifices. Such accusations were completely false. Ercole rode in amongst them, having the ringleaders beheaded. The rest of the mob quietly returned to their daily lives.

I faced a smaller outbreak while my husband was gone. I quickly ordered punishment for the offenders and protection for any Jewish families or businesses targeted. Thankfully, peace returned. I was shocked how quickly the ill-informed can turn against the Lord Jesus' own people. God said He would bless those who bless the Jewish people, curse those who curse them. God never changes. He means what He says. I sought His blessing for my life, my family, and our State. May God remember this.

One day, I took a break from the States's business. I climbed the Lion's Tower of our castle. From there, one can see every quadrant of our city and beyond. I was gratified to realize these were my people as the duchess. I never dreamed I could hold such an important position with such a loving citizenry. Over and over, God had given me much better than I deserve. His Grace is new every morning. I rejoice in Him.

My husband returned. We hoped to stay for a while. He began to strengthen the defenses of the city. We had no idea when the pope might reengage his passion to own Ferrara. Alfonso had towers built to hold new artillery. He had walls thickened to prevent breech. Then the French requested his counsel. He left. Having been to France once already, I wrote a letter to Pope Leo X to explain my husband's second visit to the pope's sworn enemy. There was a tentative peace, but the pope could easily read into the second trip as some plot to take more land from the papal authority. The letter was delivered and well received. I rejoiced in my ability to be an aid to the son of Ercole, the father of an Ercole, and the elder Este, my husband.

While Alfonso was away, I received the news the mother, Vannozza, was ill. I included the news in my letter to my sister-in-law Isabella. I called the woman in this recital, and in the letter, "the mother" not "my mother." In truth, I saw Adriana de Mila as my mother. She raised me. She cared for me. She traveled with me. She was with me in Pesaro during the days of my first marriage. She treated me as if I was her own. Cesare was closer to my mother. I believe because she felt he could be successful providing her with more benefices as my father did before him.

Only when I became the duchess of the prized State of Ferrara, did she correspond with me but only to make requests. She never wrote to me alone, but to me and "The Lord Duke." She took on debt. She would not repay. She would be threatened. She would then write for us to gain her pardon. The mother did not owe ordinary people. She used her relations with my father, my brother, and me to obtain huge sums of money from kings and cardinals alike. This was why she wrote to Alfonso (and me in the hope of my persuasion) knowing he had the clout to sway the offended.

Then Vannozza the mother died on November 24, 1518. I was stymied by what I should feel. She had never been a mother to me. She had obtained great possessions because of her consorting with my father. She had two buildings built, owned several shops, leased several rental properties, and had a fine house along with other luxuries. Yet, she sought money from others with no plans to repay. To show her heart, nearing death, she used her own wealth in an effort to purchase her salvation. She gave large amounts to her favorite church, Santa Maria del Popolo. She provided the finances for a chapel nearby. She had marble statues made for local convents. She donated a house to her favorite church to be used for orphaned and sick children. She gave a bust of my brother, Cesare, to a hospital. She had her own headstone etched listing her four children by Pope Alexander VI, accompanied by our titles to make her look like a person of significance. With her last sizeable donation to the Santa Maria del Popolo, she tied with it the requirement that a Mass be held each year so prayers would be offered for her soul.

I have struggled with forgiveness for the mother as I face the same fate in which all must go. I have decided to obey and forgive. I do not believe forgiveness is necessarily something you must feel, to do it. I believe we can forgive in obedience to God's Command. If we obey in this way, the feelings may follow. Besides, as one who has been forgiven much, how can I not forgive?

Conviction overwhelms me as I recite this. I have had to break for a moment from my recollections. How can I not forgive my mother for her abandonment yet plead with God to forgive me for abandoning my firstborn son Rodrigo? I am overwhelmed with tears again. My mother did me no worse than I did my own son. The carnal side would blame her for my transgression with the excuse, "I did what I saw modeled." This is an excuse with no ability to justify perfidy. I knew when I left Rodrigo, I was wrong. I knew all those years of pretending he did not exist, I was wrong. God convicted me, but I let my conscience callous. I perhaps understand my mother more now than ever. I pray the Lord forgives her. I pray she truly did give her heart to Him. I want to see her in Heaven, to hug her neck, and let her know I forgive her. I will ask for her forgiveness too. In Heaven, requests of mercy are immediately granted.

My Final Requests

As I finish confessing my sins regarding my mother, I am heavily laden, pregnant again. Every pregnancy has been hard on me as previously stated. With each one, I have felt the conclusion of my life was within reach. Perhaps my memory is not as sharp as in times past. Or I may correctly perceive, this is the worst pregnancy I have experienced. I am faint. I find trouble breathing. I am too weak to push, too tired to try.

Death, until the Lord returns, is a fate none can avoid. King Louis XII succumbed to it as did King Ferdinand and Queen Isabella. Emperor Maximillian recently gave way. The news reached my bedside, Francesco Gonzaga, the Marquis has passed. Our latest correspondence has been more pleasing to our righteous calling. I began to care for him as a brother, no longer a lover. I encouraged him to get his life right with the Lord. I refused to speak any longer on tender, fleshly terms. A judgement awaits us all. God has given a shelter from that judgment through His Son. I have run to His Gracious Shelter. Francesco has intimated he did the same in these last days. I pray so.

What thrilled me concerning my former "Guido", a vision of a dead nun appeared a few months back in Mantua arm and arm with a living nun in one of their convents. The witnesses to the event drew pilgrims from all over. I wrote to the Marquis that even in our sinful age, God is still God. He is not moved. His power has not been diminished. God is true. Every man is a liar in comparison. My prayer, which I wrote him, is for a spirit of repentance to break out from Mantua and spread throughout our nation and world.

I have been feeling a movement of God of late. Though I am not in agreement with the man Martin Luther, I do see justification in his attacks on the hypocrisy found in the church. He is also right to say many Christians are ignoring the Word of God. I have been of the same opinion since my dear, twelve-year-old son Rodrigo died. Pope Leo X is calling for Luther's head. I wish for him to listen to the German priest. There is some truth in what he has nailed to the doors of the Church. Perhaps, there is more truth than I can countenance at this moment.

At the Marquis' death, I wrote a letter of condolence to Isabella and to the Marquis' son.

I did not grieve as I had for my sweet Rodrigo, nor as I would have a few years before. God broke the spell evil placed upon my life concerning Francesco. My love is now at the place God has intended — The Lord first, Alfonso second, my children third. There is no love left in my heart for sin. In the flesh, I still do the things I do not want to do at times. The things I want to do, I struggle to do, but my life is being transformed. Yet, I will beat my body to please the Lord.

I am in great pain. My secretary has been faithful to capture my thoughts and confessions. My husband has been a constant companion by my side. He has heard the dreadful recollections of the sins I have committed in my life. He has wept often to hear my acknowledgements of the sordid things he feared. To hear the admission from his own wife's lips, I know has broken his heart. He says the confessions have made him love me more, knowing I am so utterly sorry for each of them.

He has had some confessions of his own to share with me which will be unrecorded. I leave it to him to decide how best to deal with those sins. Asking God to forgive is all we need. Having a priest or a loved one hear them is good for the soul. Having been brought up in the Church, being the daughter of a pope, I have a need to seek the intercession of Pope Leo X. The Lord has said we are to confess our sins one to another. This has been my desire at the onset of this journal.

The doctors believe if I can simply give birth, my health will be restored. Some have suggested aborting this pregnancy. I will not consider such a thing. If I die and my child lives, I will consider it a final gift, a fitting conclusion to my life.

In and out of consciousness, I have given birth to a little girl. Alfonso had her immediately christened Isabella Maria. My little girl is so weak. She feeds with difficultly, but we are praying. My attendants, my priest, and my husband are praying for me as well. I am not sure who is the weakest.

The doctors have cut my hair. My nose will not stop bleeding. Isabella Maria is feeding some. I have been given last sacraments. Alfonso cannot keep a dry eye. I pray for strength to complete my confessions with a letter to Pope Leo X.

I am constantly thrown into convulsions. I cannot eat. I want nothing to drink. Candles are burning all around me. Priests and nuns are in and out. There is a constant prayer vigil around my bedside and in every convent. I am told all of Ferrara is praying.

I have regained a little strength. They say I have but an hour or so left to live. I have let my family know how much I love them. I have one last thing to share before I give up my spirit to God:

Dear Pope Leo X, my beloved Beatitude,

I have enclosed a public letter for your grace in providing suffrage for my soul from the Holy Treasury that is yours as our vicar of Christ. I have confessed my sins in long form for your review and prayers to join mine for forgiveness. My hope is you will.

I now dare to risk whatever mercies you might impart. I have a great fear for you dear Pope. You have always been precious to us. Alfonso and I carry a special affinity for you. We rejoice in your kindness, though at times you have doubted our allegiance. I have done my best to write letters to you any time an action of ours could be misunderstood. You have always been gracious to respond, showing gratitude for my explanations. I thank you for this.

There are two last wishes I have for you privately. One, I pray you will keep the confessions which precede this letter. I grieve over my sins, but I do believe my experiences, and especially the enumerated transgressions of my father, can be of assistance to you. My father made grave errors as pope, seeking his own kingdom, ignoring anything of God. He took as frivolous the call of Christ, fearing no repercussions. He died, cursed by the Church and civic leaders alike. Few if any grieved his death except for me. Most celebrated his death as they celebrated that of Pope Julius II.

I do not want this for you. Jesus said if we will serve Him and all others on His behalf, we will be honored in Heaven. If we seek to be honored here, we will be the least in God's Kingdom. I pray you will be attentive to the lessons from the past. I love you as my Pope. I honor you as a man. My heart's desire is for you to be the shining example for the ones who will follow in your chair.

As you have heard, and now read, Pope Alexander VI's death was beyond horrific. His judgment, if he did not repent, is being suffered in a dark, eternal fire, none can comprehend until experienced. All who do not put their trust in the Lord Jesus Christ will suffer the same fate alongside the millions before who sought their own selfish ways. There is no prayer afterward which can deliver them from this eternal damnation. God's Word says it is sealed.

Salvation is available from the Living God. His Hand fights, not for those who carry His title, but for those who live according to His nature and commands, clinging to His dear Son who suffered on the Cross in our stead. Salvation is freely offered to each and every one.

You have seen how God has Divinely protected this State of Ferrara. Many kings and popes have sought our possession, but none have been successful. We have often been outnumbered but we have never lost. This is not because we are holy. Contrary, as you read my confessions, you will realize the only protection we have received is because of the fixed reverence my father-in-law and husband have had for the Lord. They were men far from perfect. They committed themselves to the mercy of God through the sacrifice of Jesus upon Calvary.

I know Ercole and Alfonso do not have near the Biblical knowledge you do, but with what little faith they have, they have trusted in Jesus. I have too. Our faith together may form no more than a mustard seed, but it is enough to pass us from death unto life in Heaven. I close with my ultimate plea. I have heard some say you do not believe in God nor His Son Jesus Christ. Forgive me if what I write is an insult. I am asking you to please read the Bible for yourself, not for some sermon. I am begging you to ask God to guide your understanding, even if you do not fully believe in Him. I want for you, my Beatitude, to be in Heaven one day, to find forgiveness for your sins against God. I love you. If I were in your presence, I would kiss your holy feet. I would give all I have to see your salvation as well as my children's.

I am the humble servant of your Beatitude,

Lucrezia d'Este

Guiseppe Set Free

Guiseppe stared at the last page. A tear drop fell from his eye upon the space following the final sentence. He closed the book and held it to his chest. He prayed out loud:

"Father if no one finds me, I will praise You. If I am found, I will praise You. I want to share this diary with the world, but I am content to place it back in Pope Leo X's hands, close the lid to the tomb, and leave all behind. What You have shown me is precious. I can keep it a secret, as a sweet morsel between You and me. Or I can share the diary and seek no glory or wealth from it. I worship You alone for You have saved me. You did not stop with me, nor did you start with me. Lucrezia Borgia, the supposed evil-incarnate of history, was saved by You just as I was. I praise Your Holy Name. Thank you also for letting me see there is a difference between adhering to empty rituals and clinging to a real relationship with You through Your Son Jesus Christ. Please forgive me for going through the motions on Sundays, in my prayer life, even in reading Your Word. No religion saves. Lucrezia realized this. Only the relationship You made available to us through Your Son Jesus Christ will save. I rejoice I am in this eternal relationship with You. I know what You have started with me; You will complete. I also have a confidence, Jesus, that in Your Father's Home, there are many mansions. You have a place prepared for me. In Jesus' Name I pray, Amen."

Guiseppe quietly prayed for the Lord to now rescue him. At the very moment, he heard someone near the high altar. He grabbed the ladder, but instead of climbing it to bang with the calloused flesh of his hand, he began to bang on the bottom of the memorial slab with the ladder.

Over and over, he banged. He heard footsteps come closer. He then recognized the voice of Leonardo, "Guiseppe, is that you? Are you down there?"

Guiseppe yelled back, "It's me! Can you use the A-frame hoist and get me out of here?"

Leonardo called for Federico. Together, they attached the lid to the hoist. With a strained effort, the hoist broke the lid loose from its bind.

Guiseppe squinted his eyes as the rush of light entered the dark room which had been his habitation for hours. He positioned the ladder and began to climb up with one hand. The other hand was clinging to the ancient book he had found in Pope Leo's entombment. He assumed God wanted him to present it to Father Ferrua to see how the Lord would lead regarding the blessed confessional.

Leonardo saw the ancient book, "What were you doing down there Guiseppe? And what is the book in your hand?"

Guiseppe said with a smile, "I did not realize it, but I believe this book is why God gave us this assignment."

The archaeologist promised to tell them more later. He needed them to continue their work. He was going to the rector to show him the prize from beneath Santa Maria sopra Minerva. They begged him to not leave them in suspense. He reminded them that suspense is what archaeology is all about. With his admonition, they reluctantly, went to work.

He tucked the diary in a satchel he had found in the janitor's closet. Walking out the front doors of the basilica, he looked at the elephant and obelisk. There was too much evidence to not dig for Alexander the Great's tomb. The collateral damage from the tremor would have to be evaluated before proceeding.

Guiseppe made a right turn past the elephant monument to see the ancient Pantheon. It dated back to the time of Caesar Augustus who provided the money and men for its construction. The purpose of this structure was to serve as a temple to the Roman pantheon of gods. As excited as he was to see Father Ferrua, the archaeologist stopped, thinking God might have something teachable for him. The structure was a huge, round edifice. The emperor, over two thousand years ago, who ordered its assembly was the same man who called for a census for the entire Roman world when Jesus Christ was born.

Guiseppe leaned against a building staring at the temple. He was amazed, after all these centuries, the thing still existed intact while so many others of its era had crumbled to the ground. The back part of the Pantheon stood as it appeared two thousand years ago.

Walking to the side of the edifice, Guiseppe continued his gaze as the thoughts cycled through his brain. The old part, the back part of the edifice was the temple to the gods, the front part was different in construction and form. From the old structure protruded a beautiful church building. The back part was built under the direction of the man who ordered the census. What brought about the front part?

The little boy born in Bethlehem, the one counted by Augustus, the one King Herod sought to kill after the census, survived. He lived a life like none before or since. He was crucified, buried, and rose on the third day victorious. The Roman emperor Augustus was building a temple to the gods when the Son of God was born.

The little boy who grew to be a perfect man changed the world. His power reaching through the ages transformed this Roman temple to pagan gods into a church to the Living God. Guiseppe raised his right hand to the sky to praise His Savior. God changed the nation of Rome. The satchel in his left hand was evidence of the transforming power of God in the human life of Lucrezia. God changed his trajectory too through His Son Jesus Christ.

Walking to the Vatican office, Guiseppe got lost in thought. He took a wrong turn down a side alley. He tried to correct himself by going down another side alley, hoping it would lead to the bridge over the Tiber River heading to the Vatican. Instead, he saw rows and rows of buildings and apartments. At the end of one of these, he saw an undistinguishable church of some sort.

He walked by, trying to find his way back toward the Vatican. Going almost a block, he turned back to the church. He was surprised how obscure it was. Where people packed to see the Pantheon, while large crowds visited the Santa Maria sopra Minerva, and while millions tour the Vatican each year, there was not one person visiting this church which was so easy to overlook. The archaeologist wanted to know why.

Guiseppe entered the little church. Unlike the basilica he had just escaped from, this one had three chapels on each side. The high altar had Jesus on the Cross, a fitting focus for worship. He peeked into the first chapel to his right. He was shocked to see the burial tomb of Pope Alexander VI, the former Rodrigo Borgia, the father of Lucrezia Borgia whose diary Guiseppe carried in a satchel held by his left hand!

He lingered to contemplate what this all meant. In an obscure church which he imagined hardly anyone ever sees, lies the pope who sought to be the next Alexander the Great. He cheated. He lied. He killed. All this he did to obtain the things he wanted. Pope Alexander VI was not honored by his countrymen or the

Church. He did not get an extravagant, ornate tomb. In fact, he did not even get a tomb of his own. His is shared with his uncle Pope Calixtus III.

Pope Alexander VI's son, Cesare, murdered and plotted to become the next Julius Caesar. He used Caesar's name in his battle cry, repeated often his only ambition was to equal the famous dictator of Rome. Instead, he was disrespectfully discarded for his efforts. His body was moved to a burial beneath a street to show the disgust the citizens of that town had for the man. Their intent was his body and memory would be trampled by their feet daily.

Both used Lucrezia to extend their powers. Both had terrible endings. Only Lucrezia left this world with honor. Why? Only she repented of her sins. Only she surrendered her life to Christ. Guiseppe felt as though the metaphor of his own life was held in that satchel.

The archaeologist left the church, thankful the Lord had led him there. The final thought he had as he made his way to the rector; how is it Christianity took the Roman Empire without firing a shot, just to see Christian leaders seek to live lives like the ones defeated by sin. Pope Alexander VI, Pope Julius II, and Pope Leo X all discarded Christ to reestablish the Roman Empire under their dictatorship. All three tried what the Caesars before them tried and met the same fate. Only Christ remains. Guiseppe thanked the Lord. His life grew richer still. He practically skipped all the way to the office of Father Ferrua. He was a man who had been set free — twice.

Other fine books available from Histria Fiction:

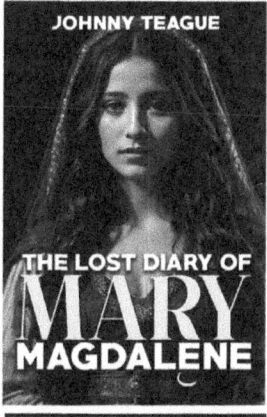

For these and many other great books visit
HistriaBooks.com

Order fine books available
from Histria Fiction

For these and many other great books
visit
Histriabooks.com